Rosa's Land

ROSA'S LAND

GILBERT MORRIS

THORNDIKE PRESS
A part of Gale, Cengage Learning

GALE
CENGAGE Learning·

Detroit • New York • San Francisco • New Haven, Conn • Waterville, Maine • London

LIBRARY OF CONGRESS CATALOGING-IN-PUBLICATION DATA

Morris, Gilbert.
  Rosa's land / by Gilbert Morris. — Large Print edition.
    pages cm. — (Western Justice Book ; # 1) (Thorndike Press Large Print Christian Historical Fiction)
    ISBN 978-1-4104-5660-1 (hardcover) — ISBN 1-4104-5660-9 (hardcover)
    I. Title.
  PS3563.O8742R67 2013
  813'.54—dc23   2013000515

Published in 2013 by arrangement with Barbour Publishing, Inc.

Printed in Mexico
1 2 3 4 5 6 7 17 16 15 14 13

ROSA'S LAND

PART ONE

CHAPTER 1

New York City, 1886
"I wish Faye would hurry up and get home. I'm starved."

Caleb Riordan was a massive individual, large and strongly built, with salt-and-pepper hair and penetrating brown eyes. He had an air of aggression about him, and his enemies had long since learned that he did not know the meaning of the word *quit* . . . or *mercy*. At the age of fifty, Caleb was indeed a successful man by anyone's standards — at least those who counted money, power, and possessions as marks of that quality.

He was seated now in the parlor of his home, and as he pulled a cigar from his inner pocket then lit a match, he looked around the room with a sense of displeasure. The parlor was decorated in cream and a muted tone the color of dry sand, with touches of cool liquid green and one splash of pale coral provided by a single chair. On one wall was a fireplace with a painting of Bosphorus looking down from a palace. Fleets of small boats plied the blue-green waters, and in the distance blurred by the haze of heat loomed a distant scene. Caleb had always disliked the picture but had said little since his wife loved it.

Eileen Riordan was almost a perfect example of opposites attracting, at least to the eye. Whereas Caleb was massive and aggressive, Eileen, at the age of forty-six, was far more gentle than her husband. She had classic features, a wealth of auburn hair, and light blue eyes. Her skin was fair, and there was a grace in her movements. Next to her husband she looked diminutive, although she was larger than the average woman.

She watched as Caleb puffed on his cigar, sending purple clouds upward toward the ceiling. Caleb knew she yearned to tell him not to smoke in the parlor. She did not speak, however. Instead, her eyes went over to the two large young men seated on the horsehide-covered sofa.

Leo, their oldest son, was strongly built. He had Caleb's size and strength, his brown hair and eyes, and some of the same aggressive qualities. Maxwell, at the age of twenty-seven, looked much like Leo. As a matter of fact, they were often taken for twins. They had the same sturdy frame, height, and coloring. Father and sons together made a picture of power that, at times, overwhelmed those they met.

"You know, Dad, I think pulling this deal with Herron was a smart move."

Caleb nodded at Leo, and a look of satisfaction scored his features. He looked at the cigar, knocked the ashes off, and then said, "He's probably sorry he ever got involved with the Riordans."

Maxwell leaned back, locked his large hands behind his head, and studied his father. "We gave him quite a going over. I think he'll go down."

The three men continued to talk about the business deal.

Eileen finally interrupted, saying, "Is this Edward Herron you're talking about?"

"Yes, it is, Eileen," Caleb said. A smile curled his lips at the intense pleasure he felt. "We had a real struggle, but in the end the three of us managed to put him down."

"What do you mean, dear, you 'put him down'?"

"Why, I mean we put him out of business. We've been trying to buy his foundry, and he wouldn't sell, so we had to put pressure

11

on him."

Eileen was silent for a moment then asked, "What kind of pressure?"

"Oh, you wouldn't be interested, dear. Nothing personal. Just a matter of business. We did some manipulating and some maneuvering, and poor Herron got into a spot where he didn't have any choice but to sell his business to us."

"And at a cheap price, too." Leo smiled. "It was a steal."

Eileen considered the three men and finally asked, "What's going to happen to him?"

"Oh, don't worry about it, Eileen. He'll be all right."

"No, I want to know. I like his wife very much, and they have three young children."

"Well, he's pretty well broke now. He had to pay off the mortgage on the factory. But don't worry. If he can't find anything else, I'll put him to work at some kind of minor job at the foundry. He knows the business. We can get him cheap."

The three glanced at each other, and finally Leo said, "Mother, you must understand. The business world isn't like your life. You've got a nice, easy way here with everything you want. But out there in the real world that Dad and Max and I have to live in, it's a matter of survival."

The brothers began trying to persuade Eileen that their dealings with Edward Herron were not immoral, but Caleb saw that she was displeased. For a moment longer, Caleb sat silent, but his mind was racing. Finally he said, "I don't want to bring it up again, but this is the sort of thing that I hate to see Faye unable to face."

"We settled that when he was one year old, Caleb."

Indeed, there had been almost a warlike attitude over their youngest son. Caleb was accustomed to his wife agreeing to anything he said, but when their third son was born, Eileen showed a streak of steel in her backbone. She had come to him and said, "Caleb, you are raising Leo and Max to be hard men. I think that's a mistake. I think a man needs some gentleness."

"There's no place for gentleness in the world," Caleb had answered.

"Well, there's going to be gentleness in Lafayette."

"Lafayette! What a ridiculous name for a boy!"

"One of my ancestors served with Marquis de Lafayette in the Revolutionary War, and my father had his name."

"Well, you should have named him *Tom*

or *James* or something sensible, but in any case I disagree with you."

"You may disagree all you please, Caleb," Eileen had said firmly, and her gaze had not wavered. "But this son is going to be mine. I'll make all the decisions about his school, his clothes. I'll raise him to be a gentleman. You got our two other sons, and you've made them hard, callous men."

Caleb Riordan had stared at his wife. "You think I'm callous?"

"Of course I do! If you listen to what people said about you, you would know that."

The argument had gone on for some time, but in the end Eileen had insisted on her way. Since that time she had thrown herself into making a different kind of man out of her son Faye, as she called him. She had chosen different friends for him, and she had talked to him from the time he could understand about the necessity for a man to be honest and gentle and not be cruel to anybody.

Caleb was thinking about that, and he wanted to plunge into the argument again, but he had learned that on this one item his wife was not to be reckoned with.

Leo said, "Mother, you're making a weakling out of him! And all this painting of

14

pictures — what good does that do?"

"He's going to be a great painter. He has real talent."

"How many pictures has he sold?" Max asked sardonically. "Not even one."

"He's learning, and his teachers all say he's going to produce great work."

They kept trying to pressure Eileen, until finally Caleb saw that his wife was upset. Despite his rough ways with others, he had a soft and gentle spot for this woman. On this one thing she had displeased him, but otherwise she had been a good wife. He rose from his chair, went over, and pulled her to her feet. He hugged her and said, "We won't argue about this anymore."

"Thank you, Caleb." Eileen looked up at him and touched his cheek, then she turned and left the room.

"You'll never win that argument, Dad," Leo shook his head.

"No, I never will, but I've got two out of three sons that'll make their ways in the world. You two will have to help me with your brother because Faye will never make it. You boys watch out and take care of him."

"Well, I wish he'd hurry up and get home. I'm starved," Max said. He stretched hugely then leaned back into the sofa and closed his eyes.

■ ■ ■ ■

The afternoon sun was fading, but Faye wanted to catch exactly that light in the painting. He had set up his easel with a canvas before him and the paints on the collapsible stool. The scene he was painting was difficult, for the vista in New York at this particular spot stretched out in a way that was hard to catch.

"My, that is pretty! I don't see how you do it."

Faye came to himself and, holding the brush poised over the canvas, turned to see that a very pretty young woman with blond hair and large blue eyes was smiling at him. "Thank you, miss. I hope to catch some of the beauty of that scene."

The young woman said again, "I don't see how you do it. Look how you've mixed all those colors together!"

"Well, I don't do it too well yet."

"Yes, I think you do. How long have you been painting?"

"All my life, it seems."

"My, ain't that a treat!"

Faye glanced over and caught a glimpse of the Riordans' driver, Pat Ryan, a hundred feet away. He was talking to a woman and waving his big hamlike hands in the air as he described something. Quickly Faye turned and said, "Well, I've got to catch this light if you don't mind."

"You mind if I watch?"

"Not at all."

Faye continued to paint the delicate leaves that clung to the trees. They kept just the right shades of green, and the young woman kept up a running commentary.

Suddenly he heard another voice and looked up to see a large, husky man wearing a derby hat. His face was blunt, and he had small eyes. When he grinned, gold flashed on two teeth in his mouth. His clothes didn't seem to fit him, for his arms filled the fabric of the shirt he wore, threatening to tear it. "Well, ain't that a pretty little picture now."

Faye said politely, "Thank you. It's not finished yet."

"That's right sweet, ain't it, girlie?"

"I think it's very nice."

"Well, you don't need to fool around with this sissy painter. Come on with me. We'll have a good time."

"Turn me loose!"

Faye twisted his head and saw that the big man had the woman by her arm and was dragging her along. "Don't do that!" he said quickly. He put down his brush and palette and moved toward the two.

"What are you going to do, beat me up?" The big man grinned. "Go back to your painting, sonny." The big man was squeezing the girl's arm tightly enough to make her cry out.

Faye reached out and pulled at the man's arm. "Don't do that, please. You're hurting her."

"You're going to stop me?"

Faye could not answer. The man was six inches taller than he was and muscular. Muscles from hard work and hands that showed hard usage. The bully was grinning at him, and he could only say, "I'm asking you to let the young woman go, or I'll have to —"

"You'll have to what? Call for a policeman? There ain't none here." Suddenly he threw his meaty hand out and caught Faye in the chest and knocked him backward.

Faye caught his balance, but the big man had released the girl and came at him. Faye took a blow directly to his face and felt the blood suddenly run down his cheek. More blows rained upon him. He could not catch his balance, and finally he fell.

The young woman cried out, "Please, don't!"

The man raised his foot to kick Faye and said, "Don't worry. He needs a lesson."

There was a sound of footsteps just as the man delivered a kick into Faye's unprotected side.

The big man turned to find someone as large as himself coming at him. He got his hands up, but he could not ward off the tremendous blow that caught him in the mouth. He again threw his fists up and tried to defend himself. "Hey, cut it ou . . . ," he tried to yell, but once again a blow struck his mouth. Then suddenly he was struck in the throat. He began to gag. Without warning, Pat Ryan kicked in the side of his knee, and the bully fell to the ground. Pat then delivered a tremendous kick that drove the man's breath out.

"You'll kill him!" the young woman cried.

"Ah, he's too mean to die." Pat Ryan knelt down beside Faye. "You all right, sir?"

Faye could only manage a moan in response.

Ryan picked Faye up as easily as if he were a child and made his way to the carriage.

The young woman followed and said, "Is he going to be all right?"

"I hope so, ma'am." He placed Faye in the backseat, shut the door, and then moved back to retrieve Faye's painting and his

19

easel. He returned and leaped to the driver's seat saying, "Get up! Get up!"

The carriage rocked back and forth as it bounced over the gravel, but Faye Riordan was in too much pain to mind.

The Riordan family had finally sat at the dining table to eat, for Caleb had said, "Well, I'm hungry. Faye can eat when he gets here."

Before anything could be served, Charles Evans, the butler, came running in. He was a tall man, very thin and balding. Now his eyes were open wide. "Sir, it's Mr. Faye. He's hurt!"

The whole family pushed away from the table.

As they got to the front door, the driver was bringing Faye in.

"What happened?" Eileen cried out.

"He got beat up."

"Quick, put him in his bed. Charles, you get Dr. Baxter quick as you can. He's just the second street down."

"Yes, madam. I'll do it right away."

"This way, Pat."

Ryan carried Faye to his room and placed him on his bed.

Eileen was trembling, for Faye's face was battered and he was bleeding freely from a cut on his eyebrow. She took her handkerchief and covered the wound.

"He looks terrible!" Max exclaimed.

"What happened, Ryan?" Caleb demanded.

"Well, sir, he was painting, and I was just wandering around, but I turned and saw this big guy was pounding Mr. Faye and starting to kick him."

"You shouldn't have let him do that."

"I'm sorry, sir. I was too far away. But when I did get to him, I fixed him good." He grinned broadly and nodded. "I busted his front teeth out, I hit him in the throat so he couldn't talk, and then I kicked his legs out from under him and gave him a couple kicks in the side. He was out, whimpering like a baby, when I left."

"I wish you had killed him," Caleb said.

"Well, sir, I couldn't do that. They put a fellow in jail for that, but he won't be fighting much anytime in the future."

"You did a good job." Caleb reached in his pocket and pulled out a roll of bills. He peeled off three or four of them and said, "Here, take this."

"Oh, you don't have to do that, sir."

"No, I want you to have it. Go ahead. If I find this fellow, I'll break his neck!"

"All of you wait outside," Eileen said.

"Faye doesn't need any more trouble."

The three men left reluctantly.

Within ten minutes, Dr. Lucas Baxter entered Faye's room. He was a slender man of fifty with black hair and dark eyes. "What's happened?" he demanded.

"Faye was beaten," Eileen said. "He's in pretty bad shape."

"Let me see." Baxter removed the bloody handkerchief and said, "I'll have to put some stitches here, and he'll have a little scar." He touched Faye, who groaned in response. "Must have hurt his ribs."

"Our driver said the man kicked him."

"Well, if those ribs are broken, it's going to take awhile to heal. But maybe they're just cracked."

He tried to get Faye to swallow something from a brown bottle and waited for a minute. When he saw that Faye was out, he began sewing the wound up. He worked rapidly. "Who did this, Mrs. Riordan?"

"Some man in the park."

"Well, if your husband catches him, he'll kill him."

"No, I don't want that. My husband has made the other boys into what he respects, strong men but hard."

"Well, Faye's not like that."

"No, he's not. I spent my life making a

gentle man out of him. He's going to be a fine painter."

Caleb was waiting with Leo and Max when the doctor came from attending Faye. "How is he, Dr. Baxter?"

"He'll be all right. I think his ribs are cracked, so he'll be moving slowly."

"Thank you, doctor. Charles will show you out." After the doctor left, Caleb turned to his two older sons and said, "Didn't I tell you? He's just a baby! He's got to have somebody to take care of him."

"We can't be with him all the time," Leo said. "You better pay Ryan more money and have him never get far away from him."

"It's a shame a man twenty years old can't take care of himself any better . . . especially *my* son."

Pat Ryan was eating a piece of pie that he had begged from Kate Evans, the cook. She was the wife of Charles, the butler, and was the best cook Ryan had ever known.

Doris Stevens, a very attractive maid, was sitting on a chair beside May Satterfield, the other maid. Both were listening to his story.

He had told them about the fight three days ago with the man who was beating

Faye Riordan and ended by saying, "It's a good thing I was there. I think that bruiser might have killed Mr. Faye."

"Did you hurt him?" Doris asked.

"I put his lights out. When I left, he wasn't talking much. He had lost some teeth, and I cracked him right in the throat and kicked him in the side."

"Oh, Mr. Faye's such a fine-looking young man," Doris said. "Really handsome."

"You been flirting with him, Doris?"

"You bet. I plan to get him to marry me. Then I'll be your boss, both of you."

"He don't pay any attention to women," May said.

"He's a man, ain't he? I'll catch him off guard. Maybe I'll be lucky enough to get caught. He'll have to marry me then, and I'll be a Riordan. I'll be your boss."

"Nah, that won't happen. Mr. Faye, he wouldn't take advantage of a maid," Pat said, shaking his head.

"No, but I might take advantage of him." She laughed and winked merrily. "In fact, I'll bet he could use some refreshment right about now."

Pat shook his head at May as he returned to his pie.

Faye was sitting at the piano running his

fingers over the keys. He turned, holding his side and wincing at the pain from his cracked ribs, when someone entered the room.

It was Doris bringing him a glass of iced tea.

Faye simply said, "Thank you, Doris. You take care of me too well."

"Well, you need someone to take care of you." She reached out and put her hand on his face. "The swelling has all gone down, and you've almost lost that awful-looking black eye you had." She left her hand on his face and said, "I'm so sorry. I wish I could take some of the hurt."

She then leaned against him, pressing her figure against his shoulders. "You need a friend. A lady friend."

At that instant his mother walked in. She took one look and said, "Doris, I think you're wanted in the kitchen."

Eileen waited until Doris left and then came over and looked down at Faye. "How do you feel, son?"

"Oh, I'll live."

She sighed. "You do realize Doris was flirting with you just now."

"Oh no. She just brought me some tea."

Eileen shook her head sadly. "You don't know women."

"I guess not, but she's a nice girl."

"No, she's a flirt. You be careful."

"Well, if you say so, Mother."

"How's the painting going?"

"I haven't felt much like painting. One good thing — I didn't hurt my hands."

"You're going to be a great artist, son."

Faye put his hands out and ran them across the keyboard softly and gently. "I'm letting Dad down, Mother. He and my brothers think I'm a failure . . . and I guess I am. Any one of them could have taken care of himself. I'm just a failure."

"You're *not* a failure! Your father and your brothers have strong muscles, but they don't have any sensitivity or gentleness."

"Well, I wish I could be an artist *and* a tough man."

"Forget being tough. There's a new teacher in town named John Arlington. He's been studying in Europe."

"I've heard of him."

"Well, I've asked him to come and look at your work, and he's agreed."

"Oh, that's good, Mother. Thank you very much. I know I need more help."

"Why don't you go lie down awhile? You look tired."

"Maybe I will." He rose, leaned over, and kissed her cheek, something Leo or Max would never think of doing. "I'll see you at dinner."

Faye went to the second floor and into his room. He liked the room, for the window went from the floor almost to the ceiling, and he could catch the morning light. He had picked his own furniture. The chairs were old, the red and blue turkey coverings were worn to center, but he was happy with it. The pictures on the walls were not expensive, mostly watercolors with a few oils and many sketches.

Faye went at once to his desk and opened it, then pulled out a book and sat down in one of the chairs and began to read. It was a book about the Texas Rangers. He had bought it at a used bookstore and was fascinated by the stories of the terrible battles with the Indians and the outlaws that the Rangers engaged in. He sat there reading for a time then closed the book and sighed, "Well, I'll never be able to do that."

He left his room and found Pat Ryan outside cleaning up the barouche. "Pat," he said, "how'd you learn to fight?"

"Why, Mr. Faye, I always knew how to fight. In my neighborhood, you had to fight."

"You think you could teach me to fight? Could I learn?"

27

"I don't think you need to. How much you weigh, Mr. Faye?"

"About a hundred and eighty-five pounds, I think."

"A hundred and eighty-five? Well, it don't show. That's big enough, but a man has to be quick." He held up his hand, palm out, and said, "Try to hit my hand. I'll try to make you miss."

To Pat's obvious shock, Faye hit him on the hand before he could even move.

"You are fast!" he said. "Try it again."

Again and again Pat held up his hand but never dodged a blow. He said, "You're the quickest man I ever saw with his fists. Hold your hand up and see if I can hit it."

But the result was the same. Pat was faster than some fighters, but he never could hit Faye's hand.

"Well, you've got quick hands, but there's this, Mr. Faye: In a fight you're going to get hurt. If somebody hits you, you just have to grin and act like it don't hurt. Some men just quit."

"Could you give me lessons on fighting, Pat?"

"No, sir! Why, your good mother would have me out on the street quick as a wink! Fighting is a hard world. You stick with your painting. I'll do your fighting, Mr. Faye."

28

Faye said, "All right" and left, thinking about how easily he had beaten Pat in the game with the hands. *I bet I could fight if I had some help!*

CHAPTER 2

A feeble light filtered down through the tall windows on the palette that Faye had placed on an easel. Carefully he dabbed his brush on the palette, mixed up two colors that he wanted, and then turned again. He glanced at the display he had, which consisted of a silver pitcher, a plate of purple grapes, and a silvery fish lying on a platter. The platter was on an ivory-colored tablecloth. Carefully he touched the tip of the brush to the canvas and slowly pulled it across the surface. His concentration was intense, but his hand trembled slightly, and he smeared the section of canvas he was working on.

"Blast it!" he shouted. He drew back his arm and threw the brush across the room. It hit the light green wall and left a purplish stain before dropping to the carpet where it left another stain.

For a moment Faye stood there gritting his teeth and staring at the two stains. He was strongly tempted to kick the easel across the room to join the brush and make an even bigger mess. He forced himself to breathe slowly, and gradually the impatience and anger, which were such a rare thing to him, began to fade away. He stared at the canvas for a long moment then picked it up by the edges, walked across the room, and stacked it against several other half-finished paintings of the same still life.

His face was distorted, which was unusual for him. Usually his expression was pleasant, and some insisted that he had a baby face, an epithet that he despised. He always admired his brothers and his father who had stern, tanned features. Indeed his own was as innocent as a cherub. His lips twisted in a disgusted expression. *I might as well give it up! Can't do anything right!*

Taking a deep breath, he shook his head with disgust then wheeled and stomped noisily across the room, threw himself into a horsehide-covered chair, and glared out the window. Raindrops were running down the glass. Ordinarily he would have found this interesting, as he did all aspects of weather, but he was so upset at his own failure that he did not notice.

"What's the matter with me?" he muttered aloud. "I can't even paint a FOR RENT sign and do a decent job of it!" He closed his eyes then leaned back, resting his head on the rough leather. The sound of the rain falling on the roof and on the outside windows made a sibilant whisper that ordinarily would have soothed his nerves, but he could not force himself into a good mood.

He had heard of writers having times when they just couldn't write, and they called those periods "writer's block." Faye had never believed for a moment that such a thing existed. In an argument once with a writer, he had exclaimed, "Writer's block? Nonsense! You never heard of a carpenter having carpenter's block, did you? Of course you haven't! When a carpenter has a job to do, he just *does* it! And you never heard of dishwasher's block, have you? If a woman has dishes to wash, she just plunges in and washes the blamed things!"

With an abrupt motion, Faye rose and walked to the window. For a moment he stood watching the raindrops run down. He was fascinated by unusual things, and he watched as two drops that were at least a foot apart at the top of the window began their journey downward. They darted to the right and to the left, and then suddenly both of them moved toward each other. They joined and made one drop. For a moment

Faye forgot his agitation and thought, *Just like a marriage. These two drops went hither and yon. Finally they found each other and came together. Now that's the kind of romance I'd like to have!*

A lightning bolt scraped its way across the darkness of a cloud and reached down and touched earth. He waited and counted the seconds, for he had heard you could tell how far away the bolt hit by counting the seconds between a flash of lightning and the resulting thunder. He counted, "One, two, three," and then he heard the rumbling. *A little closer than a mile away.*

He leaned forward, put his head against the glass, and closed his eyes. *Maybe there is such a thing as painter's block.* The thought disturbed him, for he had always been able to do any task he put his mind to as far as painting or other intellectual subjects were concerned. Even as a small boy he had been able to stick with the books that his mother provided, even when they were difficult. He had begun with crayons and graduated to charcoal and then finally paints and oils. His willingness to stick with a job, he understood, was due to his mother's careful teaching, for she had lovingly and patiently curbed his natural instinct to quit when a thing got difficult.

A sudden blinding bolt of lightning startled him, and he opened his eyes and watched as an ominous black cloud blotted out most of the sky. The woods that stretched out to the west of the house were suddenly lost in a deluge. The rain fell in fat drops making slanting lines. His painter's eye noted that, and he resolved that the next time he painted a scene having rain he would be sure that the drops were slanted, not straight down. Usually he rather liked storms, finding them a dynamic setting, but as another fork of crooked lightning clawed the earth, he suddenly realized that he was late for his lesson with John Arlington.

"What am I thinking about?" he muttered. Whirling, he grabbed his raincoat, jammed on a wide-brimmed hat, and left his room at a run. He slammed the outside door and dashed into the carriage house where he found Pat sitting down and eating a sandwich. "Pat, I've got to get to the ferry!" he exclaimed.

"Why, Mr. Faye," Ryan protested, "you can't go out in this weather. You'll drown."

"No, I must go. I'm late for a lesson. Now get the carriage ready and take me to Port Jefferson."

The burly Irishman started to protest, but seeing the stubborn expression on Faye's

lips, he shrugged, saying, "All right, sir . . .
but it ain't a good idea."

The Riordan estate was located in the
eastern part of Long Island. It was a wooded
section where rich people built their man-
sions tucked away in deep woods. It was
not too far from downtown New York City
to make the journey daily, but the setting
bore the illusion of deep woods such as was
found in the secluded parts of upper New
York State.

By the time Ryan had pulled the carriage
to an abrupt halt at the wharf where the
ferry that carried passengers across Long
Island Sound was docked, the rain was falling unchecked in what looked like solid
sheets. Faye leaped out of the carriage, calling back, "Thanks, Ryan," and reached the
gangplank just as it was beginning to draw
up.

One of the crew, a tall man wearing a
black slicker and matching hat, grinned.
"You just made it, sir."

"Thought I'd have to swim," Faye answered. He stepped onto the deck and
moved under the wide canopy that offered
shelter from the sun . . . when there was
sun. He felt the ferry shudder as the engine
took hold. The paddles began to turn, and

the huge ferry swung wide and then moved forward into the downpour. Usually Faye went inside to take shelter from the heat of the sun, but he liked the rain, and he stood watching as an occasional bolt of silver lighting illuminated the dark waters.

"You must love storms." Startled by a voice that came so unexpectedly, Faye turned to see a woman standing there smiling at him. She had a heart-shaped face and an expressive mouth that was now turned upward at the corners in a smile. Her long brown hair was exposed. She had pulled off her hat, and her hair was now turned lank by the rain. She had the most brilliant and the most beautifully shaped eyes Faye had ever seen.

"I guess so," he muttered. "I've never been scared of them for some reason. My mother found me outside once when I was only four, I think, in the middle of a terrible thunderstorm. It gave her quite a scare."

"I like storms, too." The woman's voice was deeper than most women's and had a throaty quality that somehow hinted at a passionate nature, at least so it seemed to Faye. "I'm scared of snakes and spiders but never of the weather."

"Your home is here?"

"One of them. I travel a lot. My father

and I have learned that any place we set our suitcase down is home."

"That must be interesting. You travel abroad?"

"Oh, yes. My father is an explorer, and he writes books about exotic lands. I go along to take care of him and help him when I can."

"That sounds exciting. Have you ever been to Africa?"

"Yes, as a matter of fact we just got back from there two weeks ago. We spent six months with the Maasai tribe."

"Savages, I suppose?"

"Yes, but they are such a fascinating tribe. Most of them are over six feet tall and lean. They hunt lions with spears, and they have a dance in which the men leap up into the air in a standing position. Some of them, I think, can leap as tall as their height."

"I never travel," Faye said. "I envy you. Oh, my name is Faye Riordan."

"I'm Marlene Jenson." She put her hand out as a man would do.

When Faye took it he felt the strength of her grasp. "So, you are living here now?"

"Yes, our home is in Manorville." She gave him a penetrating look. "You take the ferry often?"

"Fairly often. I'm taking lessons in Fairfield, just across the Sound."

"What sort of lessons?"

"Oh, painting lessons." Somehow taking painting lessons sounded like a rather frail thing for a man to indulge in next to a woman who had traveled among six-foot savages in the Congo.

"Well, I wanted to paint," she remarked, "but it didn't take long to find out that I didn't have the talent for it. What do you do, oils or watercolors?"

For the next ten minutes Faye answered rapid-fire questions from Marlene Jenson. She was relentless, and her interest was almost palpable. Finally she laughed, saying, "You'll have to excuse me, Mr. Riordan. Aside from accompanying my father, I'm a writer. When I find a subject, I just can't seem to let go of it. I think I would have made a pretty good prosecuting attorney putting witnesses on the spot."

"I'm sure you would." He hesitated then said, "Painting is pretty tame after your adventures in Africa."

The two were so engrossed in their conversation for the next few moments that a blast of the whistle from the top deck startled them.

"Almost to the dock," Faye said. He tried to think of some way to ask the young woman to allow him to call, but he had had almost no experience in such things. *She'd be bored to death listening to me talk about dabbling around painting pictures!*

Suddenly Marlene, who had been looking out at the waters, cried out, "Girl, don't do that!"

Faye turned quickly to see a very young girl, no more than six it seemed. She had climbed up on the protective rail that outlined the deck of the ferry. To his horror he saw her suddenly miss a step and tumble with a scream out of sight.

Faye, without thinking, started forward, shucked out of his raincoat, kicked his shoes off, and made a running dive over the side railing into the dark waters.

Marlene couldn't believe what Faye Riordan had just done. She began to cry out, "Man overboard! Man overboard!"

She heard a sailor yelling loudly, "Cut the engines!"

The engines stopped, and Marlene ran at once to the railing. It was night, and the waters were dark as a coal pit in a coal mine it seemed to her.

The deck was alive with sailors shouting, "Man overboard!" Some had lanterns, but they made little difference in the darkness of the night.

The waters were ebony, and Marlene cried out, "Where are you?" knowing that it was useless but unable to stop herself.

The ferry stopped. The captain ordered two boats put down, and sailors tumbled into them and were lowered to the waters. They started circling the ferry, but the current at this point was very swift. One of the sailors came over and said, "I seen him go over, miss. The bravest man I've ever seen!"

Marlene nodded but asked, "How will we ever find him?"

"What I'm afraid of, miss, is that they may have been pulled into the paddles. I seen that happen once on the Mississippi. I hope it didn't get these two."

It seemed like an eternity to Marlene, but finally she saw something below moving. She strained her eyes and cried out, "There! Below! There they are!"

One of the boats was close, the men straining against the oars. Marlene watched as they pulled two bodies from the water and then pulled in close to a railing. One of the sailors came on board carrying the child, who was now crying and choking. She saw Faye get up and stagger, and one of the sailors helped him up.

Marlene could not speak for a moment,

but her eyes were brilliant. She finally said to Faye, "You're coming home with me. You'll freeze in those wet clothes."

"Oh, I don't think that's necessary."

Marlene was insistent, and when the ferry docked, she pulled him off the boat, hailed a carriage, and gave the address of her home.

Faye was shaking and shivering.

She pulled him close to give him some body warmth. "We'll get you thawed out when I get you home, Faye," she whispered.

The room Faye entered with Marlene was obviously a rich man's toy. He was still shivering and the soaking wet clothes clung to him, but his eyes went around the room.

Marlene pushed him onto the couch. "You've got to get out of those wet clothes."

Startled, he stared at her. "I can't do that."

"Here. Take them off. I won't look. Don't be so modest."

Faye had never undressed in the presence of anyone, especially a beautiful young woman, but she turned her back and demanded, "Hurry up! I'll get the fire started." She kept her back to him, and quickly Faye took off his wet clothes, including his shoes and socks. Quickly he wrapped the blanket around him, which brought a welcomed warmth.

While she lit the fire in the fireplace, he glanced at the room. A George II barrister desk and matching bookshelves filled one wall. An ornate marble fireplace, where she was making the fire, was opposite with two small velvet settees facing each other across a low teak table. Along the wall, by the door, was a massive bookcase with glass-covered shelves. Several trophy heads from Africa were on the wall, including a cape buffalo that stared at Faye with glassy eyes . . . almost malevolently, it seemed. A tiger with its fangs bared watched him from another wall.

"Here. Drink this."

"What is it?"

"Never mind. It'll warm you up."

Faye took the glass that she had given him, took a swallow, and coughed.

She insisted, "Drink it all."

He drank it down, and the fiery liquid seemed to burn all the way. "That ought to warm me up."

"It should. It's ten-year-old brandy. Are you getting warmer?"

"Yes, thanks a lot."

"Well, let me hang your clothes over something." She grabbed up his wet clothes, arranged some chairs before the fire, and then came back and sat down beside him. He shivered a little, and she reached out and pushed his wet hair off of his forehead. She left her hand on his cheek and said, "Faye, I've seen men, and women, too, do some pretty brave things, but I've never seen anything more courageous than what you just did."

"Oh, swimming is about my only physical achievement."

"It wasn't just swimming. To go over in that dark water with that paddle wheel threatening to cut you in two . . . did you think about it at all?"

"Never gave it a thought. If I had, I'd never have gone."

"How did you find that girl?"

Faye thought for a moment, wiped his face with his hand, and then said, "Well, as soon as I hit the water, of course, everything was just like being in a black box with no windows. So I just began swimming around feeling with my hands. I heard the paddles churning near, but I knew the child was somewhere. Then I touched something. It was her dress. I grabbed at it, caught her, and pulled her up, but the ship had gone on by us. She was scared, and I had to hold her head up. I couldn't make much progress. It's a good thing the ship stopped and they sent those boats."

She took the glass from his hand and then took one of his hands in both of hers. "You deserve a medal for that."

"Oh no, not really."

She sat beside him, eliciting every fact about the rescue. Finally she laughed and said, "You know what I'm doing, don't you? I'm going to put this in a story. It may be in the *New York Times* tomorrow with your name and all. You'll be a hero."

"Oh, don't do that, Miss Marlene."

"A modest hero!" Her eyes arched upward, and she squeezed his hand. "That is rare."

They talked for a while until his clothes dried, and he drank several more swallows of the potion. As a matter of fact, by the time she had turned her back and he had struggled into his clothes, he was more than half drunk. He never drank alcohol other than one glass of wine with a meal. Now he felt warm and slightly dizzy.

When he stood up to leave, she put her arms around him and said, "I'll never forget what you did, Faye, never!" She lifted her face, and even a shy man such as Faye Riordan could not resist lowering his head. Her lips were soft and yielding yet firm.

Faye felt something rashly stirring between

the two of them and knew he was out of his depth with this woman. As he held her, it was as if something old and something new had come into him. There was a wild sweetness here and a shock that was completely outside his years of experience. He was also startled to feel the desperate hunger of her lips, which caused a hunger of his own to meet it. He felt himself losing control and suddenly drew his head back. "I–I'd better get back. I'll miss the ferry."

Marlene stared at him, her eyes wide. Then she began to laugh. "Well, I found a bashful hero. I didn't think there was a man in America who could walk away from me at a time like this."

"Would you — would you come and visit me, and I could show you some of my paintings?"

"Of course I will. When shall I come?"

"Would day after tomorrow be too soon?"

"Not at all." She walked to the door with him and hailed a carriage. When he got in, she said, "Dream about me, Faye."

He smiled, and as the carriage lurched off, he thought, *Maybe I'm a better man than I've always thought!*

Marlene came right on the hour, and Pat Ryan met the carriage and handed her down. She started up the steps and was greeted at once by Faye.

He smiled nervously. "I wasn't sure you'd come."

"You must think I'm a fickle woman. I told you I'd be here."

"Come in. I want you to meet my family."

Faye had not prepared Marlene for the rest of his family. He introduced her to them, and Marlene saw at once that Faye was more his mother's son than his father's.

Eileen Riordan was a beautiful woman with auburn hair and light blue eyes. She came forward and said, "It's so good to meet you, Miss Jenson."

"And a pleasure to meet you. Faye's already told me much about you."

Marlene turned to Caleb Riordan and had to look up to him.

He was much larger than Faye, a strongly built man. He smiled and said, "I couldn't believe what you wrote in the paper about my son."

"It's all true," Marlene said. "As a matter of fact, I could have been even more dramatic."

She turned to greet Max and Leo, carbon copies of their father, she noticed, and then the group went in to dinner. It was an ornate dining room, and the meal itself was ornate. Marlene was perfectly at home.

The Riordans were fascinated by her career and plied her with questions, which she answered graciously.

Max was staring at her and said, "I wish I'd been there to see Faye save that child's life."

"So do I," Caleb said instantly. "I wouldn't have been surprised if Max or Leo had done it."

"Why are you surprised about Faye? He went over the side of that boat in total darkness with paddle wheels churning just like I said. I thought he was a dead man. So did the rest of the crew and passengers on the ferry."

"He won't talk about it." Eileen smiled.

"Well, if I'd done it, I'd be talking about it the rest of my life." Caleb grinned. "I never have done anything that heroic, but I'm proud of you, son."

"Thank you, Dad. Probably the last heroic thing I'll ever do."

"Don't say that, Faye." Sitting next to him, Marlene smiled. She reached over and put her hand on his head. "Once I get my hand on a hero, I make sure he comes through. I'll find you another desperate situation."

Everyone laughed.

After a fine meal and an hour's talk in the parlor, Marlene left.

"That's some woman." Caleb shook his head. "I've never seen anyone quite like her."

"Neither have I," Leo said. "She's been all over the world. Done everything."

Max grinned. "You'd better hang on to her, Faye. With her courage and daring, she'd make you a good wife."

"Don't be silly," Eileen said. "She's rather an outgoing young lady."

Caleb nodded. "Just what Faye needs."

Later Eileen talked to Faye more about the woman, and he said, "Mother, I know this sounds foolish. I've never been in love before, but I think I might be in danger of it."

"I'd be careful, son. She's not a woman that would be easy to live with."

"You mean I'd have to go to Madagascar or some wild place and shoot game?"

"I think her husband would have to be very active."

"You don't think I could do that?"

"You proved you could when you saved that child. When the courage was needed, it was there, but her kind of life wouldn't suit your painting."

That was about as long as the conversation lasted. Faye usually paid much attention to his mother's counsel, but he paid no heed to this. He was thinking about the touch of Marlene's lips as she pressed herself against him, the womanliness of her, and knew that he would see her again.

CHAPTER 3

Sunlight shed its golden beams on the bedroom that Eileen shared with Caleb. She was sitting at a Louis XIV dressing table facing a large mirror and running a brush through her abundant auburn hair.

Most of the house had been influenced by Caleb's taste, which consisted of massive, strong furniture and rather outlandish colors. But the bedroom had been designed specifically by Eileen, and she had had her way. Silks, satins, bonnets, and shoes were arranged in a large cabinet on her left, and the ribbons, laces, velvets, swags, tassels, ruffles, curlicues, fringes, and brocades dominated the rest of the room. Sometimes she felt she had overdone the bedroom as a protest against the stark, strong, masculine qualities of most of the rest of the house.

The room was furnished with delicate furniture, including a fainting couch, which Eileen had never used, along one wall. She had thought it rather amusing that anyone would have a fainting couch and had said once to a friend of hers who had just bought one, "It looks to me, Mary, if you were going to faint, you would just fall on the floor. If you have a special couch, it means somehow you have to get across the room, position yourself, and fall gracefully. I think if I faint, I'll just fall over backward. Fainting couches seem rather strange and not at all what a woman needs."

Caleb stood across the room finishing his dressing by slipping into a snuff brown coat, one of his favorites. He liked expensive clothing, but his taste was not the best in the world. Eileen had long ago given up trying to get the idea across to him that clothes should make the wearer look somewhat distinguished.

"What do you think about this affair that Faye is having with that woman, Eileen?"

Looking up quickly, Eileen saw that Caleb was studying her, a small smile on his lips. She recognized that this was the heavy-handed humor of which he was so capable. "I'm not sure it's a good thing," she replied then returned again to brushing her hair.

"Not a good thing?" Caleb exclaimed. He shrugged his heavy shoulders and cocked his head to one side, saying, "Well, she's a

51

wealthy woman. She's got lots of spirit about her. I like that. Maybe some of it will rub off on Faye."

"I don't think so. Faye's not the kind to be influenced by that sort of thing."

"What sort of thing? What do you have against her? She's beautiful, and her father is a man after my own heart. Wades out in the jungle and fights snakes, lions, and who knows what."

"I'm sure he does, dear, and I'm sure that the woman has courage to accompany him on those safaris and journeys into dangerous places, but I don't think she's a woman that Faye could be happy with."

He came over and stood behind her and ran his heavy hand down her hair. "You know your hair is as beautiful today as it was the day I married you."

The remark was so out of keeping with Caleb's usual speeches that Eileen blinked. She felt tears come into her eyes, for she did not receive many of these compliments from Caleb. "Thank you, dear," she said. "But as far as Marlene Jenson, she's not a Christian woman."

"How do you know that?"

"Why, I asked her. She didn't make any bones about it."

"Well, she may not be a Christian, but

she's dynamic and attractive and has money."

Putting down her brush, Eileen rose and turned to face Caleb. She did not have many arguments with him, for although he never abused her in any way, his personality was so forceful that she was usually intimidated by him. "She's an immoral woman, Caleb. Don't you know that?"

"Well, I have heard that she's had affairs."

"She doesn't make any attempt to cover up her past. And another thing that troubles me . . . she thinks Faye's painting is just a hobby. That he needs real work."

Caleb blinked with surprise. "Well, that's exactly what I've always said, but you've never agreed with that."

"No, I haven't, Caleb."

"But you must see a man can't spend his life dabbing paint on canvas. He needs to step out, to take chances."

"That's the way your life has been, and Max and Leo are the same, and there is a need for men like that."

"I should say so, and I've never ceased being amazed that you don't see that Faye needs some of this in his makeup. You've made him into a helpless man, Eileen, but it's not too late. This woman might change him. He could go on some of those trips with her and her father. It'd be a chance to do something great."

Eileen sighed knowing that such conversation was pointless. She and Caleb had been going over this in one form or another for most of the twenty years of Faye's life. She shook her head and said, "We've been over this again and again, Caleb. I'm not going to change. I see that Faye's got a chance to do something . . . not heroic, perhaps, but that will bring beauty into the world. He can give pleasure to people."

"You make him sound like an actor or an acrobat," Caleb protested. "A man needs to fight in this world."

"I don't think we'll ever agree, but I'm proud of Faye just as you are proud of Max and Leo. Come. Let's go down to breakfast and not talk about this anymore."

The gallery was crowded, and Faye took Marlene's arm as they threaded their way through the mass of people that had come. The walls were full of art for sale. Faye was amused by some of Marlene's comments. They had stopped before a large painting that looked simply like the artist had stood six feet away and thrown small containers of brilliant-colored paint at the canvas and let it run down.

She turned to him and said, "Do you call that art, Faye? It just looks like a mess to me."

"It is a mess. You'll find this kind of phony art just as you'll find it in some books. They are phony books. They don't do anything. You can train a chimpanzee to throw paint at a canvas, I suppose, but it wouldn't be art."

"Well, I'm glad you think so. Let's find something we do like."

They moved along through the gallery, Marlene firing questions at Faye, and he tried his best to give his theory of art. "You see, Marlene," he said as they stood before a well-done painting of a fox hunt, "this painting doesn't speak to everybody, but to wealthy people who believe, especially the English, it captured a slice of their lives. They could look at it when they got old, too old to ride, and remember it, and it would be a warm memory for them."

"I can see that, but you don't paint fox hunts."

"I may. I've painted stranger things."

"Like what?"

"Come along. I'll show you." He led her through the crowd, and they came to stand before a series of paintings.

Marlene opened her eyes widely. "This is

55

certainly different." The paintings were real-life representations of the poor sections of New York City. Marlene stared at one of the pictures, which was nothing more than a ragged young boy, obviously from the poorest section of society.

"Why would an artist want to paint that boy?" Marlene asked. "I don't see the point in it."

"Just look at him."

She looked at the painting more clearly and saw that the young, ragged boy had a broad hilarious grin.

"Don't you see the love of life twinkling in his eyes?" Faye asked, staring at the picture intently. "He's poor, probably hungry, has been abused, and doesn't have much of a future, but he has the joy of life about him. I think people need to see things like that."

The two talked for a time about the picture and then moved on to others. In each case, in this particular group, the artist had chosen the poorest strata in American life, the sweatshops of New York. Faye and Marlene studied them, and finally they stopped before a painting of three women on a roof drying their hair.

Faye remarked, "I heard that President Roosevelt admired this painting, but he didn't buy it."

"I can see why. You can go on the rooftop of half of the tenement buildings in this city and see something just like it. It's awful. Why emphasize it?"

"It's a part of life, Marlene," Faye said. There was a gentleness and a sorrow in his voice that obviously caught her attention.

"You really feel sorry for these people, don't you?"

"Of course. Don't you?"

Marlene was uncomfortable. She had grown up in the midst of plenty, with everything she might need that money could buy, and had never really given much attention to the poorer people. They were there to serve her and were somehow in another world. "To be truthful, Faye, I've lived in a different sort of environment. I've never been around the poor, but I'm going to learn something."

"What do you mean, Marlene?"

"There's been a man who has been taking photographs of the poorer sections of the city just like these you see in the paintings. He's starting a campaign to have the politicians pass legislation to help these poor people. As a matter of fact, I'd like for you to go with me to those neighborhoods."

"We can go, but you'd better not wear

those diamonds, and you'd better get a less flamboyant dress. You won't get the right reactions dressed like the Queen of Sheba."

"I will. We'll go today."

They arrived on Hester Street, one of the poorer sections of New York City, late in the afternoon. True to her word, Marlene had dressed modestly in the oldest dress she had and was not wearing any jewelry, and Faye had changed into some clothes he wore around the house when working, so they did not particularly stand out.

They stayed until the shadows were growing dark, talking to many of the residents of the neighborhood, but on their way out of the area, they were caught in what amounted to a miniature riot. Men, and some women, too, were fighting and screaming, some of them carrying clubs. Their enemy seemed to be the police and men from the upper reaches.

"We've got to get out of here, Faye."

"Yes, this is getting grim."

They started out but were caught when a man in ragged clothes carrying a short club suddenly appeared before them. He was swinging the club at anyone who moved, and the club grazed Marlene's arm. She cried out, and Faye threw himself at the man, shoving him backward. He was immediately attacked by some of the others. Frantically he fought to free himself, grabbed Marlene, and the two managed to get out.

Faye hung his head, shaking it back and forth. "I wasn't much good at keeping you safe, Marlene."

"It's not your game, Faye. Your brothers would have broken half a dozen heads, I suppose, and your father, too."

"I wish it were my game."

They did not speak again until they were clear of the crowd and had gotten into a carriage.

Marlene turned to him, took one of his hands in both of hers, and said, "We are what we are, Faye. We can't change the really important things."

It was a tender moment, and he saw a gentleness in her eyes that was not always there. Faye had never been good with words, especially with young women. He'd had no real experience. His closest approach had been in reading a few romance novels. He knew that sort of talk would not work, but he cleared his throat and said, "Marlene, I don't know how to say this. I'm not good with words at a time like this." He halted and saw she had turned to face him and was examining him with a strange stare, almost clinical. This discouraged him, but he went on and said, "I feel something for you, Marlene, that I've never felt for any other woman."

Marlene said, "I'm sure you do, but you've never had a sweetheart."

"No, I haven't, but a man doesn't have to sort through half a dozen women and go through all sorts of the games that couples play, does he?"

"That's what most couples do, and they seem to enjoy it."

"Well, I can't do that, but I tell you right now I care for you."

A thoughtful expression washed across Marlene's face. She was silent and looked down at his hands for a long time. When she lifted her eyes and met his, there was compassion on her face, and she said quietly, "Here's the truth, Faye, so listen carefully. I could have seduced you. It would have been easy. You're so innocent any woman could have done it."

Faye was shocked. "Why didn't you?"

Marlene hesitated, then a serious look came into her expression. "I don't know why. I've done it before, but I see something in you that I don't want to spoil. I'm reminded of a section of forest I once saw in the Congo. It was beautiful . . . a rain forest. I came back later, and the timber people had cut it all down. Nothing but ugly stumps and branches. The beauty was all gone. It's something like that that I feel for you. I don't want to see you spoiled, Faye. I didn't know I had any tender spots in me. I certainly haven't proved it, but I seem to have one for you."

Faye listened quietly and did not know how to reply. Finally he said, "All that may be true, but I still care for you, Marlene."

She shook her head but said no more. When she got out of the carriage at her house, he stood beside her for a moment. She leaned forward and kissed him on the cheek. She then said, "Faye, you're nothing but a baby in things like this. And the sad thing is, I've had too much experience. Try to forget about me. I wouldn't be good for you at all. I'd spoil you as those timber men spoiled that forest."

Faye watched as she turned quickly and entered the front door. He turned and got back into the carriage, feeling somehow saddened but convinced that he would not give up. *She can come to care for me,* he thought. *I can make her do that!*

Nearly a week and a half had passed since

61

Faye had told Marlene that he cared for her. They had gone out several times, but there had been no more moments like that one. She smiled and laughed a lot. They enjoyed being together.

It was a strange delight to him to see how her mind worked. So different from his own! She was bright, intelligent, certainly physically beautiful, and he had fallen in love with her.

That morning Marlene had said, "I want us to go riding out at Central Park. It's new. We can rent some horses."

Instantly Faye felt a sudden jolt. "I–I'm not too good with horses."

"You don't have to be good. We're not going to be riding bucking horses. You know how you liked those pictures you showed me by those two men who painted pictures of the Wild West? How beautifully they brought that world to you?"

"Yes, Fredrick Remington and a man called Russell. That's what they do. They show the West as it really is, I think."

"Well, there was one with a bucking horse, and a man was on it. He was hanging on for dear life. The dust was in the air, and men were on a corral fence yelling at him and waving their hats."

"I could never do a thing like that!"

Marlene laughed and said, "Well, we won't be putting you on a wild horse. The horses they rent are fairly gentle, designed for folks who are not bareback riders in the circus."

Against his will, Faye accompanied Marlene.

When they arrived at the stables, a tall man came and smiled at them, asking, "Could I be of help?"

Marlene spoke up, "We need two mounts, sir."

"Of course. Any particular kind of animal you like?"

"Well, I like sort of a lively ride. As a matter of fact, neither of us wants to ride on horses that pull milk wagons."

The tall man grinned. "I know. That isn't much fun. Wait here. I'll bring them out."

When he had gone, Faye said, "I wish you hadn't told him that, Marlene."

"Told him what?"

"That we wanted lively horses. I've never told anybody this, but I've always been afraid of large animals."

"You mean large dogs?"

"No, I mean larger animals like horses or bulls."

"Oh, you'll do fine."

Marlene's confidence in him did not rub

off on Faye. He was feeling more and more nervous, and by the time two stable hands had brought out two saddled horses, he was ready to leave but knew that he couldn't.

"This one's for you, ma'am. A fine mare. A little bit hard to handle, but you can do it."

He handed her up.

Marlene looked back to where Faye was staring at the horse.

"He's so big."

"Well, he's a stallion," the stable hand grinned. "One thing, sir. Don't let him get the bit in his teeth."

"What — what does that mean?"

The stable hand looked up and saw that Marlene was smiling, and he winked at her. "Well, sir, as long you keep the bit pulled back where he can't get his teeth in it, he can't pull the lines out of your hands. But if you ever let up and he grabs that bit, he'll pull the lines right free and you'll have no control. Just keep a tight rein."

Faye started to get on, but the stable hand said quickly, "Not that side, sir. Mount from the left."

"It doesn't make any difference to me."

"It does to the horse, sir. Here. I'll hold his head."

Faye put his left foot in the stirrup,

grabbed the horn, and hauled himself awkwardly aboard. He looked down and thought that the ground seemed very far away.

"That's fine, sir. Just remember to keep a tight line."

Awkwardly Faye took the reins and held them tightly as the man had suggested.

"Come along. We'll start out at a walk." Marlene smiled. "These are really fine mounts. You'll like that stallion."

The two started out, and the stallion under Faye was placid enough. They kept at a walk until Marlene, always impatient, said, "Let's try just a little faster. Not a dead run. Just sort of a trot."

"If you say so." Faye was keeping his mind on the admonition of the stable hand — keep the reins tight. The horse fell into a broken rhythm that jarred him up and down. He glanced over to see that Marlene was smiling and enjoying the faster pace.

Finally she said, "Well, a gallop is easier than a trot. Let's go." She kicked her horse with her heels, spoke to her, and the mare started out in an easy gallop.

Faye tried to imitate her but somehow got confused. He released the grip on the reins for a moment and immediately felt something different. The reins were suddenly yanked from his hands, and all he could do was hang on. The horse was running at full speed, and he heard Marlene calling, but he could not tell what she said. The stallion was a powerful animal and ran at breakneck speed. The fear that Faye had always had of horses now had come alive. He wanted to cry out, but all he could do was hang on.

Perhaps under other circumstances the stallion would have tired, but at one point in the bridle path a thick branch hung down rather low. Faye never saw it, but he struck his head against it. It knocked him backward, and fortunately his feet were free from the stirrups already. He hit the ground flat on his back with a force that knocked all of his breath out of him. He lay there trying to breathe and felt that his head was bleeding.

Suddenly Marlene was there. She sat down beside him, raised him up, and pulled his head against her breast. "I'm so sorry, Faye. That never should have happened. Are you all right?"

It took a few moments for Faye to get his breath. Finally he said, "I'm — okay." He lay there pressed against the softness of the woman and said, "Marlene, I want to marry you." It had not been the kind of proposal he had dreamed of, but it was a tender moment, and she was holding him so close that it just came out.

Marlene leaned down, kissed his forehead, and pulled a handkerchief out. "You've got a little cut here. Let me wipe the blood away."

"Didn't you hear me, Marlene? I want to marry you."

She did not answer for a moment. Then she said, "I shouldn't have let you into my life, Faye. I knew all the time we would never be able to have any kind of relationship. I've had men hurt me, and I've left my claw marks on a few, but as I said before, some woman may let you down and hurt you badly — but it won't be me."

He lifted his head.

She kissed him on the lips and said tenderly, "I want the memory of one good man who loved me that I didn't hurt to hang on to."

No more was said.

She got him to his feet, and they walked back to the stable. When they got into the carriage, she said nothing even though he tried to speak to her. When she got out, he started to get out of the carriage with her, but she said, "No, stay here." She reached out and put her hand on his cheek, and he noticed a gentleness and softness in her eyes that he had never seen before. "I'd ruin you if we married as I've ruined other men. You don't understand, Faye. I'm not a good woman. There's evil in me, but I found that I have at least one tender spot, and that's for you. But you must forget me. Good-bye, Faye." She turned and hurried into her home.

Faye was despondent. All the way home he tried to think, but he could not. All his insecurities came flooding back. *Max could have won her, or Leo, but I didn't have the guts. I never will have.* He slumped in his seat.

When he arrived home, he entered by the side entrance and went up to his room, shut the door, and sat there until the darkness fell. But the darkness was not only a lack of sunlight but a darkness in his own soul.

CHAPTER 4

The sitting room of the Riordan mansion was a stately large room with three tall windows and a ceiling gracefully molded with garlands of flowers and flambeaux. The curtains were heavy plush, a hot crimson with thick gold fringes and ropes, which Caleb liked immensely and Eileen disliked with equal fervor. Every foot of space was crammed thick with furniture — tables incongruously jostling a mahogany chiffonier, heavy tables crowded with ornaments, Sheraton bureaus, Chinese vases, and alabaster lamps. In short it was a room filled with Victorian junk.

At least that was Eileen's idea, but Caleb had enjoyed bringing home items that he thought might please her, and she felt it necessary to show some appreciation. It was a room without taste or moderation but a part of Eileen's life with Caleb.

Caleb and Eileen had led the way to the

sitting room with Max and Leo following. They all found seats in overstuffed furniture. Almost at once Caleb said, "I can't understand Faye's behavior."

"I can't either, Dad," Max said. "It's like he's a walking dead man."

Leo lit a cigar and sent purple clouds toward the ceiling. "It's that woman. She done him in somehow or other."

"I thought he was doing so well with his courtship." Caleb sighed. "He just doesn't have it in him to finish anything."

Indeed, although Eileen did not join the conversation, she was more aware than her husband or her sons of how different Faye's behavior had become since his separation from Marlene Jenson. She had noticed it almost at once, for the first sign of danger was that he, who had always been so eager, seemed to have lost his taste for painting. Whole days went by when he would not touch a brush, and when she had suggested he might try a new subject, he had merely shrugged and said, "Perhaps you're right, Mother."

He had not done so, however, and had spent his days in his room reading. He took his meals with the family, of course, but he had almost nothing to say. When his brothers or his father mentioned Marlene, he

70

simply said, "That's all over," which closed the door finally and abruptly in a manner not often seen in Faye Riordan.

One day when Faye had been walking for long hours on the property, he got back to his room and found a periodical — and the picture on the front leaped out. It was Marlene with a famous stage actor. She was looking up at him with what appeared to be adoration. His arm was around her, and he was looking down. Even the coldness of print could not conceal the fiery ardor that the two seemed to feel.

From time to time throughout the day, Faye would decide to throw the article in the wastebasket, but each time he would go back and take it out. That night at supper he was almost mute, and he went up to his room as soon as the meal was over. He was aware that his family was puzzled by his behavior, and he himself could not explain it. When he got to his room, he began to read some of the books he had begun to collect. One writer that he had read almost ceaselessly was James Fenimore Cooper, whose books reflected the sort of vigorous heroism that Americans liked to read about. His heroes were physically strong, emotionally tough, and were willing to fight to the death to overcome all obstacles. The present book was a novel called *The Deerslayer.* Faye loved reading the adventures of Cooper's famous hero, Natty Bumppo, and he also loved reading about his home state during the frontier days.

It was past one o'clock when Faye finally finished the book. A strange feeling had come over him, and he fondled the book in his hands thinking of the hero. He was still not sleepy, for his whole being was stirred by the heroic adventures of the fictional character. He finally put his head down and held it with his hands. "Why can't I be a man like Bumppo?" he whispered. The answer immediately came back that he did not have Bumppo's physical strength. He also was suddenly aware that he did not have the determination to win even if it killed him.

For what seemed like hours Faye sat in the chair, the book in his hands, his head bowed, his mind swarming with thoughts of Marlene, the failures in his life, how he had been overshadowed by his father and his brothers. A grim despair seemed to grip him, and he threw the book aside, stood, and began to pace around the room. Finally he stopped and found himself gritting his teeth. *I may not be a hero like Natty Bumppo, but I can do something!*

He prepared for bed, but once he lay down he was suddenly possessed by an idea. It came to him as clearly as black print against a white wall. "I can do something!" The idea took root, and he tossed and turned and finally got up, walked to the window, and stared out on the moonlit gardens and grounds of the estate. The idea seemed preposterous, but he was living in a desperate state since he had lost Marlene and could not face a future that only held more of the same.

He went over and picked up the paper and stared at the picture of Marlene and her lover. "I can become a man she would admire." He spoke the words aloud, and the sound of his words seemed to startle him. He fixed his eyes on Marlene's face and the poor reproduction, and the real memory of her came to him. *I can be the kind of man that she would learn to love.*

He moved quickly to his desk and pulled out a sheet of paper and a pen. He began to write, and what he designed was a list of achievements that he would have to conquer in order to be a real hero. He listed the books that spoke of such men then jotted several physical activities. His mind worked rapidly as he thought of what all he would have to achieve. "I can do it!" he said through gritted teeth.

The sun was lighting up the east when he finally put his list aside. He picked up the newspaper, stared grimly at Marlene, and then his eye caught a story he had not noticed. He began to read it. The story concerned Judge Isaac Parker who had been appointed judge in a large territory that included the Indian lands of Oklahoma as well as parts of Arkansas. The story was well written, and Judge Parker's choice of marshals had been outstanding. The marshals were described in vivid detail, all of them hard-bitten men, fearless, expert with a rifle or a side gun, ready to face danger and endure the hardships of the blistering heat and crippling snows as they pursued the criminals. He read that only the marshals were permitted to enter the Indian Territory. One of them was a man called Heck Thomas. Thomas was a family man but had sent his family away because his wife could not bear the stress of knowing that her husband was out facing killers, both red and white, in the Territory. As he read this, Faye put the paper down and thought about the stories he had read of the West. "That's the kind of man I'd like to be. One who could be a federal marshal under Judge Isaac Parker!" he decided.

The next morning Faye got up, dressed, ate a hurried breakfast alone, and went to downtown New York. He made inquiries and found a gym on the east side that he was told produced some of the best pugilists in the state. When he went in he was met by a man who had beetling eyebrows, a beefy red face, and hands the size of hams.

"My name is Kelly, sir. What can I do for you?" the man said.

"My name is Faye Riordan, and I want to learn how to box."

"Oh, do you now? Are you intending on winning the championship?"

"Nothing like that," Faye said. "Just enough to take care of myself."

"Well, if you've got the money, we've got the men who can train you."

"I can pay whatever you ask."

"All right. We got some fighting togs. Come along."

Faye followed the husky man to a dressing room that smelled strongly of smoke and human sweat and other things even more vile. He stripped, and the man watched him carefully. "How much you weigh?" he said.

"About a hundred and eighty-five."

"I wouldn't have taken you for that much. You're all packed in. Come along," he said, seeing that Faye was dressed.

He took him upstairs, and Faye found himself in the middle of rather fervent activity. There were three rings, and in each one two men were battering each other. There was a *rat-tat-tat-tat* from suspended punching bags, and men were punching them with fierce rapidity. Other men were striking at huge punching bags being held by trainers. There were sounds of grunting and cries when men were hit, and some of them were knocked completely down.

"Well, let's see. I'll tell you. It's not strength in this game, Mr. Riordan. It's speed. If a man is fast enough, he don't have to be no Samson. Now look. I'm holding up my hands, you see, and I want you to try and hit one of them."

It was the same game that Faye had played with Pat Ryan. His fist shot out and caught Kelly's big beefy hand with a sharp *splat.*

"Ho! That's the fastest I've seen in a while. Try it again."

It was the same with Kelly as it had been with Pat. If a hand stayed still for one second, Faye's hand shot out and struck it.

"Well now. You're the fastest thing I've seen around these parts. Hold your hands

76

out now and let's see if I can hit yours."

The experiment was the same as it had been with Pat Ryan. The big man simply could not hit Faye's hands.

"Well, that's one part of being a fighter, but there's more to it than that. A man has to be able to take a punch. You're fast enough to miss most of them, but you're going to get hit. That pretty nose of yours is going to get flattened."

"That's all right. Just put me with somebody who can show me."

"Come along. I got just the fellow for you."

Faye followed Kelly to the back section of the room where a man was punching a bag. He had a wealth of curly black hair and an olive complexion — and his hands were very fast.

"Hey Tony, this here is Riordan. He wants to learn how to box. You take him in hand, will you? Don't hurt him now. He don't know nothing."

Tony nodded. "Sure, Mr. Kelly. Come along, Riordan. We'll try a little sparring."

Faye had never sparred with anyone. He had been in only one fight and had lost resoundingly. He put on big padded gloves and watched as Tony did the same.

"We'll just skip around and throw some

light blows. Nothing heavy. Don't try to knock me out."

"All right."

Faye did not know a thing about footwork. He pretty well stood still, and from time to time Tony would throw a punch, which he easily avoided. He learned that when a punch came at his head, his hands were fast enough to reach up and deflect it.

"Say, you've done this before."

"No, I really haven't."

"Well, let's go at it a little bit faster, okay? This time I'm going to throw some harder punches, and you try to hit me, too."

"All right."

The Italian came in and shot a hard left, which caught Faye by surprise. It grazed his head, but immediately he threw out a hard right that caught Tony full on the forehead.

"That's a good counter punch!" Tony exclaimed. "Well, I'm not going to believe you've never had boxing lessons."

"No, I never have."

"Well, you're not going to need a whole lot of them. Come on. Let's just go at it now. I'll have to show you a few things, but you've got the speed and the build to throw a good enough punch to make it. Here we go . . . !"

Faye had been back for three lessons at
Kelly's gym, and on Tony's advice he had
started running. "You've got to build up
stamina. If you ever go up for the championship, you'll have to go fifteen rounds. Just
try sometime walking around for fifteen
three-minute rounds just holding your
hands up not trying to hit. What kind of
exercise you like?"

"I like swimming."

"That's the best! Swim all you can. Run
all you can. You're doing great, Mr.
Riordan."

Faye reduced his visits to the gym to once
a week. Both Tony and Kelly told him he
had it in him to be a professional fighter,
but he had laughed that off. "No, nothing
like that for me. Just to be able to handle
myself, that's all I want." They had both as-
sured him that he could, and he was satisfied.

All the heroes he had read about were
experts with guns of some type. He had
begun learning how to shoot by enlisting
Pat Ryan and buying his own set of equipment for skeet shooting. They had gone out
one day far from the house, and Pat, who

had done this often for his brothers and his father, set up the equipment ready to shoot. "You holler 'Shoot,' and I'll let it go. You try to hit it. Wait a minute." Pat quickly came over and looked at the gun. "That's not a shotgun."

"No, it's a Winchester. I just bought it."

"Why, you can't hit skeet on the move with a rifle. Nobody does that."

"Well, I'm going to try."

"All right. If that's what you want, Mr. Faye."

He went back and Faye called out, "Shoot!" The circular clay pigeon flew through the air. Faye got off one shot, but the pigeon was not harmed.

"You see. I told ya. You wasted your time."

"Let's just keep going. You throw them as fast as I call. Now, shoot!"

He missed again, and for the next half hour he missed consistently. Finally he hit one, and Pat said, "Well, that's an accident."

Faye smiled. "With enough practice you can do anything, Pat."

Indeed, practice he did, until finally he became so adept with the Winchester that he could hit three out of four of the clay pigeons. By then, he knew he could hit anything on the run.

Next he knew he would have to handle a

pistol. He went to a gun shop in the center of the city and looked for quite a while at guns.

The owner's name was Abe Lemmons. He seemed curious. "What will you be doing with the gun, Mr. Riordan?"

"Oh, I just need to handle a gun."

"Well, I tell you what. Most men these days want one of those .44 Colts." He reached into a glass case and said, "Here. Hold that."

"It's pretty heavy."

"Yes, it's heavy, plus your hands are small and that handle's big. Most of these are single action."

"What does that mean?"

"It means when you fire the gun you have to use your thumb to pull the hammer back before you can shoot again. As I say, you've got small hands."

"What do I need, Mr. Lemmons?"

"Well, I'd say a .38 would just about fit your hand. Here. Try this one for size."

Faye took the .38, and it did feel very comfortable. "Yes, I can hold this."

"Well, it has another advantage. It has a double action. You pull the trigger, you can fire again immediately. You don't have to cock it again before each firing."

"But it's a smaller gun than the .44."

81

"That it is, but let me tell you something, sir. A .38 will stop a man as quick as a .44 . . . if you put the bullet between his eyes."

"Well, I'll take this one. You have a belt and a holster?"

"You're going to wear it?"

"Well, when I go into the woods, it'll be a handy way to carry it." This was not what Faye had on his mind, but it was a good enough story for Mr. Lemmons.

"Well yes, of course, we have all kinds of belts." He fitted him with one that would work fine. Faye put it on and slipped the .38 into the holster. It was about even with where his hand was hanging.

"See how quick you can get it out. That's what those big lawmen out west do."

Faye's tremendous speed came to his aid. He pulled the gun and leveled it so quickly that Lemmons batted his eyes and took a step backward.

"Heaven help us! I've never seen a man so fast! Well, you got what you need. I hope you don't ever have to use it."

"So do I. How much?"

For the next two weeks Faye went deep into the woods carrying a leather bag full of .38 bullets. He carried targets and practiced drawing his gun and shooting at them. At first he would miss the whole tree, but he had a quick, steady eye and a steady hand, and soon he was able to at least hit the tree. He improved daily, both with the speed of his draw and accuracy of hitting the target. Finally the day came when he put six bullets into a six-by-six-inch piece of paper from forty feet away. He smiled, pulled the gun up, and said, "Well, I've done that."

The next few days he went to the public library and found all the writings he could about Judge Parker and his court and especially about the marshals that represented the law in Indian Territory. He had made up his mind that this would be a good place for him to be a man, but how to tell his mother he could not imagine. *She's going to have a terrible fit, and she's going to say no, but it's something I've got to do.*

"You want to do what, Faye?"

"I want to prove myself to be more than just a painter."

"Why would you want to do that?"

"I feel like I'm only half a man, Mother."

"You're just measuring yourself against your father and your brothers."

"I'm sure that's true and also against some other people. They're bigger than I am and stronger, but I want to prove to myself that

83

I am a man. That I'll survive."

That was the beginning of the argument. It went on for a week but never in the presence of his father or his brothers. Always the battle took place between Faye and his mother.

As for his mother, she was shocked so greatly she could not even speak for a while. She was completely against the idea.

Finally Faye said, "I'm going away for a few days. Maybe even a month."

"Where are you going?"

"Oh, I've never gone anywhere. I want to wander around and learn to take care of myself. When I come back we'll talk some more about what I want to do."

"Yes, you think it over carefully. It would be the wrong thing, I'm sure."

CHAPTER 5

The next morning Faye left his house before breakfast, leaving his mother to explain his vacation to the family.

He took a train to upper New York State and got out at a small stop where there seemed to be nothing but three or four buildings. The trees were huge, and it was a large enough forest to intimidate him.

He went at once to the livery stable and said, "I want a very tame horse. No bucking broncos."

"Why, I've got just the horse for you, Mr. Riordan. Name is Patsy. She's just as gentle as a mother. She's never thrown a man in her life, I don't think. You're not going to win any races with her, however."

Indeed, Patsy was a gentle horse. She was strong enough and could carry his weight easily. He led Patsy down the street to a general store, and when he left he had bought a frying pan, a saucepan, salt, a knife

85

to hang on his belt, a spoon, and matches. He already had a blanket, some soap, a fishing line, and some hooks. He also took a toothbrush, and the biggest part of his load was feed for Patsy.

That afternoon he loaded Patsy and stepped awkwardly into the saddle. "Well, Patsy, we're going out into the woods, and I'm going to stay there for about a month. The only food I have will be what I shoot with this .38. I'll sleep on the ground, and if I don't learn to hit something with this pistol, I'll live on grass and leaves." He suddenly felt good about the whole thing and slapped her on the neck. "Come on, girl. Let's go make a man out of Lafayette Riordan!"

It was cool but not uncomfortable as Faye walked through the woods. It was two weeks into his experiment, seeing if he could survive, and now he was feeling doubt, for he had not been able to secure much in the way of food. He had learned that squirrels are quicker than a man's hand. Even when he would see one behind a tree, the creature could scoot around on the far side of the tree quicker than Faye could draw a bead on him. Up until this time he had caught two frogs and forced himself to eat them, but the only animal he had killed with his revolver was a porcupine who was a slow-moving beast to say the least. He had almost given up, but he had turned the porcupine upside down and dug out enough meat to at least fight off his hunger pangs.

Suddenly Faye heard what he thought — and hoped — was a flock of geese. Looking up, he could barely see them through the trees. They were in a familiar V-formation and crying their familiar *"K-whonk! K-whonk! K-whonk!"* To his delight, they descended quickly, and although Faye knew little about wild geese, he assumed late in the afternoon they were looking for a place to spend the night. He was fairly sure that they stayed near water.

As he moved forward, he realized that he was famished and beginning to feel a bit weak from hunger. More than once he had been tempted to give up his plan, but he had doggedly stuck with it. Once while out there, he had found a tree with berries on it that he could not identify. Hoping they were not poisonous, he ate them. They had filled his stomach, although they provided little nourishment. The other meal he had supplied himself was one he had never thought to sample. He had been moving through the woods when he heard a rattle. Whirling around he saw a huge snake in a coil, ready to strike. He had pulled his .38 and got off three shots. One of them had hit the snake in the head.

Now as he moved cautiously forward, Faye remembered how he had considered the monstrous snake. He had heard of men eating snakes but had never thought he would be one of them. Hunger had won out. He had cut the head and the rattles off, skinned it, and toasted the white meat on a stick over a fire. To his surprise it had been rather tasty and had filled his stomach at least for a period.

Trying to walk silently as the Indians did in the stories by James Fenimore Cooper proved to be a problem. According to the books, they could walk silently through a forest unless they happened to step on a twig. But now the leaves had fallen. Some of them were crisp and made a crackling sound each time he stepped on them. Taking a deep breath, he started shoving the leaves aside with the toe of his boot so he could step on the bare ground. It was a slow method, but finally he came to what seemed to be a ridge of some sort, about six feet high.

The sound of the geese came to him clearly as they were splashing, and their honking came to him on the afternoon air.

They're right over this rise down in the water.
The thought touched him, and he knew he was still too far away to get an easy shot, but he eased the pistol out of his holster and took a deep breath. *God, don't let me miss.* Faye didn't even realize he was praying, but then in one motion he came to his feet and scrambled to the top of the rise. As he had surmised, a pond fed by a small creek was filled with geese, and as he had also known would happen as soon as he stood up, a warning honk filled the air, evidently a signal. *I'm too far away for a good shot. Wish I had my rifle, but it's too late.*

The large birds rose with a flapping of wings and a hoarse cry. Faye lifted his pistol, tried to aim at one, but when he fired he hit nothing. They were rising rapidly and going farther from his range. He fired again, counting his shots, and despair filled him as he fired his last bullet. He lowered his gun, disgusted. Then he saw one of the geese falling in an awkward fashion. Quickly he shoved the .38 into the holster and ran headlong into the water. He hit the edge of the pond running, his eyes fixed on the goose, recognizing that the bird was not dead but apparently hit in the wing.

The water was shallow, and by lifting his

feet high, Faye plunged rapidly toward his goal. The goose hit the water and began floundering, swimming away. Faye was breathing hard, but when he came within six feet of the wounded bird, he flew himself forward in a dive, stretching his arms as far as he could, and managed to grab a handful of feathers. The goose struggled, but quickly Faye came to his feet and wrung the bird's neck. The bird quivered once and then was still. For a moment Faye stood there holding the dead goose, and a feeling of pure joy came to him. "I did it!" he shouted.

Turning quickly, Faye made his way to the shore then ran at a trot toward the camp he had made. It amounted to little more than a lean-to he had made of saplings cut with his hunting knife and covered with branches with leaves to throw off the worst of the rain. His blanket was in there, and the fire he'd made earlier was blackened. He had, however, made sure that he always had kindling, which meant small pieces of dry wood and larger pieces to make a fire for warmth and for cooking. As he stood in the middle of his small camp, he tossed the goose down and stared at the mare, who lifted her head and considered him.

"I did it, Patsy!" he shouted again, and his voice echoed through the deep woods. "I killed it, and now I'm going to eat it."

Patsy considered Faye seriously then complacently lowered her head and nibbled at the grass at her feet.

Quickly Faye built up a fire. He had done poorly at keeping his fire at first, but practice makes perfect, and now he kept plenty of dried wood on hand and had learned how to get it started quickly.

Picking up the goose, he moved out of the way and began pulling the feathers off. It was a difficult business. The feathers closer to the breast were light and easily pulled, but getting the long ones off was a problem. He suddenly grinned and shook his head. "Well, I've eaten chickens and turkeys all my life, but never once did I think how they got dressed, cooked, and put on my plate. Now every time I eat a chicken leg, I'll think about someone having to pluck and cook the thing."

Faye spoke aloud, which he had begun doing soon after arriving in the depth of the woods. He had brought two books with him, and at times he would read aloud. One of them was the Bible, and the other was a book of the history of the southwest. The silence of the deep woods had proved to be intimidating, almost ghostly, and Faye had found that even though no one heard him, there was a consolation in the sound of his own voice.

"Now, how do I cut this fellow up?" He drew his hunting knife and began hacking away at the goose. "Bloody mess, that's what it is," he said in disgust. Finally when he had cut small pieces off the bird, he brought a small frying pan out to where the fire was now crackling merrily. He took the parts he had sheared off to the creek, washed them off, and came back. Carefully Faye placed chunks of meat into the pan. "I'm having fried goose for supper, Patsy."

Soon Faye discovered that the meat in the frying pan was burning. He turned the pieces over with the point of his knife and stirred in some water. "Hey Patsy, too bad horses don't eat goose." He laughed aloud, but his stomach had an ache in it.

As soon as the meat in the frying pan was half cooked, he stabbed it with his knife and bit off a bite. "Ow, that's hot!" he yelped. He blew on the meat, and when it was finally cool enough, although it was burned on the outside and half raw on the inside, he bit off small parts of it and chewed them with delight. "I never tasted anything so good," he murmured.

He ate slowly, devouring about a quarter of the cooked goose, and saw that the parts in the pan were softened up. "I guess I'd better save something for tomorrow." A thought came to him, and he gingerly poked through the inner parts of the goose that he had thrown aside. He found what he thought was the liver, pulled it out, and dropped it into the frying pan. When it was brown, he picked it up with his knife and waited until it cooled. Cautiously he tasted it. "Tastes kind of like chicken liver," he murmured.

Finally he spoke to the horse. "Guess I'll clean up, Patsy." He washed his pan and his knife, wrapped the remains of the goose in a piece of heavy cloth, and then sat down in front of the fire, enjoying the sensations of a full stomach. After a while he grew sleepy. He built up the fire, rolled up in his blanket, and lay down.

For a while he lay awake listening to the noises of the forest. He heard all kinds of night birds calling, and somewhere a fox was yipping at the moon. "Well, maybe Natty Bumppo could kill a wolf or a bear, but I'll bet he couldn't hit a goose on the wing like yours truly." He felt pleased with himself and quickly fell asleep, for the first time sleeping a dreamless, placid, sweet sleep.

■ ■ ■ ■

"Well, girl, about time for us to head for the house."

Stepping into the saddle, Faye settled and turned the mare's nose to the southeast. He spoke to her, and she started out on an easy walk. As they left the camp, he looked back at it. It had been home for him for quite some time. "It makes me feel a little bit sad," Faye murmured, "but it's time for other things."

The sun was coming up in the east, and as Faye swayed with Patsy's movement, headed toward civilization and a life he wasn't sure about, he thought about the time he had spent alone. He remembered how it had taken him two and a half weeks before he hit a squirrel with his .38. That seemed to unlock some sort of ability, for he became a dead shot. He also had learned to shoot rabbits. He had missed the first ten he shot at. They were fast, and he had to learn to shoot slightly ahead of them. As soon as he found this out, he knew that he was going to be all right. He had eaten several rabbits during his stay in the woods.

He thought of the biggest kill, which had been a four-point buck he had stalked for an entire day. After standing absolutely still within the shadow of a huge tree, the buck had cautiously come out of hiding. Faye had remembered the deerslayer remaining perfectly still, making himself one with the forest. Finally when the buck stepped within twenty feet, he drew his gun with one swift motion. The bullet caught the buck just behind the front leg, killing him instantly. Now Faye smiled as he remembered the difficulty he had had dressing the deer out, but he also remembered how the animal had fed him and how he had learned to cook venison. He thought of other kills he had made, and, as usual, when he thought of the snake, he was disgusted. "Snakes are dangerous. I don't know why God made them, but they're not bad eating. Though I wouldn't want to have snake meat as a steady diet" — he smiled — "it was better than porcupine."

All morning Faye rode steadily, crossing a logging road and going past a few cabins. Finally he reached the small town where he had bought Patsy and left for the woods all those weeks ago.

When he stepped down, the owner came out to greet him. "Well, sir, you came back."

"Sure did. Got a favor to ask of you."

"What's that?" The man was instantly on

his guard, which caused Faye to smile.

"Do you know a young girl who could use a mare of her own? Maybe someone too poor to buy her own horse."

Instantly a smile came to the lips of the owner of the stable. "I sure do. My niece. She's just eighteen. She wants to be a schoolteacher. She has to walk four miles to get to school and back. Why you asking?"

"I'd like for you to give Patsy to her. Will you?"

"You mean sell her?"

"No, I mean just give Patsy to her. I can't take her with me."

"Well, mister, I sure will. That's mighty handsome of you, sir."

"What time does the train come through headed southeast?"

"About noon." He pulled out a watch about the size of a turnip. "It'll be about two hours now."

"I haven't had a good meal in a while. Is there any place around here I could get something?"

"Why, of course you can." The owner smiled. "You come eat with us. I just killed the finest pig you've ever seen. How does fresh pork chops, homemade biscuits, and beans sound?"

"Like heaven." Faye grinned. "Lead me to

it." He slapped Patsy affectionately on the rump, went up, and rubbed her nose. "Thanks for the ride, Patsy."

"What about your saddle?

"Goes with the horse. Give it to the young woman."

"Why, she'll want to thank you."

"Not necessary. Just tell her I wish her good fortune with her teaching."

Two hours later Faye was sitting in the window of a narrow-gauged railroad passenger car. Cinders came in through the window, and from time to time the whistle made a shrill scream. Faye leaned back, pushed his hat down over his eyes, and wondered, *Now I've done something, but convincing Mother of the next step won't be this easy.* He thought for a while how he would tell his mother his plan and came up with nothing. Finally the clickety-clack of the wheels lulled him into a slight sleep, and as he slept, he smiled as he headed back toward his life.

CHAPTER 6

Eileen was in the kitchen talking to Kate about the following week's menus when Doris, the downstairs maid, rushed into the kitchen, her eyes wide with excitement. "Mrs. Riordan, it's Mr. Faye! He's come home!"

"Where is he, Doris?"

"He's in the foyer looking for you."

Eileen rose at once and hurried out of the kitchen. She turned down the wide hallway that divided the big house, and when she saw Faye standing in the foyer she cried, "Faye!" and ran to him.

He caught her, picked her up, and spun her around. He laughed at her protest then set her down and kissed her cheek. "How's my best girl?" He smiled.

"Why didn't you tell us you were coming? I ought to turn you over my knee and spank you!"

"You've done it before, Mother, but not

since I was about six."

Eileen was almost weeping for joy. "I've missed you so much, Faye. Why didn't you write?"

"Well, to be truthful I was a long way from a post office."

"Well you shouldn't have been." She began to fuss at him to cover her emotions but was studying him carefully. His skin was an even golden tan — something she had never seen before. His hair was long, the clothes he had on were ragged and dirty, and he seemed to have lost weight. There was, however, something new in his expression — the look in his eyes, the set of his lips. Something about him was different. "Well, come into the parlor and sit with me for a while." After catching him up on news of the family, Eileen asked Faye where he had been.

"Mother, I wanted to learn how to hunt a little, so I've been out in the woods. It was really an interesting experience for me."

"Well, I don't want you going back and doing that again." *He was heartbroken over that woman. Thank God he's gotten over her!*

Faye got to his feet. "I really need a bath and a change of clothes."

"Yes, you go bathe, change clothes, and lie down. Take a nap before supper. Your father and brothers will be glad to see you."

As soon as Faye left the room, Doris came back. "He looks like a different man, Mrs. Riordan. My, he's so tan! He must have been outside a lot."

Eileen said, "Go get Kate. She's out in the garden. We've got to have a fine meal tonight to celebrate his homecoming."

"Yes, ma'am, I'll do that."

Kate did a fine job with the meal. She had fixed a large beef roast with potatoes, carrots, onions, and garlic, but few noticed it.

Caleb and his sons were shocked at the changes in Faye and told him so. Leo asked, "How did you get so tan, Faye?"

"Well, as I told Mother, I decided to learn how to hunt a little bit. So I was out in the woods a lot. I just wanted to travel and see the country."

"You look like you've lost a little weight," Leo said.

"I don't think so. I'm about the same."

"Did you get that woman out of your system, brother?" Max smiled.

Everyone stared at Faye who did not blink. He said, "You know, Kate makes better meals all the time. I haven't had a meal this good since I left home."

It was obvious that he was not about to discuss his personal life. Suddenly he turned to his father and said, "How have things been going at the factory, Dad?"

Caleb blinked with surprise. Eileen knew he was surprised at their youngest son's question, as Faye had shown little interest in the factory before. Caleb finally said, "Going well, son." Hope lit up his face, and he asked, "Are you thinking about coming to work with me and your brothers?"

"Not just yet, Dad. I've got a few things I need to do."

They all retired to the large parlor, and Faye talked a little about the country he had seen but not in enough detail to tell them anything. For the rest of the evening, Caleb, Leo, and Max tried to get Faye to say something about his plans, but he simply avoided their inquiries. Finally Caleb said, "Well, it's about bedtime. I can see we're not going to get anything out of you, Faye."

"I had a good time out there, Dad."

"We'll talk about it tomorrow. Will you come to the factory and see what we've been doing?"

"I'll be glad to."

This pleased Caleb, and he left at once along with Leo and Max.

"You've gotten rather closemouthed, Faye," Eileen said. "You're not telling a

101

thing about where you've been. It's had us all worried, and I think it's unfair of you to keep us in the dark."

"Mother, I'll tell you more about it tomorrow. All right? I'm tired now and need to go to bed."

Eileen put out her cheek to receive his good-night kiss, the same as they had done for years. Yet she couldn't help but wonder if she had lost the gentle son she had always known.

The next morning, Faye rose early and ate breakfast with the family. He promised his father to come to the factory later and lingered at the table drinking coffee while his father and brothers left.

Eileen got a cup of coffee and sat down beside him. "Now, you've got to tell me what you've been thinking. You've got to tell me where you've been."

"All right, Mother. This is going to be a shock for you, but I hope you'll listen carefully until I get through. Then you can ask me anything."

"Go ahead, son." Eileen leaned forward, her lips slightly parted, as Faye began to talk.

"I had gotten to the point when I realized that I wasn't everything a man should be."

He saw her start to protest and shook his head. "Just hear me out, Mother. I know my painting is important. Art is important. Many things are important, but I had taken one part of my life and ignored the rest. I think Father and Leo and Max have ignored the opposite parts of themselves, too. They work at the big things in their lives and ignore art, music, drama . . . things like that."

He continued to speak for a long time, and then he finally said, "Well, Mother, you're not going to like this, but here it is. I've been reading about Judge Isaac Parker out in Fort Smith, Arkansas. You know anything about him?"

"No, I don't even recognize his name."

"Well, he's a judge in that district. He's over the Indian Territory in Oklahoma and part of Arkansas. He has two hundred marshals to keep the area protected. Only a federal marshal can go in and settle. It's become a hideout for bad men. Judge Parker has to send in his marshals to get them. I've been studying what they do, and I've decided to go to Fort Smith and ask Judge Parker to make me one of his officers."

Eileen stared at Faye as if she had not heard him correctly. "You mean to become a marshal?"

"That's exactly right, Mother. To become

a federal marshal. I want to see if I can be any part of a man, and that's a good test, I think."

Eileen began to speak rapidly, telling him the reasons she could think of why what he had suggested was just a terrible idea.

He listened carefully and did not interrupt, but finally when she had finished, he said, "Mother, I know you're worried about me. To tell the truth, I don't think I'll ever paint again until I get this out of my system. I've got to become a whole man."

For quite some time, Eileen argued with Faye, but her pleading didn't work, and she was terribly disturbed.

"I hate for you to feel like this, Mother, but this is something I must do." He rose, went over, and put his arm around her. "Don't worry, Mother. It may not work at all. I've got an idea that the judge has pretty strict standards. I doubt if he'll have me."

"What if he won't?"

"Then I'll come home and do this thing another way. I don't know how, but I'll try to get back in the painting mode again."

The conversation ended like that. Faye knew his mother was terribly disturbed, but there was nothing he could do about it. *I'll just have to wait a few days until she accepts it.*

■ ■ ■ ■

Eileen had not mentioned Faye's plan to her husband or to her sons. For several days, she was unable to do her work. She had difficulty following a train of thought, for all she could think of was her boy hunting a bunch of outlaws and in danger of being killed.

She had prayed about it for a long time. Every day. And finally she had an idea. It seemed simple enough, so she called Faye to sit with her. They went into the parlor and sat down.

Faye asked, "What have you decided, Mother? I hope you'll give me your blessing."

"I've decided to go along with you on this matter, son, if you'll promise me one thing."

Showing surprise that her surrender came so easily, he said, "What is it, Mother?"

"I ask that you take any job the judge gives you and stay with it, no matter how low it is, even if it's washing dishes."

Faye was obviously caught off guard. He finally smiled and said, "Why, Mother, I'll be glad to promise that."

"Good, son. Now, we'll just wait a few

days, and then we'll tell your father about it."

The next day Eileen set the rest of her plan into motion. She sat down in her bedroom at the desk with paper and pen and began to write:

To Judge Isaac Parker:

Dear Sir,
I'm sure you get many letters asking you to do things for people. I suppose that's the penalty of being a public figure. I am no different, Judge Parker, and I am writing this letter with a prayer in my heart that you will at least listen.

I have three sons. Two of them are real satisfied to be in their father's business. My other son has gone another direction. My two older sons are outdoorsmen. They are tough, as their father is. They hunt and shoot and ride, but my youngest son, Lafayette, is not that kind of man. He has been a student all of his life. He is twenty years old now, and that's all he's ever known, that and his painting. I'm convinced he will be a great artist one day.

That's why I'm writing this letter. I

hear that your men are in danger in their work. My son has no training, and as far as I know, no ability with a gun. I know he cannot ride a horse well. I'm afraid he will come out and waste his life and be killed, perhaps, and that would be the tragedy of my life.

Please consider this in almost the nature of a prayer, Judge. I hear that you are a father, and I know you treasure your sons. I know you wouldn't want to send one of them into a situation that would be almost impossible and dangerous. Please consider what I ask you to do, which is simply this: When my son comes to ask you to make him part of your force, agree to take him but give him the most humiliating, dirtiest job you can possibly think of. Keep him at it, and I'm sure in a short time he'll become discouraged and change his mind.

My prayer is that God will be with you as you read this letter and that you will give it your prayerful consideration.

Respectfully yours,
Mrs. Eileen Riordan

She blotted the ink, put it in an envelope, addressed it, and then left the house. She went at once to the post office and mailed the letter herself. Turning, she went back home again and felt that she had solved her problem.

Judge Isaac Parker had brought a letter home with him. He sat down with his wife and said, "Dear, let me read you this letter." He read Eileen Riordan's letter and then handed it to his wife and let her think it over. "What do you think we should do about this young man?"

"Why, it's clear enough." She smiled. "We have to do what she asked. This young man isn't fit to send out into the wilds of the Oklahoma Territory with the drunken Indians and outlaws. You know how many of your marshals you've already lost. It would be murderous to send this young man."

"Yes, I would never have sent him anyway, but she wants us to keep him until he gets full of this dirty side of life."

"Well, we will pray about it, Isaac, but I feel this mother's plea, and we must help her all we can."

Eileen opened the envelope, her heart pounding. She quickly read the brief letter from Judge Parker.

My dear Mrs. Riordan,

My wife and I have read your letter together. We both sympathize with you, and as concerned parents of a son, we know your heart aches. Never fear. I will do exactly as you ask, Mrs. Riordan. I will give your son such a hard time that he will not last long if he's like other young men. He sounds like he's rather spoiled, perhaps, so it will be easy to discourage him. I'll have him washing dishes, cleaning stables, all the things my men hate to do. We will pray together, my wife and I, that your son will return to his life with you.

Yours respectfully,
Isaac Parker

Faye had been escorted to the railroad station by his family. It had been a hard few days for him, for when his father and brothers found out his plan, they all were incredulous. All of them warned that he was being a fool.

"You could stay here and learn to ride and shoot if that's what you want," Caleb said earnestly.

"Yes, we'll help you," Leo said. "Don't do this crazy thing."

Faye had listened patiently, but here they

were at the railroad station. The train had pulled in. The conductor was calling, "All aboard!" He shook hands with his father and then hugged his two brothers.

Faye went to his mother and said, "Don't worry, Mother. I know you'll pray for me and I'll be all right. Besides, it's likely that Judge Parker won't make me a marshal without some training. He'll probably have me learning to ride a horse better and how to track, things like that. He won't let me go out until I have some experience and can make it as one of his men."

He hugged her, kissed her on the cheek, and then mounted the train steps. Minutes later, the train left the station. His last view was of his mother and his father, both looking despondent.

He grew restive during the long train ride to get to Fort Smith, Arkansas. He read a great deal, all he had been able to find about Judge Parker's court and the marshals.

When he finally arrived at Fort Smith, he went right away to Judge Parker's office. To his surprise, he was admitted at once.

Judge Parker was standing at a window looking down at the gallows that were in plain sight. "What can I do for you, young man?"

"Judge, my name is Riordan. I've come to

ask you to take me into your marshal force."

"Tell me your experience."

This did not take long, for in effect, Faye had none. Finally he fell silent, and Judge Parker said, "Young man, I have a great many volunteers. I can only take those who are experienced, and you are not."

"Just let me work. I'll do anything you say, Judge, and I'm a quick learner. I don't expect to be sent out right away to Indian Territory."

"You mean what you say, young man, that you'll do anything?"

"Anything, sir."

"Very well. You may join my force." He lifted his voice, saying, "Mr. Swinson."

The door opened, and a short, stocky man stepped in.

"Riordan, this is Chester Swinson, my chief of marshals." He then turned to the chief. "I want you to put this young man to work."

"Doing what, Judge?"

"Whatever needs doing."

"Come along. What is your name again?"

"Just call me Riordan."

"All right, Riordan, come this way."

Carrying his suitcase, he followed the man. He had given merely his last name because he was ashamed to be called Faye,

111

which sounded feminine to him. He always had hated the name and now determined just to be called Riordan.

Swenson led the way to a large rectangular building. He opened the door. It smelled of sweat and other nasty things he didn't want to know about. "Clean this building up until it's spotless. Clean the windows, mop the floor . . . everything. I want it shining."

"Yes, Marshal Swinson."

"All right, Riordan. When you finish this, you've got another job out in the stables. Shovel out all the stalls and put the refuse into a cart. The judge uses it for fertilizer in his garden. Dirty and nasty job. Nobody wants to do it. It'll be your job from now on."

Somehow Faye knew that he was being tested. He thought that the two men had some idea of how to make things hard on a recruit. He made up his mind right then. *No matter what they do to me or ask me to do, I'll stick it out!* "Yes sir, I'll do a good job."

After Swinson left, Faye looked around at the terrible condition of the room and then began to whistle. "I'm with Judge Parker's marshals. Maybe it'll be rough for a while, but one of these days I'll ride out with Heck Thomas and some of the other men."

Part Two

CHAPTER 7

The Mexican settlement had no name and was not legally a town, just a collection of adobe huts and wooden shacks built from castoff lumber located a few miles west of Amarillo, Texas. At night the liveliest place in the village was Pepy's Cantina. Pepy's was an exciting place for young men looking for female companionship, or vice versa.

At one end of the large room, three men were playing guitars, and a small space had been set off for those who wanted to dance. Now three couples, laughing and pawing at each other, moved around the floor. The room was filled with the shrill laughter of women, the coarse mirth of men, and the hum of constant loud voices. Rough tables and chairs were scattered around, all of them filled, and a bar ran along one wall — on the wall behind it were pictures of half-dressed, over-endowed women. One very fat man was serving at the bar, sweat pouring over his face. His filthy apron had once been white but now was a leprous gray.

The customers at the tables were served by two young men and by Rosa Ramirez. She was wearing a full skirt and a white blouse that clung to her sweaty body. Fatigue lined her face. She had been busy for over four hours, and now it was well after midnight. Most of the clientele were either drunk or soon would be.

As Rosa Ramirez threaded her way across the crowded floor, she paid no attention to the scents of raw alcohol, thick cigarette smoke, and unbathed bodies. When she reached the bar, she had to raise her voice to say, "Four cervezas and a bottle of red wine, Leon." She waited until the fat barkeep moved to fill the order.

Without warning she was roughly seized from behind, two arms pinning her. Her captor ran his hands down her body and whispered, "Rosa, you need a man to love you!"

Without hesitation, Rosa moved her head forward then flung it back and felt a satisfaction when she felt flesh crush.

A strangled voice cursed and said, "You broke my nose!"

Wheeling quickly, Rosa saw Viro Lopez, a heavyset man with dark piggish eyes, glaring at her. Blood was running from his nose, over his mouth, and dripping off his chin, and from there making an ugly blot on his emerald green shirt. Lopez cursed and reached for her but halted abruptly when he saw the six-inch blade of bright steel in Rosa's hand glittering under the yellow light of the lamps suspended over the bar.

"Touch me again, you pig, and I'll cut your liver out!"

The clientele of Pepy's Cantina was well accustomed to violence, but most of them turned now to see the knife in Rosa's hand, her face contorted with anger, and Viro Lopez, a man of blood who had killed and battered women until they could not walk.

Suddenly, almost magically, the owner of the cantina, Pepy Garcia, appeared like a ghost. He was short but broad of chest and shoulders, and his neck was thick. His eyes glittered under the lamplight, and he said quietly, "Time for you to go home, Viro. Maybe you can come back some other time." He waited for the larger man to act, but Lopez cursed, pulled out a bandanna, and began wiping the blood from his face. Pepy nodded. "That's wise. Go now, my friend. This is not your night."

Rosa had shown no fear, but she was aware now that her legs were unsteady. She showed nothing in her face, however, but a slight smile. "*Gracias,* Pepy," she said then added, "but I lost you a good customer."

"He'll be back." Pepy shrugged. He hesitated, stroked his mustache, and then said, "I don't like it when things like that happen in my place, Rosa. My customers are all drunks, and I can't control them sometimes."

"I don't complain."

"You never do. Take the rest of the night off. You look tired. Go get some sleep."

"Thank you, Pepy. I am tired."

"How is your father, Senior Ramirez? Any improvement?"

"No, sir, my father never seems to improve."

"Too bad! Too bad! I always admired him. I knew him when he was a young man and able to whip any man in the Territory, and his word, it was always strong. Whatever he said, he would do. Give him my best wishes, Rosa."

"I will, Pepy, and I'll see you tomorrow night."

Rosa left the cantina and made her way down the dark streets of the village, warily watching for men who might be lurking in the darkness. She reached the outskirts of the village and turned into a yard that housed a squat clay adobe house. Two lights were shining through the windows, a feeble yellow, and even as she reached out to knock on the door, she heard the raucous laughter from Pepy's Cantina. The distaste at the thought of the place where she had worked for two years seized her.

There was no need thinking about that, so she knocked on the door — two knocks then a single knock. This was the code that the family had created. Rough men and women were common here in the village and in Amarillo, and blood had been spilled often enough. The door opened a hair, and she pushed it open saying, "You still up, Juan?"

Juan Ramirez was a handsome boy of sixteen, tall and thin as though undernourished. He had dark hair that needed cutting and the dark eyes of his half-Crow mother. "I was worried about you, Rosa."

"You shouldn't do that. You should get some sleep."

"I saved you some supper. Raquel was sleepy and went to bed early.

Rosa reached out, hugged him, and smiled. "Good! I'm hungry." As she sat down wearily at the rough table, she looked around at what had been her home for several years and, as always, was depressed. The house had only two rooms. One was a bedroom used by her parents, and the other room was for living. It contained a kitchen, of sorts, a table for meals, and three cots with blankets, which were used as seats and beds for Rosa, Juan, and Raquel.

Juan moved toward a cabinet and brought out a plate covered with a cloth and a bottle. He set both on the table before Rosa, moved back, and got two glasses. "I saved you some beer," he said, "but it's not cold, sister."

Rosa smiled and patted his hand. She removed the cloth, picked up a tortilla, and filled it with meat. She ate without hunger, but Juan was watching her, so she said, "This is very good. What did you do tonight, Juan?"

"Nothing." The boy shrugged eloquently. "What is there to do in this place? I played cards with Chico and Carlos. We went over to see the new horse Arturo's father had bought."

Rosa listened as Juan spoke and was glad that he talked to her. They were the two that held the family together, and it broke her heart that he had so little chance to become something. She had given up on a good life for herself to work at Pepy's to bring in money for the family. Once she had had dreams, but they had faded a long time ago, and now she had to concentrate on making it through a single day at a time. "How is Papa today?"

"Not so good." Juan's smooth face showed a troubled mind. "I wish I could help him, Rosa."

"You're helping him by being a good son."

"No, that's not enough. I need to do something else. I need to get a job and go to work."

"No, there's no proper work here. We all know you would work if you had a chance at it. Just help Mama with the house. Be sure she has plenty of wood and water. You're a good son."

He shook his head and said stubbornly, "No, that's not enough."

The two sat at the table under the corona of flickering yellow light cast by a single, stubby candle. Finally Juan looked closely at Rosa's face. "You're tired, sister. Go to bed."

"Well, I am tired." She rose and put her hands on Juan's shoulders, startled to feel how thin they were. From lack of nourishing food she knew. "We have each other, Juan, you and me. I couldn't make it without you." She saw her words pleased the boy and brought color to his face. She ruffled his hair, kissed him on the cheek, and whispered "Good night, brother."

The two of them went to bed on the cots, and in the ebony darkness Rosario Ramirez tried to pray that God would give them a better life. But she had prayed in that fashion for so long that her faith was small.

The sun had lifted in the west, sending pale yellow beams through the two small windows of the hut and through a large crack over the primitive woodstove. Raquel, a trim fourteen-year-old girl wearing a tattered dress too large for her, had started the fire with bits of wood that she and Juan had collected, and, as usual, the smoke made her eyes smart. "I hate this stove, Mama!" she exclaimed.

"Be thankful we don't have to cook on the floor or in a rock fireplace." Chenoa Ramirez was grinding corn with a pestle in a hollowed-out stone. She wore an ancient dress long ago faded to a dull, neutral, noncolor and held together with patches. The sunlight touched her, revealing her unusual racial heritage. Her father, Frank Lowery, was a tall American trapper, but her mother had been a full-blooded Crow Indian. The mixture of races had made Chenoa a beautiful woman. She had lost that early beauty, for now at the age of forty, after years of hard living since her youth, her face showed lines that revealed her age.

She glanced at Raquel, whose dress was almost as worn as her own, and marveled at the blossoming beauty of the girl. *Not a child. She's on the verge of womanhood.* She glanced over at Rosa, and a sadness came to her. *She's so beautiful, but what does that get her? The men of this place chase after her but for evil purposes, and it will be the same with Raquel.*

A door hinge creaked, and Chenoa turned quickly as her husband Mateo entered the room. She rose quickly and walked with him to the table. "Sit down, Mateo. I'll fix you a good breakfast."

"I'm not hungry, Chenoa."

As her husband sat down, Chenoa was suddenly reminded of how handsome he had been when she had first seen him. She had been a mere girl, and to her the young, pure Spaniard with dark eyes and lively features and an aristocratic air had been the finest-looking man she had ever seen.

A bitterness came then as she thought of how good their life had been until Mateo had fallen ill with cholera. He had been in charge of a large property owned by a wealthy citizen of Amarillo. She longingly thought of the fine wood house that came to the Segundo and how she had had a new dress for herself from time to time and how the children, who were very young, had been clothed in finery. Food had been plentiful, and she had thought this life would last forever. Mateo had finally recovered but had become so weak he was unable to work. He had lost his position, and everything from that time had become difficult.

As Chenoa began to heat a pan full of rice, she turned to see Rosa rise from her cot and throw the thin blanket back. She was wearing a thin undergarment, and Chenoa remembered how long ago she had been as shapely as this oldest daughter of hers. She turned back to the boiling rice, stirred it, added salt and a little butter, then put it in a bowl and set it before her husband. "Here. Eat this. You've got to keep your strength up."

Mateo began to eat, but he took only small bites. He did finish the bowl and smiled. "Very good, wife. You were always the best cook in the village."

Juan coughed, groaned, and rolled out of bed. He wore a pair of worn, patched jeans too small for him and a shirt that had once been colorful but now was faded. "Is there any of that pork left, Mama?" he said, yawning hugely.

"Yes, you can share it with your sisters."

They ate quickly, and then the children left the room — Juan to go fishing in the river, Raquel to visit her friend Sofia, and Rosa to work in the cool of the morning in the garden behind the house.

Chenoa had made a cup of weak tea and put it down before Mateo.

He looked at it, smiled, and tasted it. "That's very good," he said.

They sat silently, and finally Mateo said heavily, "I don't like the way our children are living." He made a thin shape as he sat watching Chenoa's face. "Juan and Raquel, they've been running with bad companions."

"Their friends are not as bad as some."

"Maybe not, but I don't like it. And I hate it when Rosario has to work in that hellish cantina." Rosario was the name given to Rosa, but her nickname had become almost second nature. Only her family used her full name at certain times now.

"I hate that she has to fight the men off. She's a good girl, Mateo."

"I know that. But what's going to happen to them, Chenoa? What in God's name will become of them? There's nothing good in this place." He lowered his head and whispered, "I failed you all."

Chenoa moved at once to his side, put her

127

arm around him, and held his head. "You have not. You've been sick. When you are fully recovered, you will get work and things will be better." They both understood that such a future was highly unlikely, for his weakened condition grew worse, never better. "Don't worry," she said, stroking his hair now streaked with white. "The good God, He will take care of us." Her words, she saw, gave Mateo no comfort, nor did they make the sadness and hopelessness in her own breast go away.

It was two days after this that the Ramirezes had a visitor. It was late in the afternoon when they heard a knock.

"Who could that be?" Mateo asked.

"One of the neighbors maybe," Chenoa said. She got up and opened the door. She stood there for a moment in shock. "Is that you, Gray Hawk?"

"Yes, your uncle has come for a visit." Gray Hawk stepped inside at her invitation. He was full-blooded Crow, a handsome man. The Crows were the most handsome people among the Plains Indians, and he was a good example. He was near fifty but erect as a pine tree, and his muscles were still limber and strong.

"I'm glad to see you. Come in and sit down. We have some food left."

"I will eat, and then I will talk."

Gray Hawk sat down, and the family watched him as he ate. When he finished, he sat back, belched loudly, and said, "That was good. Now I'll talk. You listen."

"All right, uncle," Chenoa said. "Why have you come?"

"Your father. He is sick. He wants you to come and live with him."

The family had heard Chenoa speak of her father, who was, by all her reports, a fighting man admired among all the Indians.

"Live with him?" Chenoa said. "How could that be? He has another wife now, not my mother."

"She is dead. He has a woman to keep house for him, and he needs you he says. He has a fine ranch, a big house."

"Well, why don't you help him, Gray Hawk?" Mateo asked.

"Ah, I'm a wild hawk. I do not always keep the law. I sometimes buy whiskey and sell it." He laughed then slapped his chest. "The Choctaw Light Horse is after me."

"What is that?" Chenoa asked.

"Indian police."

For a time he talked about the house, the ranch, and what was there.

Finally Mateo, who had remained silent,

said, "You are not telling us everything, Gray Hawk."

"No, I am not. Your father's ranch is in Indian Territory, which has more outlaws there than there are fleas on a dog. Evil men everywhere! Your father fought them off while he was well, but he can't fight now."

"What's wrong with him, Gray Hawk?"

"Bad heart. If you come," he said, "you will have to fight for what you have."

For a while they talked about going, but it was obvious to Rosa that they really had no other choice. "There's nothing for us here."

"Yes," Mateo said, "I can do nothing, but perhaps you can help the old man."

"But how will we get there?" Chenoa said.

"Your father has given me money. He told me if you will come to buy a team and a wagon. Some of you will ride in the wagon with your goods, and I will buy horses for the others."

"You will take us there?" Rosa said quickly.

"Yes. I must say this, though. In the mission school they talked about heaven where everybody is happy and there's plenty of food." He paused, and a grim look swept across his face. His obsidian eyes seemed to glitter. "This place where you're going, it's not heaven."

CHAPTER 8

"I'm worn down to the bone," Mateo groaned.

It was late afternoon. The sun had been beating down on them all day long, draining the strength from the horses and riders alike. They had started early in the day and had paused only an hour or so at noon to eat a quick meal. Now the party had stopped beside a small stream that gurgled over smooth stones and made a pleasant sound in the ears of the thirsty travelers.

Chenoa stood up and arched her back. She had driven the wagon all the way, and Mateo had lain down, for the most part, on the bed they had made for him in the wagon. Now she went over and dipped a small pail in the stream. As she did, she saw a group of minnows flashing silver. They all darted away then broke and made a left turn. *I wonder how they all know to turn at the same time?* The thought had occurred to her before.

She straightened up, ignoring the ache in her back, walked over, and reached down into a box in the rear of the wagon. Taking out a quart bottle, she handed him the water then picked up another glass and carefully poured brown liquid into it. "Drink this," she said.

"I hate that stuff."

"I don't want you to drink it because you like it, but it helps you to feel better, to feel stronger."

Mateo shook his head, making a face. He swallowed the painkiller then quickly downed the entire contents of the glass. He handed it back to Chenoa and looked around at their surroundings. "This is bad country," he muttered. "I don't like it."

Indeed, this part of Texas was not known for its beauty. The land stretched away endlessly, so it seemed, flat, dull, and without any interesting hills or mountains. The strange mesquite trees that twisted their branches looked like black ghosts reaching to heaven.

Chenoa sat down beside him, put her hand on his shoulder, and kneaded his thin, wasted muscles. "It will be better when we get to Oklahoma."

"I don't think so. From what I remember

of that place, it's just about as stark as this."

"It's been a long time since we've been there, and Gray Hawk says my father's ranch is much better country than this."

"I don't think that Indian would know good country if he saw it."

The two fell silent and watched as the three young people were laughing and splashing water on one another. They had taken their clothes down to the creek and were washing them, working up what soap they could from the yellow bars they had bought before they left their home.

Gray Hawk had been given enough money by Chenoa's father to buy them clothes. *He must have known,* she thought, *that we had nothing to wear except rags.* They had all outfitted themselves, and she felt better wearing a respectable dress and good shoes.

"Maybe I should try to get some firewood and build a fire for supper," Mateo said.

"No, Juan's already done that. I'll go light it. Gray Hawk ought to be back, but if he's not, he said to eat without him."

Going over, she piled small sticks into a pyramid, took a match she had brought from the wagon, struck it, and held it steady. The smoke began to rise, and as the flame caught, yellow flames leaped upward. She added larger sticks, and the fire began to

133

crackle with almost a malevolent sound in the silence of this deserted country.

When the fire was going, she built a small base out of bricks that they moved each night. On top of it she put a steel piece of grill. It made a passable stove, and now she put water on to boil for the coffee, and right on the grill itself she put chunks of beef. Almost at once the fat began to sizzle, and the smoke billowed upward almost furiously.

"It's about time for Gray Hawk to shoot another cow," Mateo said. "This last one is almost gone."

He had no sooner spoken when Gray Hawk came in riding a small pony. He used no saddle. He slipped to the ground, tied the halter to a mesquite tree, and came over. He looked down at the meat and nodded, "I'm hungry."

"It's about time for you to shoot another cow," Mateo said.

"You better not shoot one that belongs to someone," Chenoa warned. "We'd be in a bad way if we didn't have you to lead us home."

"These cattle are wild. They're not branded. I'll shoot another one at noon tomorrow." They were pretty tough, but the beef was a welcome addition to the meat-starved diet of the Ramirez family.

"It was thoughtful of Father to send money to buy food," Chenoa said. "He must have known we were struggling."

"I think he did," Gray Hawk said. "Did you write and tell him?"

"No, I haven't written him for years."

"We left under pretty bad circumstances, Gray Hawk, if you remember," Mateo said. "He didn't want me to marry Chenoa. I thought he was going to take a gun to me."

"It was unpleasant," Chenoa said, "but evidently he's mellowed."

"I think he has," Gray Hawk muttered. He squatted beside the fire until finally the meal was ready.

Chenoa hacked off a big chunk of the beef, put it on a tin plate, and handed it to him. He dipped into the pot containing beans and scooped out a heaping spoonful. "Good," he said. "Lots of pepper. A white man don't know how to do that."

Chenoa called, "Children, come and eat."

The three came at once, bringing the wet clothes.

"I'll have to tie a line up and hang them out to dry," Rosa said. "But we'll eat first."

They all sat down and filled their plates with the spicy beans and chunks of beef.

"How much farther is it?" Mateo asked.

"A few more days. It's not too far. Not

too close either." Gray Hawk looked up in the sky. "It will rain tonight. Cover everything up in the wagon with that canvas we brought." He walked over to his horse and began rummaging through the pack on the animal.

"Do you believe him, Chenoa?" Mateo asked.

"Yes, he never was a liar unless he had to be."

They all ate hungrily, dipping beans out of the pot that was boiling hot.

"These beans need more pepper," Juan said. He reached into the pocket of his new shirt and pulled out a large red pepper. Taking out his pocketknife, he cut off some small round fragments and dropped them into the beans. His eyes widened with the heat, and he said, "That's better."

Gray Hawk came back shortly with a bottle. He sat down, took a long drink from the bottle, and said, "You want some whiskey, Mateo?"

"No, it burns my gut."

"How about you, Juan?"

"Don't offer him whiskey," Rosa said. "He doesn't need it."

"Don't be foolish, woman. Every man needs a drink. What about you, Rosa?"

"What do you mean what about me?"

"You look lonesome."

"I'm fine."

"No, a woman needs a man. That's what you need. I'll find you a good one when we get to the Territory."

Rosa gave Gray Hawk a look of disgust. "I can find my own man."

"She doesn't have to go hunting men," Juan said. "They come hunting her. I think she had to take a knife to one or two of them."

"Well, a knife wouldn't discourage a good man," Gray Hawk said. He continued to drink, and quickly the alcohol made him sleepy. He went over close to the wagon, stretched out flat on his bed, and soon was snoring.

"You think he's telling the truth about these cows that wander around?" Juan said. "I thought all cattle belonged to somebody."

"It's always been that way he told me," Rosa said. "They're just wild steers. Sometimes ranchers round some up, but there are so many of them and not many ranchers. And he's telling the truth. None of these cows have brands, so they're just wild."

Soon the rain started, just a drizzle at first, and then the tiny drops began to form fat ones pattering down on the earth, settling the dust. They covered the wagon up with the canvas, and then all of them got under the wagon, out of the rain as much as possible. They had brought slickers, and each had put one on. Now they sat, waiting.

"You know, it's kind of nice sitting here with the rain falling down. I always did like that sound," Rosa said.

"It was nice of grandfather to send money for clothes," Raquel said. "Maybe he'll buy me some pretty dresses when I get there."

Chenoa's face turned sour. "He didn't buy me any when I was your age. He's stingy."

"But Mama, he's giving us a place to live. He bought these clothes for us."

"He needs us, Raquel."

"Look at Gray Hawk," Juan said.

They all looked to see the Indian lying flat on his back. His mouth was open, and the rain was falling in.

"He's going to drown."

"You better go pull him in, Juan," Chenoa said. "We couldn't do without him."

Rosa and Juan went out and dragged the drunken man under the shelter of the wagon. He coughed and snorted then went back to sleep.

Mateo began to cough, and Chenoa put a blanket over him. "We'll get you a good doctor when we get to the Territory."

"I doubt if your father will pay for that.

He never cared much for me."

"I think he's probably changed. People do when they get older."

"Or when they get sick," he said.

The rain continued. It had a soporific effect. Finally Mateo dozed off. Chenoa felt her eyelids closing as sleep was coming on. She saw her younger daughter move to her older one through her half-closed eyes.

Raquel tugged at Rosa's sleeve. "Are you glad to be going, Rosa?"

"Yes, it's better than what we had." She paused for a moment and then laughed bitterly. "It couldn't be worse," she said. "Now go to sleep."

Chenoa prayed Rosa was correct as she drifted into sleep.

"How long before we get to grandfather's place, Gray Hawk?" Rosa asked. They had been traveling steadily all day, and she was tired. Riding a horse for long hours was a new experience for her. She had no split skirts, and at first the saddle had chaffed the insides of her legs, but she had taken one of her old dresses, cut it down the middle, and sewed it so that it had, in effect, legs. She had put ointment on the raw places and bound them up with underwear so that it was bearable.

Gray Hawk was riding along in front with Rosa at his side. "We've been on his land for the last hour."

"This?"

"Yes, this is all his."

"The land looks better than I expected." She had expected it would look much like the barren, sandy plains near her home, but here there were rolling hills, none of them large, but at least they broke the monotony. Some trees were scattered around, not tall, but at least they added color.

They had crossed one wide creek. Gray Hawk had told her, "That creek is spring fed. Ain't a very big creek, but it never goes dry. Got fish in it, too."

Rosa looked eagerly forward as they moved up a hill, noting the cattle running free. "Look, they've got a brand. What is it?"

"That's an anchor. I didn't know what an anchor was. He told me sailors used them to stop a ship. Don't know why he chose that." They crested the hill, and Gray Hawk motioned with his hand. "There's the ranch."

Rosa's eyes swept the vista. It made a pretty sight, at least to her. She was used to the squalid village, and here was space with trees and grass. There on a rise was a house and outbuildings. The house was wide and had tall windows. A veranda stretched all the way across the front. The roof was made of some sort of metal, for it caught the glint of the sun. "What's the roof made out of, Gray Hawk?"

"Tin. Makes an awful racket when it rains."

"I've always liked that."

When they drew closer, she saw that there were two large barns and several corrals, all of them containing horses. The cattle were running free, and she saw two men moving around among the horses. "What is that thing?" Rosa asked, staring at a strange-looking structure.

"That's what they call a windmill. The wind blows it, turns some machinery, and pulls water up from a well. I remember when your grandfather had it built. Everybody said he was crazy, but I was there when it first started. We had to wait for a breeze. It started clanking and making noises, and then water came up from the ground. He had some troughs built so the stock could always have fresh water. The workers on the ranch use it, too."

Rosa called out, "There's our new home, Mama, Papa!"

Chenoa looked over the ranch. She turned

to Mateo and said, "He added to the house. It's bigger than it was."

All of them looked eagerly at the house. There were only the two workingmen they saw, but as they got closer, they saw a man was sitting on the front porch in a rocking chair.

"That's my father," Chenoa said. She pulled up in front of the house and got down from the wagon.

Mateo crawled down, and the rest of them dismounted from their horses.

The old man got up carefully, slowly, and came down the steps. He was frail.

Rosa had never seen him, of course, nor a picture of him. He was not a tall man, and his flesh was wasted. His face was lined, but his eyes were bright and active. He carried a cane and leaned on it slightly. His eyes were on his daughter.

Chenoa stepped forward and said, "It's been a long time, Father."

Frank Lowery studied this daughter of his whom he had not seen for years. "You look like your mother when she was younger. Not quite as pretty, though."

"I never was."

Lowery moved forward and stuck his hand out to Mateo, who shook it. "Good to see you, Mateo."

142

"We appreciate your having us."

"We didn't get along too good the last time you were here."

"No, the last I remember you threatened to shoot me if I ever set foot on the place." He smiled and said, "Now's your chance."

"No, I'm past that. I can see you're not well. Well, that makes two of us." He grinned suddenly and laughed. "We'll see which one of us lasts the longest."

Rosa had been watching the scene, taking in her grandfather. Suddenly he turned and looked her up and down. "You look like you might strip down nice."

Rosa had heard her mother speak about how awful her grandfather's talk was.

Chenoa snapped, "That's no way to talk to your granddaughter!"

"I like that. Your grandmother was like that. She didn't mind speaking right up." He studied Rosa and said, "You're a good-looking squaw."

"I'm not a squaw."

"Well, you're part squaw. What I figure is you're one-eighth Crow. Anyway, you're good-looking enough to draw some men to help us. But you keep yourself clear. I don't need no great-grandchildren right now."

"Don't worry about me. I'll be fine."

"And who is this?"

"This is Raquel, our youngest daughter," Chenoa answered.

"Are you a good girl, Raquel?"

"Sometimes."

Lowery laughed. "I like that. Someone asked me once when I was just a boy, 'Are you a good boy?' and I said, 'No, I was born in sin when my mother conceived me.' " He laughed at the thought and said, "I don't know how I knew that scripture. I guess it about sums me up." He turned and looked at Juan carefully. "You look like your pa did when he was a young man, which is good. Hope you're as tough as he was when he came courting your mama."

"I've come to help you all I can, Grandfather."

"Good. Well, let's go in the house." He moved slowly up the steps. Rosa noticed he held himself carefully.

"Are you feeling bad, Father?" Chenoa asked.

"No, don't feel bad at all. I had me a severe spell with my heart. Never was scared in my life, but that scared me. Thought I was a goner, so I move pretty careful now. Don't want to stir that up again." He made it up the steps, opened the door, and said, "Come on in. I got a passel of bedrooms. You can take your pick, except for mine."

They all filed in, and Lowery yelled in a big voice, "Ethel, get out here!"

A big woman in her forties came through the door. She was plain but strong looking.

"This here's Ethel. She's been taking care of me since I got too old. I done asked her to stay around. She makes the only good biscuits in the Territory. Ethel, I want you to fix us up a good meal. The prodigal sons and daughters done come home."

Rosa said at once, "I will help. My name is Rosa, Miss Ethel."

"I'm glad to see all you folks. He gives me trouble, but he gives me a home, too."

"You children go out and look the place over. I want to talk to your folks," Lowery said.

Juan and Raquel left at once, and Rosa went off with Ethel. She quickly discovered that the woman was blunt and plain spoken but seemed to have a kindly nature. "We got all kinds of stuff to make Mexican food. That's what he likes best. His wife was good at it, but I never was. I can do the regular cooking. If you'll do the Mexican, I'll do the rest."

"Why, you've got all kinds of things here. We can make a fine meal."

The two women set about preparing the meal.

Rosa asked finally, "How about my grandfather? He seems very weak."

"Well, he nearly died with that heart problem. He was in bed and couldn't hardly move for a long time. He had a hardworking foreman who took good care of the stock. But when some outlaws were taking our cattle, he tried to stop them, and they kilt him. I think that's really why your grandfather sent for you folks. I don't see how you can help with the killers hangin' out around here."

"Can't the law do something?"

Ethel was making a crust for a pie. She stirred the batter quickly and worked the flour in until it was pliable and said, "We're in the Territory, Miss Rosa. The only law here is the federal marshals. Judge Parker's court's got about two hundred of them, but they got the whole of Indian Territory to take keer of. They can't do everything. Then there's the Choctaw Light Horse."

"Choctaw Light Horse? What are they?"

"Indian policemen. But they only deal with Indian trouble. Don't have nothin' to do with white men." She worked quickly and efficiently.

"How did you happen to get here, Ethel?"

"A drunk Cherokee killed my husband. I didn't have no place to go, no money,

146

nothin', so Mr. Lowery brought me out here. That was four years ago. He was a strong man then. He kept the outlaws thinned out, but now they've been movin' in, taking what they want." She gave Rosa a direct look and asked, "What kind of place do you come from?"

Rosa told Ethel how poorly they had been living. She looked up once and said, "Ethel, I'll do whatever I have to on this ranch. If anyone tries to run us off or take it from us, I'll put a bullet in his head if I can."

"That's a good thought. You hang on to it. I keep a shotgun handy by the door. In case they ever try to come in, I'll blow their heads off. Now, let's get this meal going."

Lowery was reveling in the supper. "Look at all this! Chicken quesadillas with red sauce, burritos, tamales. Everything I like and all delicious. Miss Ethel, that's the best meal I've had in a long spell."

"Well, I didn't have nothin' to do with it. Miss Rosa did all that."

Rosa said quickly, "My mother's a much better cook, Grandfather."

"Don't see how she could do much better than this."

All during the meal, Frank Lowery kept asking them questions about how they'd been living. Rosa and her mother did most of the talking, and finally Lowery said, "It sounds bad."

"It was worse than we're telling it," Chenoa said. "We needed a home badly."

"Well, I'm glad you're here."

Rosa spoke up. "Ethel's told me about your foreman getting killed by outlaws."

"His name was Sam Butterworth. He was a good man, tough and hard, but he wasn't harder than the bullets they put in him. He tried to stop Henry the Fox from taking some of our stock. Henry just gunned him down."

"Henry the Fox?" Rosa asked. "Is that his real name?"

"Partly. His last name is Beecher, but mostly he gets called the Fox."

"Did you send word to the law?"

"I sent word, but I couldn't go in person. I was too sick by that time."

"I can't really understand why you sent for us," Mateo said. "Chenoa can take care of the house, but how do you think we can help with the outlaws?"

"It's just a start. We've got to build up a little army around here. It don't have to be all that big, but they gotta be tough men." He turned and looked at Rosa and said, "Rosa, I wish you was a man, but you ain't.

But you're gonna have to do a man's job. And Juan, you are second in command. We got three good hands left. They're tough hairpins, and they've stayed with me when it would have been easy to ride off. Now, you two have got to learn how to shoot, and you've got to learn horses, how to ride 'em and how to take care of 'em. You've got to be willing to shoot a man if you have to. I've talked to Captain Canno of the Choctaw Horse Brigade, that's the Indian policemen. Since you got Indian blood in you, Rosa, his band can help you, at least with Indian problems. But he's got no authority over the white man. So that's our problem."

"What can we do, Grandfather?" Rosa asked.

"Well, Mateo and me are too sick to fight. Raquel is too young. So you two are gonna have to take care of it."

Juan at once said eagerly, "I can help, sir. I can shoot a little, and I'm a good rider."

"Good boy. Now listen. Today I want you to pick out your weapons, rifles and pistols. From this time forward I don't want you to be without 'em. Sleep with 'em if you need to. I've got 'em in a room in the back of the house. We'll get you gunned up, and then I want you to go out and get Ned Little to teach you how to shoot. Blinky knows all there is to know about horses. So ask him to give you lessons, and you've got to learn quick. The first time any man comes to do us harm, shoot at him. If you miss him, fine. If you hit him, good. And listen to Ringo Jukes. He's tough as barbed wire and ain't afraid of nothin'. If you back off," he warned, "they'll walk over you. So we got four men, counting Juan, and one woman. That's our army right now. But if we make a good show, that'll keep the worst off of us until we can draw some more men. You may have to throw a wink or two at somebody, Rosa, to make 'em want to come out."

"I won't have to do that, Grandfather." Rosa smiled. She was getting used to the old man's teasing and liked him a great deal.

He was silent for a time, and then Rosa said, "I have something to say, Grandfather. I've never had a home, not a real home, but I want this to be a home for us. I wish I were a man, but a man who takes a bullet from a woman is just as dead as one who takes a bullet from a man. All of us are grateful to you, and we want to be your family."

"I can't ride or fight, Father," Chenoa said, "but I can make life easier for you."

Lowery was silent for a while, and then he said, "You know, I won't be long on this

150

earth. I got to thinking one day what I'd be leaving behind, this house, this land, a few cattle. It'll be all gone. But then I thought a man needs a family of his own blood, and that's why I sent for you. I realized I hadn't been the man I should have been with my family, but if you give me a chance, I think I can do better."

"Lead us to those guns," Rosa said.

He led them down to a room in the back of the house where, indeed, there was a small armory. Rosa and Juan found holster belts and .38s to put in them.

"The .44s are too big for your hand. You hit a man in the brain and that'll make him dead enough," Lowery said. "Now, you go down and tell them worthless hands of mine they gotta teach you how to shoot, how to ride, and how to keep this place up."

Rosa and Juan left the house and headed for the corral where three men were sitting on the top rail. Brother and sister were both conscious of the pistols in the men's holsters and that they were holding repeater Winchester rifles. They halted, and the three men stared down at them silently.

The biggest of the men said, "You Mr. Lowery's kin?" The speaker was a tall, lanky man, around thirty, with yellow hair and hazel eyes.

"Yes, I'm Rosa Ramirez, and this is my brother Juan. Get down off that fence while I'm talking to you."

Startled, the three men leaped to the ground, and Rosa asked, "What are your names?"

"I'm Ned Little."

"My grandfather says you know guns. Your job is to teach us to shoot pistols and rifles."

Little grinned. "Who you exactly plan on shootin', missy?"

"Anybody who gives trouble to this ranch." She turned to a short rider with red hair and a mustache that was a mistake. "What's your name?"

"Blinky Mullins."

"You'll be teaching my brother and me all about horses. We don't know very much, but we can learn." She turned to face the third man who was watching her curiously. He was six feet tall, strongly, built with handsome features. His hair was chestnut with a slight curl. "I'm Ringo Jukes." He smiled suddenly. "What am I going to teach you, Rosa?"

There was a suggestion in his voice, and Rosa said, "Nothing, until I teach you some manners. You see yourself as a ladies' man?"

"Pretty much."

"All right. You call me Miss Ramirez. You

touch me, I'll make you sorry."

Jukes sobered. "You ain't too friendly, are you, Miss Rosa?"

Rosa knew she had to bond with these men. "I don't mean to be hard. I'm very grateful to all three of you for staying with my grandfather. I realize I'm just a woman and Juan's just a boy, and you three can do things that we can't. My grandfather's a helpless old man, and so is my father. Gray Hawk has told me how hard this country is, and right now Juan and I aren't able to take care of this ranch by ourselves."

She paused, dropped her head, and considered what to say next. The silence ran on, and then she lifted her head. "I don't want to sound hard, but the job is too big for us. Only if you three help us can we survive. So I'm asking you, will you help us?"

Ringo Jukes said quickly, "I didn't mean to get on the wrong side of you, Miss Ramirez. I like your grandfather. I'll be glad to help any way I can."

Rosa smiled. "Thank you, Ringo, and my friends call me Rosa."

"I'll be glad to teach you about horses," Blinky spoke up.

Ned Little shrugged. "I don't claim to be no sharpshooter, but I think I can show you how to put a bullet where it will discourage

153

a man. You ready to start?"

"Yes. Blinky, you start teaching Juan about horses while I learn how to shoot horse thieves."

CHAPTER 9

Eileen began a letter to Faye late in the afternoon before the menfolk came home from work. She wanted to have time to reread it and make sure it was worded well, for his letters to her always seemed to touch her deeply. She put the letter away in a drawer in the bedroom and went downstairs to make sure dinner was ready.

When the men came in, they had to clean up. Finally they came to the table. Their talk was of the factory and things that she knew little about, but she did sense that there was something about the way her husband did business that seemed cold and calculated. Knowing little enough about the world of business, she picked up on the fact that he was a hard man when it came to business tactics. She knew he did not mind using his power to crush a smaller and more vulnerable business opponent, and this disturbed her. But she could think of no way to change it.

When the meal was finally over and the men went to the study to smoke and finish their talk, she went upstairs, took the letter from the drawer, and then went to the parlor. Sitting down, she unfolded it with hands not quite steady. She was not a woman easily disturbed, but the problems of this youngest son of hers occupied her mind. She prayed for him every day with all the power she could muster and hoped her letters reminded him of the home she longed for him to return to.

Faye blew on the completed letter to his mother to dry the ink and then read it over to check for any errors.

Dearest Mother,

I wanted to get this letter off to you as quickly as possible because I have missed a few days. I hope you have not been worrying about me, as I am absolutely in no danger here. As I told you before, Judge Parker saw to it that I had a job, and the head marshal, Chester Swinson, sees to it that I have plenty to do.

I am learning a great deal about horses. As you know, I have never been comfortable on a horse. To tell the truth I've always been afraid of large animals, but that has been changing here. It is my job to take care of them, which includes cleaning up after them, grooming them, and seeing that they are fed properly. I've picked up quite a bit from the stable hand here. His name is Josh. He's a black man and a fine Christian. He's been after me to go to church with him, and I went last Sunday. It was a black Methodist church, and the preacher was very eloquent. The singing was nothing like we have in our churches. The people all sang at the top of their lungs, some of them raised their hands, some clapped their hands. They had the best time I've ever seen any congregation have. I understand the Methodists are like this, the old-time ones anyway. Maybe I can find a Methodist church that has some of the early beginnings in it.

I've been getting plenty to eat here. There is no shortage of good food. The marshals come in at all hours after long trips. They're always hungry, dirty, and tired, so it's my job to see that they get good meals. I've even helped out by cleaning their boots and little things like that. I haven't gotten to be friendly with any of them because it's sort of like a men's club. The marshals make a close confederation and stick together, and I can see that you have to buy your way in with deeds and not just words.

I get up before daylight and work on preparing the breakfast with the cook. Afterward I clean up the dishes. Then Marshal Swinson puts me to some work that usually takes me the rest of the day. As a matter of fact, I hardly ever finish the list he gives me.

As I was saying, I have never been comfortable around horses. I told you about Patsy, the one I rode on vacation. She was a sweetheart, but there's a horse here that I've grown rather close to. Her name is Maggie, and none of the marshals will have her, or at least she's always the last choice. I found out that she's gentle, too lazy to buck, and the men think she's not tough enough to go on the scout with them. That's what they call it, "going on the scout." But I've learned she's very patient and never bucks. I've learned how to throw on a saddle and put on a bridle very quickly. I've learned to get on a horse without any problem and stay on. Well, there's no triumph there, Mother, because any ten-year-old could stay on Maggie, but

I've grown very fond of her.

I must close this letter and get it in the mail. One of the men is going to the post office, and he said he would drop it off for me. I miss you a great deal, and once again I tell you there's no point in worrying about me. I'm doing nothing more dangerous than washing dishes and cleaning up after horses.

I did make one friend here. A big dog that's been hanging around, they say, marshal headquarters for a long time. He has one eye, no tail — it's been chopped off — and three legs. His name is Lucky, which I think is really poignant, but he's a good dog. I save him scraps from the kitchen, which nobody ever did, and he and I have a good time together.

I'll close this letter by asking you to continue to pray for me. Sooner or later I will be going on the scout, but I will let you know. Just give my regards to Dad and my brothers, and tell them I'm thinking of them.

With warm regards,
Faye

Faye quickly folded the letter, slipped it into an envelope, sealed it, and went to find

Clyde Jordan, one of the marshals, who was headed for town. "Would you mail this letter for me, Clyde? Here's the money for the postage."

"I reckon so." Clyde was a big, bulky man, good-natured, and not as standoffish as some of the other marshals. "This to your sweetheart?"

"In a way. It's to my mother."

Clyde nodded approvingly. "That's good, Riordan. You can have lots of sweethearts, but you only have one mother, and I'll bet she's a dandy."

"Yes, she is. Thanks a lot, Clyde. I'll save you some pie tonight before the gluttons eat it all up. What kind do you like?"

"Any kind." Clyde took the letter, and he left.

Almost at once Faye ran from his room, which was nothing more than a space above one of the stables. He had made a fairly good bed there and kept his belongings nearby. He came down the steps quickly and went to help with the breakfast. The cook was a fat, greasy man, good-natured enough except when someone crossed him. His name was Davis Beauregard. He was a French Cajun and a pretty good cook.

As soon as Riordan entered, Beauregard said, "Get started on them pancakes. You

160

know how these sorry lawmen eat 'em up quicker than we can make 'em."

"Sure thing, Beauregard."

The men came trooping in, and Riordan put plates down and big cups. They were all hollering for breakfast, and he carried in a huge stack of pancakes and divided them up. He went back and brought another stack in and then filled their coffee cups. He ran back and forth, and finally, when the last pancake had been devoured and the last marshal had left, he drew a sigh of relief. "Well, I guess that will keep 'em fed, until noon anyway, Beauregard."

"They ain't got no manners. You sit down and eat something, Riordan. You've got to be hungry."

"I'll fix it."

"Shut up and sit down. I'll bring it to you."

Riordan grinned, for beneath the crusty manner of Beauregard was a heart that was fairly good. He ate five pancakes along with fried ham and downed several cups of coffee. He got up, took his dishes back, and said, "You make the best pancakes in the world, Beauregard."

"You'd think I was feedin' 'em hog feed, them marshals. Back where I come from in Bastrop, Louisiana, we had a few manners.

161

We'd tell the cook he done good. They never say a nice word."

This was true enough, so Riordan always made sure he managed to say something nice about the food to the cook. "I'd better get these dishes washed," he said. For the next hour he worked hard scrubbing the plates and the silverware and putting them away. He was just finishing when Chester Swinson came in.

The marshal's face was red, as it usually was when he was upset — which was most of the time. "Quit loafing here, Riordan! You got to clean out the stables. Take the refuse over to the judge's garden. I'll be watching you to see that you don't go to sleep."

"Sure thing, Chief Swinson."

As always, Riordan was careful to give a quick word to the marshal. He had done that ever since he had been there. Never once complaining. Always ready to go.

He went out at once, and for the next hour and a half he shoveled the stalls of the horses.

He whistled and continued to work, and when he finally finished, he walked over and washed his face and hands but knew there was no point in changing his clothes, for Marshal Swinson would have another dirty

162

job for him.

The judge and Swinson were talking over the cases on the docket and deciding which men to send out on the scout. After they had settled all this, the judge suddenly asked, "How's that boy doing? Young Riordan?"

"Well, Judge" — Swinson scratched his head, and a puzzled look came into his face — "I've treated that boy like a dog. He should have hit me and left here. He's got determination if he ain't got nothing else."

"Well, I thought he would have quit by this time, Chester. Just keep pouring it on."

"His ma still worried about him? I don't think she has to worry. He's good at mucking stalls and washing dishes and other dirty jobs, but that ain't what we need out in the Territory."

The judge was thoughtful for a while. He tapped his chin with a pencil then ran his hand over his hair. "I'll tell you what, Swinson. Heck is going out to serve a paper on Sudden Sam Biggers. Why don't we send Riordan along?"

"Why, he ain't ready to go out on the scout."

"It's not much of a scout, as Biggers is pretty small-fry. He won't give any trouble.

163

And you know how Heck wears his partners out. Riordan might get worn down to the knees trying to keep up with him and give up this idea."

"But he could get hurt. He might meet somebody worse than Sam."

"Well, you tell Heck to look out for him."

"Maybe you're right, Judge. Maybe a taste of what marshals have to do will discourage him. It makes me nervous when a grown man don't get mad when he's put on the way I put it on Riordan."

"Okay. You talk to Heck. Be sure you make it plain. We don't want him shot up."

"No danger of that. Sudden Sam never shot nobody. Ain't nothing but a two-bit thief."

"Well, there are other rough ones out there besides Sam. Just make it clear to Heck I don't want the boy hurt."

"All right, Judge. Maybe it'll work."

A hand grabbed Riordan, who was in a deep sleep, and he came up fighting and striking out.

"Keep your hands to yourself!"

Riordan sat up in bed, and by the lantern that the man was holding, he saw that it was Heck Thomas, probably the best of Judge Parker's marshals. He always got his man, though not always alive. "What is it, Marshal?"

"Get up. Get your clothes on and get your gun."

"What for?"

"You're going to ride with me on a little job. I'm going to give you a taste of what it's like on the scout."

Riordan at once came off the bed and began to throw his clothes on. He strapped on his pistol, his rifle, and followed Heck out.

"Get yourself a horse."

"I know which one I want, Marshal. Maggie over there."

"That ain't no horse. She's just a big pet."

"Well, she's not mean and she doesn't buck, and you know, Marshal, I'm not very good with horses."

"Well, throw a saddle on her. She looks strong enough. I guess she can keep up."

Quickly Riordan saddled up.

Heck, who was sitting down smoking a cigarette, said, "Go in the kitchen there and get us some grub. Enough to last two or three days."

"What kind?"

"Anything we can keep down."

Quickly Riordan went into the kitchen, grabbed two sacks, and filled them with things they might use on the trail. He threw

165

in some dried beans, bacon, some hard rolls, some salt meat, and several other things.

When he returned outside, Thomas said, "Okay, let's go."

They left before the sun peeped over the western ridge. Riordan kept waiting for Thomas to tell him something about what they were after, but Thomas said nothing.

All morning all Riordan heard was, "Catch up! Put the spurs on that nag. We ain't got all day. You ride like a squaw!"

Since this was fairly well true, Riordan could hardly answer, so he kept up as best he could. When they stopped for a meal, he did the cooking, which amounted to frying some bacon and slicing some biscuits he had brought and breaking out a bottle of honey. They ate the crunchy bacon, poured honey all over the biscuits, and got their hands all sticky. As soon as they were through, they sat there drinking coffee.

Heck stared at him for a moment then said, "We're out for Sudden Sam Biggers."

"Is he an outlaw?"

"Well, not much of one. He's pretty small potatoes, but we've got to pick him up."

"You think there'll be any shooting?"

"No, Sam ain't a killer." He took another bite of biscuit and then wiped the honey

166

from his lips and mustache. "But he's got a brother who is. His name's Hardy. He's a mean one, and they got a cousin, Dent Smith, that's rough enough to suit anybody. If we catch them, we'll serve the papers on Sam, get the cuffs on him, and bring him home."

"What if his brother's there or this cousin of his?"

"Well, we'll have to do it anyway."

Riordan began cleaning the frying pan and then stored it away, for he knew they would leave as soon as possible. "Has this Sudden Sam ever killed anybody?"

"Nope."

"What's he wanted for?"

"He's wanted 'cause he robbed Jim Tyler's widow." Heck's eyes glinted with anger. "He was my partner, Jim was, as good a man as I ever had. He got killed by Henry the Fox. I'm going to stop that gentleman's clock. You see if I don't! I'll get him sooner or later."

"Henry the Fox? What is he?"

"He's the roughest outlaw in the Territory. His real name is Henry Beecher."

"And he's the worst man in the Territory?"

"Yeah, I reckon he is, and that's saying a lot. He's got some pretty bad ones working

167

for him. Sal Maglie, Hack Wilson, Red Lyle. A couple more. When they get together it'd take an army to stop 'em. They're all tough. They can all shoot."

After putting the remnants of the food and the utensils away in the pack and tying it on the saddle horn, Riordan climbed on his horse. When Heck came up beside him, he said, "How much did Sudden Sam steal?"

"Two hundred and fifty dollars . . . and two chickens."

The report amused Riordan. "So we're out after a chicken thief?"

"No," Heck said, his voice hard, "we're after a low-down skunk who stole from my partner's widow, and I intend to have his hide for it. We'll put him where the dogs don't bite him."

"Is he fast with a gun, this Sudden Sam?"

"Not a bit. He's slow as mud." He laughed harshly. "Why, you could get a shave and a haircut while he's pulling a gun. But his brother, Hardy, he's fast as lightning, and so is their cousin, Dent. You just let me handle them if we happen to run into 'em. They'd shoot you before you could pull a gun."

Riordan was cooking the last of their bacon and heating the last of their beans. They had traveled hard for three days with no success. Heck had spoken very little, so Riordan had kept his own counsel. Now he put the beans and bacon onto the tin plates and poured the coffee into the tin cups and walked over. "Marshal Thomas, got the grub."

Heck had been lying down taking a nap. He got up stiffly, stretched, and looked down at the meal. "That ain't much," he said.

"It's all we got, Marshal."

"Well, we got to have grub. I'll tell you what." He picked his plate up and began shoveling the beans into his mouth at a fierce rate and washing them down with boiling coffee. He seemed to have no feeling in his mouth. It was said that Heck Thomas could drink coffee boiling straight out of the pot. "We'll go over to Mason Peterson's store. It ain't but about ten miles. We can get what we need."

Riordan made sure the fire was out, climbed on board Maggie, and said, "Get up!"

Heck was amused. "One thing. There ain't no danger of that horse gettin' a bit between her teeth and runnin' off with you."

"No, she's a lady, she is."

"I never rode her, but she holds up pretty good."

"She's a strong girl."

"What are you doing out here anyway?"

Riordan was surprised. "What do you mean . . . out here in the prairie with you?"

"No, why are you washing dishes and shoveling refuse when you could be doing something easy? You got some education. You been to college?"

"Yes, a little."

"What you doin' out here then? You could work in an office."

"I did help out some in an office at my dad's factory when I was younger. Couldn't stand it. Got bored stiff."

Heck suddenly grinned. "If we run into Henry the Fox you won't be bored stiff."

"Well, have you ever gotten close to him?"

"Oh yeah. Traded shots with him, but both of us missed. He's a slick one, he is. Not very big. He's got small eyes, and they're green. He's not heavy. He's kind of built like a — I don't know, like a panther or something. That's why they call him the Fox, I guess."

They rode on for a time as Heck Thomas described Henry the Fox in his wrongdoings, and finally he said, "You ought to quit this. Go on back and do something that

170

pays more. You're not going to be shoveling out horse stalls the rest of your life, are you?"

"I hope not."

"Why do you want to be a marshal?"

"I've never done anything hard. Everything's come easy to me, and I wanted to find out if I could do something hard."

"Well, you picked a good one. Not what you're doing now, washing dishes, but if we run into some of these outlaws, or wild Indians, you'll find out if you can take it hard. What if you can't?"

Riordan took a deep breath and looked over at Thomas. "Well, I'll have to spend the rest of my life doing something I don't want to do."

"Most of us do that anyway."

They reached the makeshift store a few hours later. Mason Peterson served them himself. They were able to get coffee, beans, salt meat, and a few other things.

After they had acquired all the goods they could think of, Thomas said, "Mason, we're on the scout looking for Sudden Sam Biggers. You seen him?"

Mason was a well-built man. He had lost most of his hair but was not bad looking. "Why, it's funny you should ask, Marshal. He was in here yesterday with his brother

171

Hardy and Dent Smith."

"Aw, we just missed 'em."

"Well, I can tell you where he's going. I heard 'em talking. They're going for Sam's cabin."

Heck looked glum and shook his head. "I was hoping to catch Sam alone. It'd be easier to take him in."

"Well, Dent and Hardy won't take easy, but you know that."

"Thanks a lot, Mason."

The two went outside and loaded the grub and other supplies. Heck was quiet.

"What's the matter, Marshal?"

"Blast it! Seems like everything goes wrong. It'd be easy to take in Sudden Sam, but there'll be three of 'em. If we bump up against 'em, and it comes down to facin' 'em off, you try to keep Sam. Even you can outdraw him."

"You want me to shoot him?"

"Well I don't want you to powder his nose! What do you mean? Don't you know what we're up against here?"

"Well, what about the other two?"

Heck was silent. "I can't beat 'em both. I don't know what it'll be like, but that's what it is bein' a marshal."

"I wish you had a good man along instead of me."

172

"You keep Sam off of me, and I'll take care of the rest."

For the next few hours they rode in a westward direction. There was no question of getting lost because Heck knew exactly where Dent Smith's cabin was.

They stopped late in the afternoon at a stream on the lee side of a mountain. As they watered their horses, Riordan pulled some cheese and crackers out of the sack, and the two munched on them. After they had finished, Thomas brushed the cracker crumbs from his mustache and said, "We're getting pretty close. We'll reach the cabin before dark. I don't want to take 'em on after nightfall, so we'll get 'em out before then."

They continued riding, passing a herd of deer feeding off the bark of saplings, and after a while Thomas threw up his hands and said, "There it is."

"I don't see any cabin."

"That's it."

"That's not a cabin."

"Well, I guess you might say it's a cave. A dugout."

It was a small structure only about ten feet by twenty. Half of it was sunk back into a clay bank. The part that was sticking out was poles and sod and a roof of sod supported by a center pole. There was a shed adjoining it, and the horses were stamping and blowing out their breath.

"Look there. They got a fire going. Must be cooking." He suddenly said, "Take that coat off."

Surprised, Riordan took off his coat.

"Now, take a side approach. Climb up that hill, get up on top, and put that coat on that pipe sticking out up there where the smoke's comin' out. That'll go back and smoke 'em out. As soon as you get the pipe covered, come back here. We'll catch 'em as they come out the door."

Quickly Riordan did as he was ordered. The slope was not steep. He stepped out upon the sod roof carefully. It held his weight, so he put the coat over the pipe sticking up. He saw it was going to drive the smoke back, so turning he made his way back to Thomas.

"Don't stand close to me. Get over there about ten feet away."

Riordan's nerves grew tense. Soon he heard coughing, and the door burst open and two men came out.

"One of 'em is still in there," Heck complained. "That's Sudden Sam on the left and his brother Hardy on the right. You watch out for Sam. I'll take care of Hardy."

174

Suddenly Thomas raised his voice. "This is Heck Thomas, Sam. I'm takin' you in!"

"You ain't takin' nobody in!" The voice was rough, and it was Hardy who spoke. "Sam ain't done nothin'."

"Hardy, you stand away. I've got no trouble to pick with you, but I'm taking Sam in."

"No, you ain't."

What happened then was so quick that Riordan could not logically follow it. He was watching Sam, but then out of the corner of his eye he saw Hardy draw his gun. Heck must have drawn his own because he got his shot off first, which drove Hardy backward.

Riordan then saw, at almost the same moment, another man come out of the cabin. He knew it must be Dent Smith. He was holding a rifle up, aiming right at Heck when Heck shot Hardy. Without thought, Riordan pulled his gun and in one practiced motion got off a shot. It caught Dent Smith in the throat. He dropped the rifle and fell back gurgling. He grabbled around on the ground, trying to speak but making only unintelligible noises.

Heck went over and kicked Dent's rifle away and looked down. "Well, you've kilt your last man, Dent Smith."

Riordan looked down at the man he had shot. He was sick, but he knew that he had done what had to be done. "I didn't want to kill him," he said hoarsely.

Heck shook his head. "You didn't have no choice." They watched as Dent Smith died, finally stiffening into that attitude of death. Heck Thomas turned and said, "Well, this bothers you, don't it, boy?"

"Yes, sir, it does."

"You never shot a man before?"

"No, I never did."

"Well, it'll bother you some. It goes like that. It did when I got my first man. But Dent Smith is a bad one. He's killed four men and one woman, and he would have added me to his score if you hadn't got him. I know it's going to be hard for you, but you done good. As good as any marshal could have done." He sighed then nodded at Sudden Sam and said, "Let's get this worthless critter in the pokey."

CHAPTER 10

Judge Parker stood at his window, staring down at the gallows. He had been responsible for condemning many men, knowing there was no appeal from his decisions. Every time there was a hanging, he stood at this window, staring down. He never missed a hanging. Most thought he enjoyed watching the men die, but only a few knew he took no pleasure from it. He just felt it was his duty. If he was going to command the ultimate sentence, he should be able to face its carrying out.

His attention was drawn to a man riding up to his building. He watched as Heck Thomas stepped out of the saddle, took a deep breath, and then made his way across the dusty street. Within a few minutes, Heck knocked on his door. "Come in."

Heck entered with his hat in his hands.

"Hello, Marshal. Have a seat."

Heck sat down heavily.

The judge poured two glasses of water and handed one of them to Heck. "You look dried out."

"I am. This summer's got the best of me. I read a book about Eskimos living on top of the ice. I wish sometimes I had the luck to be born there."

"Well, you'd be just as unhappy there, I guess, wishing you were down here in Fort Smith with the sun burning your brains out. Well, tell me about the scout. Did you catch up with Sam?"

"We sure did, Judge, but the trouble was he had his brother Hardy and Dent Smith with him."

"That's a bad horse." Judge Parker frowned. "Were you able to sneak up on 'em?"

"Well, Judge, we had to hunt 'em pretty hard. Finally found out from a store down there that they'd gone to Sam's cabin. We took out after 'em and got there just before dark. I didn't want to tackle 'em in the dark, so I sent young Riordan to cover up the smokestack and force 'em out."

"Has that young fellow been able to keep up with you?"

Heck scratched his head and said thoughtfully, "You know he did. He's got more stamina than you'd think. He looks like he's little, but he must be made out of steel wire."

"What happened then?"

"Well, he got on top of the dugout, covered up the stovepipe, then he come back down, and we waited. Just like I knowed would happen, the smoke backed up into that dugout, and pretty soon Sam came out, and Hardy was with him. I didn't see Dent, so I told Riordan to take care of Sam. He's a slow draw and a coward anyway, but Hardy's different. So I kept my eye on Hardy. That was sort of a mistake. He went for his gun, and you know how quick he is. I pulled at the same time, and I got off a shot. But then I heard Riordan yell, 'Look out!' and knew Dent had come out of that dugout. As soon as I fired at Hardy, I started to turn, but right on top of my shot came another one. I thought Dent had missed me somehow. I turned around, and there was that young fellow Riordan with his gun out. He had hit Dent right in the throat, and that done him in. He fell down and gurgled for a while, and then he died."

"You mean that young man beat Dent to the draw?"

"I don't see how he done it. But Dent is a bad guy, and he's killed his share of folks. I wasn't sorry to see him go."

"How did Riordan take it, killing a man?"

"Not good. He's tough enough to keep up with me, and he can pull a gun quicker than I thought, and he must be a good shot 'cause he hit Dent right where it done the most good. But he was kind of green."

"Did you ask him?"

"Sure did. He said it made him kind of sick, but I remember when I killed my first man. I didn't take it too good either. But let me tell you this, that young man is better than he looks. I'll partner with him anytime, Judge."

Parker listened as Heck talked for a while. When Heck left, Parker sat down, pulled a paper from his desk drawer, took the pen, and dipped it in the inkwell. He began to write:

My dear Mrs. Riordan,
I take this opportunity to write with what I think is very good news. I think I've told you we followed your advice and poured every dirty, hard job we could on your son. It didn't do any good, however, not from your standpoint. He stayed cheerful and did everything that Marshal Swinson put on him. Never said a word, always with a smile. Well, that impressed me very much. I

180

know you may not agree with this, but I think he's at least learned a little bit about how to become a man. He's got all kinds of determination. What I would like is for you to consider letting me give him more responsibility. I don't mean to make a marshal out of him and send him out on dangerous missions, but there are other things he can do, for example, delivering summons, and I'd like to try him for that. I will, however, await your reply, and whatever you decide will be the way it is.

Respectfully yours,
Judge Isaac Parker

He sealed the envelope, put it on the desk with other mail he had answered, and then smiled. "That young man has come a long way, and I know his mother will be proud of him."

Rosa was sitting in the parlor, mending one of her sister's dresses. Her grandfather sat across from her. She looked up when he cleared his throat, obviously wanting her attention.

"Well, time for a little foolishness, I guess."

"What kind of foolishness, Grandfather?"

"Olan Henderson, a rich rancher on the

Arkansas side of the Territory not far from Fort Smith, is throwing a big wedding. He's making a celebration out of it. He's going to have dancing and drinks and food and entertainment. I think you ought to go."

Rosa had heard about the wealthy rancher and how he was marrying his daughter off. He lived so close to Judge Parker's court that for the most part the bandits stayed away from him. He had only the one daughter, and he decided it would be an event that the Territory would never forget. He had instructed his hands to build a six-inch platform, which would be the venue of the wedding ceremony itself and also be a dance floor after the wedding. He had made arrangements for music and had killed two heavy beef critters to barbecue and cut up into different sorts of meat dishes. He was a drinking man himself and would provide strong spirits for those who drank and lemonade for those who didn't. He sent out general invitations to as many of his neighbors as he knew, and one of those had come to Frank Lowery. "I'd like to. Could I take Raquel with me?"

"Why, of course. You two probably need some pretty dresses."

"I don't have much and neither does Raquel, but we'll get some material, and we'll deck ourselves out like the Queen of Sheba."

Indeed, it was a big job, but Rosa and Raquel had Chenoa and Ethel to help. They were all good seamstresses, and they had plenty of time.

When the day of the wedding came, they had the dresses ready. They put them on, and Frank and Mateo admired them.

"That's a beautiful dress, daughter," Mateo said.

Indeed, Raquel did look beautiful in a mild green dress. Her waist was tiny, and the bodice was crossed over in the front.

"Thank you, Father." She turned. "Grandfather, isn't Rosa beautiful?"

"She certainly is," he said. "You look sweet, darling."

Rosa was pleased that her grandfather was now saying gentle, kind things he would never have thought of before.

He looked at Rosa and smiled. "You are as beautiful as any woman in the Territory."

Rosa didn't think that was true at all, but she did feel pretty in the blue dress with a tight bodice defining the high richness of her bosom and the elegance of her waist. The tight sleeve of the upper arm flared out with ruffles, and the skirt flared out at the hem.

She smiled. "Oh Grandfather, you just think that because we are your granddaughters."

"Well, all I can say is you two better take your guns along. You're so pretty them men are going to try to run off with you."

"Well, they won't do that," Rosa said. "I wish you would both go."

"Somebody's got to stay here and take care of the place."

"That's why you hired two new hands." Indeed, they had hired a man called Whitey Ford and another called Felix Mantilla. This would allow Ringo and Ned to escort her and her sister to the dance. Blinky had no interest in going. He said he would stay around and watch the place.

Finally it was time to go, and they got into the wagon. It was quite a long ride, and they were glad to arrive at Henderson's ranch. They met his daughter, Hettie, who was marrying a man named William Logan.

"We're glad to see you ladies." Olan Henderson smiled. "Don't you look pretty! I can't answer all these young fellows that are coming. Some of them will be up to no good. You just watch yourself."

"Thank you, Mr. Henderson. We'll be careful."

The wedding came before the dance, so

when Henderson had gotten the preacher in the front, everyone gathered around to listen as he talked about the sanctity of marriage. Finally he was through, and the bride came forward.

"Isn't the bride beautiful?" Rosa whispered to Ringo, who was standing next to her.

"All women are beautiful," he whispered back.

She laughed at him. "You don't really think that."

"Sure I do." He moved closer and put his arm against hers. "When are you going to have your wedding?"

She liked Ringo Jukes very much indeed. He was a bit forward, but she knew he admired her as a woman. They both had senses of humor, and now she said, "Well, I'll have a wedding when I find a man who will do everything I tell him."

She expected Ringo to scoff at that, but he said, "Why, you know I feel the same way."

"You don't really."

"Why, I do. You know there's a verse in the Bible that I'm partial to."

"I didn't know you knew anything about the Bible."

"Well, I know this one. It says, 'When a

man hath taken a new wife, he shall not go out to war, neither shall he be charged with any business: but he shall be free at home one year, and shall cheer up his wife which he hath taken.' " He grinned at her and winked. His eyes were full of fun. "Ain't that a doozy? So you see, if you take me for a husband, I'll do nothin' but cheer you up for a whole year, Miss Rosa."

"I don't know how you found that in the Bible," she said. She was amused but also impressed that he knew such a verse. "Well, I'll tell you more about my plans after this wedding is over. Come on. The dancing's starting."

Rosa discovered that, as she expected, Ringo Jukes was a fine dancer. He was handsomely dressed in a gray suit she had not seen before, and she felt the eyes of many women taking him in. For a moment she found herself wondering what it would be like to be married to him. She was sure that he was speaking playfully about staying home for a year, but no man she had ever talked to had even such an idea as that.

Rosa was enjoying herself tremendously. She seldom lacked for a partner, if she wanted one. She did sit out a couple of dances as she needed some time to catch her breath and get a drink of lemonade.

The dance had been going on for some time when a tall man suddenly stood up in front of Rosa. "Don't know anybody to introduce me, and I don't want to be brash, but I'm Charles Rhodes. You're Miss Rosa Ramirez, I understand."

"That's right. Glad to know you, Mr. Rhodes."

"Just Charles is fine." He hesitated and said, "I've been meaning to come over and welcome you. My ranch is about twenty miles west of yours. Could I have a dance?"

"Of course." The two moved around the floor. After a couple of minutes, he asked, "Are you Frank Lowery's granddaughter?"

"Yes, I am."

Rhodes looked uncomfortable for the rest of the dance. When the music was over, he led her to the refreshment table. He seemed to be searching for words. After offering her a glass of lemonade, which she declined, he took one himself. After a long drink, he said, "I've been meaning to come over to your place, but your grandfather wouldn't like it."

"Why not?"

"Well, we had a little trouble quite a few years back. Frank got peeved at me, and of course, I got peeved at him."

"What was the quarrel over?"

187

"Oh, it was about a horse that we didn't agree on. But you know your grandfather holds a grudge pretty well."

"Yes, I've heard my mother say that. He's stubborn."

"Well, what I would like to ask, Miss Ramirez, is if I could come over and call on you, and maybe you could get your grandfather to forgive me about that horse?"

"Why, of course, Mr. Rhodes. You just come. Grandfather is older now, and he's mellowed quite a bit."

"Well, you can look for me then." He looked around and said, "I don't get around to many things like this. Before my wife died, we used to go out to dances and such things quite a bit. Been kind of lonesome without her."

"How long has that been?"

"It'll be four years now. She was a wonderful woman."

"I'm sorry."

"So am I. It's hard to lose someone, isn't it?"

After the dance, Ned Little, one of the hands she'd come to like, came over and spoke to her. "I saw you talking to Rhodes."

"Yes, who is he?"

"A big rancher. His wife died a few years ago. He and your grandfather had an awful

188

ruckus."

"He told me about it. Said it was a fuss over a horse."

"Well, it was a little bit worse than that. I never knew the ins and outs, but your grandfather despises him."

"I don't know, Ned. He asked if I'd try to make Grandfather listen to him. I think he was wanting to apologize. I told him to call on us. Maybe I can get Grandfather to forget the quarrel."

"Well," Ned said, "your grandfather hasn't set any records for forgiving folks, but now he's old and not too long for this world, I guess. Wouldn't hurt to have a friend. He's a rich man, and when trouble comes, all of us need to stick together. There's enough bad men that the good men need to do their thing together."

A week after the dance, Rosa answered the door and was pleased to see Charles Rhodes. She smiled and greeted him warmly. "I'm glad to see you, Charles. Come into the house. I told Grandfather you might be coming."

Charles looked slightly sheepish. "Did you take his gun away from him?"

She smiled even wider. "No, but I told him he had to be civil."

Rhodes shook his head. "I was in the wrong about that horse deal, and I'm just too stubborn to admit it when I'm wrong."

"Well, you're doing the right thing now. Come on in."

They found Frank and Mateo, as usual, playing checkers.

Rhodes said at once, "Hello, Frank. I ask your pardon for calling without permission."

"No, my granddaughter said you might be coming." He got to his feet and stared at him and said, "Been a long time since we spoke."

"Well, it was my fault, Frank. I was wrong about that horse, and I want to apologize to you. As I told your granddaughter, I don't apologize good or easy, but I felt bad about it. Not many of us left. We need to stick together."

Frank stepped forward and stuck his hand out. "That's good enough for me. This is Rosa's father, Señor Ramirez."

"I'm glad to know you, sir. Your daughter graced the dance last week. The prettiest woman there."

"Now, that's enough of that." Rosa smiled. "Will you have some refreshment?"

"I'd really rather you show me around the ranch and any horses you might have. I'm always in the market for a good mount."

"He's got lots of money, Rosa. Be sure you gouge him." Frank smiled.

"Oh, Grandfather, I won't do that. Come along, Charles."

The rest of the afternoon was pleasant. She found herself liking Rhodes very much. True, he was a willful man. She had found that out from several sources, but he wasn't that way with her. His manners were perfect.

When he left he said, "I thank you for making the way for your grandfather and me to bury the hatchet. Next time maybe I can come without a guilty feeling."

"You're welcome anytime, Charles."

"I'll take you up on that, and I'll be back to pick up that bay stallion that I liked so much." He swung into the saddle and rode away.

She watched him go and wondered what it would be like to be married to him. *That's what all women do,* she thought. *When they see a man, they wonder if he'd make a good husband. This one's rich, good looking, got good manners. Got a quick temper, they tell me — but so do I.*

She thought about him often the rest of the day and even dreamed about becoming his wife that night.

The next day she went riding on the edge of the property, just looking things over. She was returning to the house when suddenly she saw a man riding close.

He announced himself. "My name is Henry Beecher."

Henry the Fox, she thought. *He doesn't look like an outlaw.*

Indeed, as she studied him, she saw he was well dressed. He had a gun at his side, as most men did in the Territory, but he had removed his hat when he spoke to her.

"I'm Rosa Ramirez."

"I'm glad to know you. I've come to look over your horses. I've bought several from your grandfather over the years."

Rosa did not know whether to mention she knew he was an outlaw.

He said, "I'm in the market for another mount."

"My grandfather doesn't do much business. That's why he sent for me and my family."

"Well, maybe you can show me a good horse. I'm partial to mares."

"Come this way." She rode down to the stables.

He kept beside her, speaking favorably about the ranch. She showed him the horses and named a rather high price on the mare that he liked.

He reached into his pocket, pulled out a sack, and said, "I've got these gold coins, just about the right amount." He counted them out and put them into her hand.

She slipped them into the pocket of her riding skirt.

They talked for a while, and even though she knew he did terrible things, she found herself enjoying their time together. He was a bad man, everyone had told her that, but somehow he just didn't look it. His face was pleasant. He was handsome with fair hair and pale green eyes such as she had never seen on a man.

He suddenly said, "I see they've told you about me."

"Yes, I have heard of you, Mr. Beecher."

"Just call me Henry. Well, I don't deserve any medals, but half the things they say about me I didn't do. Every time there's trouble they say, 'Well, that Henry's been at this.' I know my reputation's bad, but I hope you'll give me a chance to get to know you."

She started to speak, but then more quickly than she thought a man could move, he reached forward, put his arms around her waist, and drew her close. He kissed her before she could even react. She finally struggled back and pushed him away. She was angry and said, "That was not a gentlemanly thing to do!"

"I'm no gentleman." Henry laughed at her. "I'll take the mare with me." He went into the corral, put a loop over the mare's head with a practiced motion, and led her out. As he left, he lifted his hat. "I'll be seeing you, Miss Rosa."

As soon as he was gone, she turned and saw Ned stepping out from behind the barn. He had a rifle in his hand. "I was just about ready to shoot him."

"Is he really as dangerous as they say, Ned?"

"He's worse. You know he's smooth. Don't let that fool you. Don't ever let him catch you alone."

Rosa thanked Ned and went about her way. All that day she thought about how a man could be that attractive and be such a villain.

Three days after the Fox bought the mare, most of the crew had gone to take a herd to better grass. Blinky had stayed back, along with Whitey Ford, the new hand.

Rosa was in the house talking with her father when suddenly they heard gunshots.

Then the door opened, and Blinky said, "It's raiders! They're after the horses!"

Instantly Rosa and Juan grabbed the rifles that they kept by the door and stepped out onto the porch. At least half a dozen men were opening the corral gate. Without hesitation, Rosa raised her rifle and sent off a shot.

One of the men hollered, "Shoot 'em down! Shoot 'em down!" and the men began shooting at the two, who took cover.

She was aware that Blinky and Whitey were dodging across the open ground, firing and looking for shelter. Suddenly she recognized George Pye and the two men who had tried to take their horses before. They had three more men with them and were leading some of the horses out. She was also aware that her father and grandfather had stepped outside, both with rifles, and they were pouring a withering fire. One of the outlaws cried out and grabbed his side. Then another one took a shot. Someone yelled, "Let's get out of here!"

Rosa saw Pye raise his rifle and fire, and the shot struck Blinky who was knocked over backward. All of them on the porch kept up their fire, but the men got away with half a dozen horses.

Quickly Rosa ran to where Blinky was lying. The shot had taken him in the heart. He had probably died before he hit the ground. Tears came to her eyes, for the little man had been kind to her.

Whitey came limping back.

"Did you get hit, Whitey?"

"Just pinked me in the leg. Missed the bone."

"Let's get Blinky in the house, and then I'll put a patch on it."

They carried the body of the rider into the house. She washed Whitey's wound and put a bandage over it.

There was nothing to do but wait for the crew to return. Three hours later they returned.

As soon as he stepped out of the saddle, Ringo Jukes saw her face. "What's wrong, Rosa?"

"There were raiders. They killed Blinky and shot Whitey."

Ned said, "Scatter out. They may come back."

"I don't think so. They took six of our horses."

"We'll nail things down here, and then we'll go after 'em."

"We've got to take care of Blinky first."

They buried Blinky the next morning, and it was a solemn chore. They had all liked the small man.

An hour later, Rosa called Juan to one

side. She had saddled her horse, and she told him, "I'm going to Judge Parker's to get marshals."

"You can't do that. Not by yourself."

"They won't catch me on this horse. She's the fastest one we've got. Don't tell Grandfather or Father until I've left."

"Let me go with you."

"No, they might come back. They'll need all the help they can get here. I'll be fine."

Juan argued with her for a time, but she knew what she had to do . . . for all of their sakes. She mounted her horse, waved goodbye to her brother, and rode away from the ranch.

CHAPTER 11

Judge Parker leaned forward, opened an envelope, removed the letter inside, and spread it out. His wife sat across from him, and he looked up from time to time. She was cracking black walnuts on the face of an iron with a hammer and putting the nuts into a small jar.

Parker read the letter carefully then leaned back and stared thoughtfully across the room. Finally he said, "Dear, do you remember the woman named Eileen Riordan?"

"Of course I do. She's the one who had the young son who wanted to become a marshal. How is the young man doing?"

"Well, we're very pleased with him. As you know, she insisted we give him the worst jobs we could, hoping he would get tired of it and return home. But just the opposite happened. No matter how hard or dirty the work, or how difficult it was, Riordan got at it, always smiling, never complaining. We're very pleased with him."

"Well, that's good news."

"Actually, there's better news than that. Heck usually wears young men out, the marshals that go with him. He's tireless himself, and he thinks everyone else is. So, we sent him out on what should have been an easy job. You've heard of Sudden Sam. He's a crook but not a vicious one. Never killed anybody. Never shot anybody that I know of. But he's a burglar and a robber. Heck hated him because he robbed the widow of his partner of some money and two chickens. So, we sent him out. We decided Heck could go arrest him and bring him back — and he took young Riordan with him."

"Did they catch him?"

"Well, they did, but he had two rough gunmen with him. They tried to kill Heck, and this young man shot the man that was about to do the job. Heck said he would have been dead for sure if young Riordan hadn't been there. He was amazed that the young man was so quick with his gun. And so am I."

"That sounds like he's ready for something else."

"That's what I felt, too. So, a few days

ago I wrote Mrs. Riordan a letter and told her all about her son. This is her answer:

"Dear Judge Parker,

What you tell me is encouraging, although it frightens me a little. As you know I'm partial to my youngest son, Faye, and I hesitate to do anything that would put him in danger. However, it sounds to me as though he has done everything we both asked, and if you think well, I would encourage you to give him more responsibility. I'm sure you know better than I how to handle this matter. I can't tell you how much I appreciate your consideration, and as you say, your wife concurs with this in the decision to help me bring my son to a higher part of manhood than he felt he had. So, please do your best for him.

Sincerely yours,
Eileen Riordan"

He put the letter down and said, "She's changed her mind."

"Yes, she has. Do you have any idea how you can help the boy more?"

"Well, I'm going to find some way to get him out on the field. Nothing very difficult, but I'd like to help the young man. I think he has great potential."

"Well, you must do it, Isaac. She kept the boy close, and that's the way we mothers are. But he wants to prove that he is a grown man. If I remember correctly, he had a father and two brothers who are very manly, and he feels that he's failed them."

"I can see how that would affect the boy. We'll do that. I'll give him a chance."

Riordan stepped inside the judge's office and was somewhat intimidated. Judge Parker, however, smiled and said, "Sit down, young man. There's something I want to tell you."

"Have I done anything wrong, Judge?"

"No — no. Quite the opposite. Let me tell you what I've done. We were so happy with the way you conducted yourself on the job with Heck Thomas that I wrote to your mother and told her how well you had done. I told her you had completed every dirty, hard job we gave you without complaining, and then when we sent you on the scout you saved Heck Thomas's life. I told her how proud we are of you."

"Well, thank you for writing her, Judge. I've got a lot to learn, but I'd like to try a real job."

"All right, Riordan. How about this? The

first request we get that I think you can handle without putting yourself in much danger, we'll send you on a scout."

"Oh, that's fine, Judge. I appreciate it."

"It won't be a big job," Parker warned, "but you need to learn how to work in the Territory."

"I promise I'll do the very best I can. Thank you for this opportunity, Judge."

Riordan did not change his ways. He stayed under Marshal Swinson's orders, still cleaning out the stables, washing the dishes, and helping the cook when he could.

He had been out one afternoon hauling the fewmets, as they called the stable sweepings, to the judge's garden and was sweaty and filthy from head to foot. He had on a floppy-brimmed hat that came down over his ears so he knew he was not much to look at.

Heck Thomas stopped him to say, "Well, Riordan, the judge tells me he's going to put you to work."

"Yes, sir."

"I wish you could go with me on this job, but it's a little bit rough."

"Maybe I can go with you some other time, Marshal Thomas."

"I'm sure you can. I told the judge so. Hang in there, young man. Your opportunity is coming."

For the next hour Riordan kept hauling the refuse of the horses' stalls to the judge's garden, which was blooming well from so much fertilizer. He was pushing a wheelbarrow toward the garden when he saw the judge and Marshal Swinson come out of the courthouse, joined by some of the other marshals. *Maybe I'll get to go on a scout soon,* he thought.

He looked up to see a young woman in a riding outfit such as he had never seen ride in at a gallop. She pulled the horse up to an abrupt halt and dismounted. Being curious, Riordan moved closer to where he could hear what was said.

Rosa climbed off her horse. It was a longer ride than she had anticipated, and she was exhausted. She had met Judge Parker at the wedding, and she glanced around to see that not much was happening. One man in filthy clothes was hauling something with a wheelbarrow. She ignored him, well aware that everyone was staring at her.

She walked right up to the judge and said at once in a loud voice, "Judge Parker, our ranch has been raided, and a man has been killed. I saw the men who did it. The leader was George Pye, and two of the men with him were Vernon Epps and Boog Powell. It was the same three men who tried to take the horses from us earlier. We took their guns from them, and George Pye swore he would get even. He killed one of our hands, and I want him and the others hanged on your gallows. We need a posse of your marshals to run them down."

Parker removed his hat and ran his hand over his hair. He was disturbed and shook his head saying, "Well Miss Ramirez, it's not quite that easy."

"Why isn't it? I saw the men who did it. I'll testify against them. I've heard you have over a hundred marshals."

"But they're out in the Territory. Our men don't stay here long, Miss Ramirez. They do their jobs, they come in, they get other assignments, and they're gone again as soon as possible. I'll tell you what, we'll send a man out to your place as soon as one comes back. Right now we don't have anybody."

"Don't tell me you don't have a single marshal to catch a cold-blooded murderer."

Parker's glance fell on Riordan, who had stopped and was listening to the conversation. He turned to Swinson and said under his breath, "We can send Riordan. He can stay at their ranch until some of our men are available to track the killers down."

"That's right, Judge. He can't get hurt just looking out for these folk. The killers have gone underground by this time. It's going to take some good men to root 'em out."

Parker nodded then put his hat back on. "Miss Ramirez, I'm sending you the one man we have. He'll stay close to your ranch and guard your folks, and then as soon as I get a few men, I'll send them. They can run down Pye and his band."

"Thank you, Judge," Rosa said. "I knew you would help us."

Judge Parker called out, "Riordan, come here!"

Rosa turned to see the man who was hauling compost in a wheelbarrow come forward. He was filthy from head to foot, had on a floppy hat, and looked young and inexperienced.

"Riordan, this is Miss Rosa Ramirez. You go with her and guard her family. We'll send a posse out as soon as some men get back."

Rosa stared at the sorry figure that stood before her. Then she turned and said, "You're sending that fertilizer hauler to help us?"

"He is better than he looks, Miss Ramirez."

Rosa was fighting hard to hold back angry tears. "I thought you'd give us somebody to help . . . a marshal. That dirty clodhopper might as well go on hauling refuse for the garden!" She turned, went to her horse, and started to mount.

Parker went to her quickly and said, "Just a minute. Let me explain."

Swinson ran over and said, "Riordan, saddle up, get your guns, and go with this woman."

"Don't I have time to clean up?"

"Nope, she's mad as a hornet. You stick with her. You can clean up when you get there."

Rosa waited, hardly listening to the judge who was trying to explain that Riordan was new and not yet ready for a full-time marshal's badge but that he'd help the best he could.

When Riordan rode up on a sorry-looking horse still in his filthy clothes and his floppy hat, Rosa stepped into the saddle and gave him a withering look. "You might as well stay here and clean up after the horses."

The man did not blink or smile. He said, "Wherever you lead, Miss Ramirez, I'll go with you."

She snorted and kicked her horse's flanks and rode out. Riordan followed her on his placid horse.

■ ■ ■ ■

Marshal Swinson and Judge Parker watched Riordan and Rosa riding off toward her ranch.

"That young woman's pretty fierce, Judge. By the time Riordan's listened to her for a couple of days, he'll probably be ready to come back and clean up the stables."

Judge Parker shook his head. "She'll give him a hard time, Chester, but you remember we gave him a hard time. He never flinched. They're like fire and water, those two, but I hope they can live with each other long enough to do some good. Riordan is better than he looks, but all Miss Ramirez can see is that he doesn't look good. They'll just have to live with each other long enough for us to send some men who might do better."

"I just hope they don't kill each other," Marshal Swinson said. "I don't think it's going to work."

"It'll have to work," Judge Isaac Parker said. He gave a final look in the direction of the two who had disappeared into the distance, shook his head, and went back into the courthouse.

PART THREE

CHAPTER 12

The ranch was in sight now, but when Rosa turned and looked back over her shoulder, she saw that Riordan was far behind, his horse plodding slowly. Anger seemed to bubble within her, and she waited there, the mare shifting under her weight, flaked with sweat. She let him get close and then said, "Spur that worthless horse!"

When he did not advance any faster, she waited until he was even with her, his eyes watching her cautiously. He gave her a mild answer, "Miss Ramirez, Maggie here does the best she can."

Twilight had begun to creep over the land, the low hills to the west turning dark against the sky while the flatlands of the east slowly shadowing as night crept over them. The day had been blistering hot, sharp and bright, with no clouds to bring any relief from the sun's rays.

Now as Rosa stepped off her horse, the

sun had settled westward and seemed to melt into a shapeless bed of gold flames as it touched the faraway mountains. She advanced to the porch, having seen her father and her grandfather sitting there in their cane-bottom rocking chairs. Pearl shadows had come on the eaves of the house and the barn, and the dusty road took on soft silver shadings. Soon evening's peace would magnify the distant sounds, but all the beauty of the sunset meant nothing to Rosa, for she was still furious over the treatment she had received from Judge Parker.

Shaking her head with disgust, Rosa spurred the mare, which despite being hard ridden, still had some spirit left. She rode up toward the house, and as she drew near, she saw Ned walking across the front yard. She pulled the mare to an abrupt halt, stepped out of the saddle, and said in a spare tone, "Ned, this mare is overheated. Would you please walk her until she cools off?"

"Sure I will, Miss Rosa." He started to ask how her trip went, but seeing her face set with anger thought better of it. He took the lines and moved away.

Rosa gave one disgusted glance backward over the road and saw that the man was still dragging along. She mounted the steps and seeing Ethel standing at the door said, "Ethel, I'm parched. Would you get me some cool water, please?"

"Yes ma'am, I'll do that."

Rosa looked at her father and her grandfather, but her lips were so dry it was difficult to talk. Both of them were sitting in rockers with the checkerboard in front of them. Rosa knew they were both men who were quick to pick up on the moods of others, and her mood at that moment was definitely not favorable.

Ethel appeared at the door with a large glass and a pitcher of water. "I'll just set this here, and you can drink all you want, Rosa."

"Thank you, Ethel." She drained the glass slowly, letting the coolness and the moisture of it seek out her dry tissues. She then poured a second glass half full and then put the glass down on the table.

Frank glanced at Mateo then asked Rosa, "How was your trip? Did you get to see the judge?"

"Yes, I saw him, but precious little good it did me!"

Frank exchanged glances with Mateo. It was her father who asked, "It didn't turn out well, I take it?"

"No, it didn't turn out well! I rode as hard

as I could, and when I got there the judge was out in front of the courthouse. I got off my horse and walked right up to him. He was very polite, but then I guess he always is. He asked me what I wanted."

"He didn't ask you in his office?"

"I didn't give him a chance. I told him about the raid and how we lost a man to the outlaws, killed, shot dead in the dust. I told him how we were plagued with outlaws.

"What did he say?"

"Oh, he was sympathetic," Rosa said. "He said he was sorry and that he hoped he could do something."

"I told him flat out what I wanted. I said, 'Judge, we need some of your marshals to run the outlaws down.' He gave me a story about how the marshals stayed out for a long time, sometimes coming in one day and going out the next. Said he didn't have any men right now."

"Well, I expect that's true," Frank said. "This is a big territory. He's had almost two hundred marshals, but he's had about fifty of them shot down. He's got a hard job."

Rosa was beyond reason, however. She turned and looked out at the road and saw that the rider was moving along at the same pace. In a tone dripping with anger, she blurted out, "There's what he sent us."

The two men watched as the rider got off his horse, tied up at the rail, and came to stand on the ground in front of the steps.

"This is the famous marshal," Rosa said. "He claims his name is Riordan, but I just call him fertilizer hauler."

Both men were shocked at her anger, and she smiled in a humorless, bitter expression. "That's what he was doing. Dressed like he is now in filthy clothes and hauling refuse out of the stables."

Frank cleared his throat. Finally he said, "Well, Riordan, have you been a marshal a long time?"

"Just since three o'clock, sir."

His answer shocked both Mateo and Frank, but it was Rosa who snapped bitterly, "Well, he's been a marshal now for at least four or five hours, but that ought to be plenty of time to make him into a great hunter."

Mateo now cleared his throat and turned to look at the man more closely. "Didn't they have any more experienced men, Riordan?"

"No, sir, they didn't."

Rosa spoke up at once, disgust in her tone. "All they had was this famous stable cleaner, and I found out he's also able to wash dirty

215

dishes." She slapped her hands together and knew it was not difficult to read her mood. She was still furious and gave Riordan a look of utter disgust, saying, "Go back to Judge Parker. I'm sure he misses your services. A hauler of fertilizer! I'm sure that'll be handy when Henry the Fox brings his band and kills all of us!" She whirled and went into the house, slamming the door behind her.

Frank got to his feet and walked to the edge of the porch. "She's a little bit upset, Marshal."

"Yes, sir, I can see that. I don't blame her much, but she's telling the truth. All of the marshals were gone at the moment. I've been working for the marshals for some time now, but this is the first time the judge has sent me out on any kind of a job."

Indeed, Riordan looked young and inexperienced, and his clothes were filthy, his face was dirty, and the shape of his hat shed an innocent face not at all like the hardbitten marshals that Frank had seen coming out of Judge Parker's court.

"Why don't you get settled in, Riordan. I guess you could use a bath and some clean clothes." He lifted up his voice and said, "Ned, come here a minute, will you?"

Ned Little came quickly to stand beside Riordan, giving him a cautious look.

"This is Riordan. He's from Judge Parker's court."

"Glad to know you, Riordan. I'm Ned."

Frank said, "Ned, why don't you help him get settled in. Find a place for him to sleep, and maybe he can change his clothes and get cleaned up by suppertime."

"Yes, sir, I'll take care of that."

From the time Ned had laid eyes on Riordan he had been filled with questions. He managed to ask a few as he led Riordan around to the side of the house toward a long, low structure. "That's the bunkhouse where you'll be staying. You been with the marshals long?"

"Not too long."

"I've seen a few of the marshals. You seem younger than most of them."

"I guess that's right. The judge agreed to take me on. He let me do a few odd jobs while I was getting ready for the big ones."

"Well, this is a big one all right." He entered the door, and when Riordan followed him, he gestured with his hand. "Take that bunk over there."

The place was a mess, Ned knew, but Riordan made no comment. He simply said,

"Thank you, Ned."

"Tell you what. Why don't you wash up a little bit and change your clothes. Supper will be ready soon."

"Well, to tell the truth I don't have any more clothes. Miss Rosa left in such a hurry, and the judge shouted at me to follow her. All I had time to do was get my rifle and my pistol and get in the saddle. She was almost out of sight as it was. The horse I rode is not very fast."

"So, you don't have any clothes except those?"

"Yes, this is all I have."

"Well, we lost a man in a raid. That's what Miss Rosa went to see the judge about, and that's why you're here, I guess. His name was Blinky. I'd known him for five years. Mighty good man." Ned shook his head. "He was about your size. Nobody's had the heart to clean up his things. As far as I know, he don't have any kin around. I believe his clothes would fit you; at least it's better than what you got on." He walked to Blinky's bunk and gathered a few items.

"Thanks, Ned. Where can I wash up?"

"Come here." He walked to the doorway and pointed outside. "See that windmill over there?"

"Don't see many of those."

"Well, it pumps water. There's several buckets there and a big tub. You can go splash around, get yourself as clean as you can, and put on some of Blinky's clothes. You'll be all right."

Riordan picked up the clothes and nodded. "Much obliged, Ned."

Ned stepped outside and watched Riordan walk toward the windmill. He didn't walk like most cowboys. There was nothing bowlegged about him. His legs were straight, and he walked quickly toward the windmill.

Ned turned and went to find Ringo, who was currying his horse out in the stable. "The marshal came in from Judge Parker's court."

"Well, I guess we can use him. What's he like?"

Ned leaned against the wall and watched as Ringo continued to curry the horse. "Well, you can see for yourself at supper. He's not a big man, and he looks terrible."

"What do you mean 'terrible'? He's ugly?"

"No, I reckon he looks fair. I couldn't see him, as he was wearing a floppy hat, but he looks about like a shoe clerk. You know, kind of innocent."

Ringo straightened up and stared at Ned. "All the marshals I've seen are pretty tough.

This one sounds different."

"Well, he is different. But you know looks are deceiving. Remember Dirk Patrick?"

"Sure do. He was a bad one."

"Bad as they come, but you remember he had a kind of a prissy look about him, a sissified way. That got a lot of men in trouble. He didn't look like he would fight, but when someone crossed him it was like a stick of dynamite going off. He left a trail of blood all the way across Oklahoma and Texas."

The two men talked about the marshal, and finally Ringo said, "Well, he may look like a schoolboy, but maybe he's better than he seems."

"You ought to see the horse he rode in on. I watched him coming. He's just plodding along like he was on a plow horse."

"Well, there again not all gunfighters are great riders."

"Yeah, but something else bothers me, Ringo. He carries a .38 by his side."

"That's different."

Indeed it was different, for Ned knew every man in the Territory, certainly all of the marshals, carried a larger caliber, with most of them being Colt .44s.

Ringo shook his head. "Well, those little .38s won't knock a man down unless you put a bullet in his brain. Doesn't sound like

Miss Rosa got a very good man out of the draw."

"No, she was mad as a hornet when she rode in. I started to speak to her but figured I'd better not."

"Well, we'll find out more about this fellow. What's his name?"

"Riordan is all I heard. Don't know his first name. I'm going to go in and tell the cook to throw on some more steaks, or whatever he's cooking, on the stove. This fellow won't eat much. He's too undersized for that, but I can eat what he leaves."

Rosa came out of a fitful sleep slowly, for she was still tired after the long ride she had made, but she was aware that dawn was coming. As she sat up in the bed and put her feet on the floor, she thought of her trip to Fort Smith and how the judge had seemingly not been willing to help her. With that came the thought of Riordan, and just that one single thought seemed to trigger all the anger she had had yesterday. "What are we supposed to do with a fool like that?" she muttered.

She got out of bed, walked over to the table, and poured tepid water from a ceramic pitcher into an enamel washbowl. Stripping off her nightgown, she washed her face and hands and arms and then went over the rest of her body as well as she could. It was not a bath, but it was her habit to do this every day.

She dressed, putting on her underclothing, her divided skirt, and her white blouse. She put on the vest with the gold coins for buttons, which she had grown fond of. It had four pockets that held small things. Besides the buttons and the pockets, she thought it gave her a rakish look.

She walked over to the window and looked out. The sunrise was slow, and she had noted that the night left the land so gently that things were dim and only an outline. Now the earth was beginning to take form, the distant hills barely visible. Even as she watched, a bird began singing. She did not know what kind. "What have you got to sing about?" she muttered.

Now that she was fully dressed, she went downstairs.

As soon as she entered the kitchen, Ethel turned and said, "Breakfast will be ready soon, Miss Rosa. It's biscuits, gravy, eggs, and ham."

"That sounds good." She began moving around, setting the table, although she knew it was possible that the older men would not get up. She knew they awoke early, but many times they would just lie in their beds resting.

"Mr. Frank said you brought a man back from Judge Parker's court. What's he like?"

"He's not a man. He is little more than a dishwasher."

Ethel blinked and stood staring. "You don't like him."

"I went to get a tough man or about a half dozen to run these killers down. What do I get? A stable cleaner! That's all he's good for, that and to wash dirty dishes. Well, I told him to go back, but I suppose he's still here."

"Well, that's too bad, but maybe if we give him a chance he'll be of some use."

"He'll be of use cleaning the stable," Rosa snapped.

The food was soon ready, and she sat down and ate with Ethel. Her mother came in and joined them. When they were eating, Rosa spoke with bitterness to Chenoa, and Chenoa listened to her silently. "Better not be judging a man. He may be better than he looks."

"Well he couldn't be any worse! Filthy clothes, hands and face all smeared with dirt, and who knows what else. And you should have seen the horse he rode! I had to wait on him. I think he was riding a plow horse."

"Well, you need to give him a chance," Chenoa said, echoing Ethel's words.

"I'll give him a chance. Our stables need cleaning, and there's always dirty dishes."

She fell silent, and the other two women began to talk of other matters of the house. Her mother soon left to wake Juan and Raquel and tell them to come for breakfast. As Ethel brought in some more food for her brother and sister, an idea was forming in Rosa's mind. She finished eating and said, "I've got to go talk to the hands. I'll see you later."

Leaving the house, she noted that the sun was now climbing in the west, throwing its lambent beams down over the earth. She found Ringo, who was coming out of the kitchen shack, which also included the tables for the hands. "Hello, Ringo."

"Hello, lady. You should have been here. That Riordan, he's a better cook than we've had. Made some of the best pancakes I ever ate."

"We don't need a cook. We need a man who can shoot somebody."

"Well, Ned and me talked about it. Sure enough he don't look like much, but you never can tell."

224

"He rode in on a plow horse. What good is that to us?"

"Well, maybe that was all they let him have at the judge's."

"No, you can tell the way he sat on the plug he's not a rider. I want you to give him some lessons."

"Riding lessons?" Ringo laughed. "What do you mean by that? You said he rode in."

"I want you to teach him how to stay on a fast horse. Start him out with Chief."

Ringo's eyes opened wide, and he passed his hand over his face. "Chief? Why, that's a plum bad horse. He's throwed me and Ned both, and everybody else that I know of."

"Put Riordan on him. He's got to learn somehow."

"Well, that marshal might get hurt. Don't that bother you?"

Rosa smiled, but there was little humor in it. "Of course it does, Ringo. But he won't last against the outlaws if he isn't ready for it. Sometimes you have to endure unpleasant things to get toughened up to complete what needs to be done. I wish we could take it more slowly, as you all did with Juan and me, but we just don't have the time."

Ringo stood looking at Rosa, apparently searching for something to say. Finally he said, "You know, Rosa, you look sweet, but you got some toughness in you."

"All women are like that. Haven't you noticed?"

"Well, not all look as good as you, but all of 'em have a little toughness, I suppose. I don't like this, though. That horse can be plum mean."

"Don't tell Riordan he's a bad horse. Just get him in the saddle and then get out of the way so you don't get stomped."

"Well, it's your say so, Rosa, but we may have a busted up marshal on our hands."

Riordan came out of the kitchen shack. He had helped wash the dishes. The regular cook had left a week earlier, so Riordan had been glad to plunge in to fix pancakes. That was simple enough. He found Ringo Jukes waiting for him.

The husky rider said, "Need to give you some riding lessons."

"Why, I can ride."

"No, I don't mean that old pokey horse you rode in on."

"Maggie is a good horse."

"Look, sooner or later we're either going to be chasing after some outlaws or they're going to be chasing us. In either case that horse is no good. You've got to have a fast mount."

"I haven't had a lot of experience."

"Well, you're fixin' to get some. Come on. I'll pick you out one to start on."

Riordan followed reluctantly, and when they got to the corral he saw that all the hands had gathered, including Ned, who was leaning against the corral post rolling a cigarette. "Want to ride a little bit, Riordan?"

"Sure he does," Ringo said. "Here. Let me saddle this horse up for you."

Riordan had a quick mind. He saw that the men were all grinning, and when Ringo led a beautiful black stallion out of the stable, he was sure that he was in for a thumping. *I've got to do it. No other way out. I hope he doesn't kill me.*

"That horse is named Chief. He's plenty fast," Ned said. "Easy to saddle. He stands just nice and still. You see?"

Indeed, Chief did stand still while Ringo put on a blanket and saddle. He then put the bridle on. Ringo turned and said, "Okay."

Riordan approached slowly. The horse was very large and muscular. He turned and looked at Ringo, and there seemed to be a gleam in his dark eyes. "This horse is pretty hard to ride, I take it?"

"Oh, he's fine. A good horse is always a

227

little harder to ride than your plow horses. They're lively," Ringo said. "But you'll need a lively mount around here, Riordan. Now you just go ahead. Just ride him around the corral here a few times until you get used to him."

Riordan clenched his jaw as he readied for this newest challenge.

Rosa had positioned herself at one end of the corral. She had a clear view of Riordan and saw the apprehension in his eyes. She heard the men talking about him.

One of the new hands, Charlie Jones, said quietly, "Ned, that's a pretty bad horse. He plowed me up."

"Yeah. He plowed me up, too. He's a good 'un."

"I wouldn't call him a good 'un," Charlie said. "This poor fellow looks like a tender-foot."

"Well, you know how Ringo is. Always playing a joke."

A sudden impulse came, and Rosa felt that she should try to stop what was about to happen, for it could be dangerous. Still she said nothing. *He shouldn't have come here if he wasn't ready to work.*

She watched as Riordan put one foot in the stirrup then swung his leg over the horse. He grabbed the reins from Ringo, and as soon as he did, Chief exploded with raw strength. Humping his back, he went straight up in the air and came down stiff legged. She saw Riordan jolting up and down in the saddle. He made a wild grab for the horn and missed. He was thrown sideways as Chief twisted and turned like a corkscrew. Three more jumps from Chief and Riordan lost all control. He sailed up in the air, his arms flailing, and turned a complete somersault. He landed flat on his back with a distinct *whump.*

Grandfather, who had come to stand beside her, said, "That was a bad fall."

"Sure was," Father agreed. "I hope he ain't bad hurt."

Ringo bent over the fallen man and said, "You okay, partner?"

Riordan did not answer, as he was trying to suck air back into his lungs.

"Well, that was a pretty bad fall. No fun having the air knocked out of you. You'll be okay. Here. Let me help you up."

Rosa watched as Ringo pulled the smaller man to his feet.

"Well," Ringo said, "maybe we'd better give you a gentler horse."

"No, that's the one I want," Riordan said.

"Oh, come on now, Riordan. This was just

kind of a trick. You don't want that horse. He's a mean one. You could get hurt."

"That's the one I want."

Rosa heard a stubbornness in Riordan's voice and saw that his mouth was drawn into a tight line.

"Catch him up for me, will you, Ringo?" Riordan asked.

"What in the world is he doing?" her grandfather demanded.

"It looks like he's determined to ride that horse," Father said.

"Why, he can't ride Chief. None of the men can. You'd better stop it, granddaughter."

"Let him ride."

"He's liable to get hurt."

"None of my business," Rosa said. "You break it up."

"That fellow is more stubborn than he looks." Father nodded.

Rosa saw that Riordan was stepping back into the saddle, and she watched with shock as twice more he was thrown, each time getting up more slowly.

Finally Grandfather shook his head. "This ain't right, Rosa." He entered the corral and came to where Riordan was getting up, his face pale. "That's enough of this horse, Riordan."

"I'd like to try again."

"You can try later." He turned to face Ringo and said nothing, but Ringo's face grew red. "That's all the entertainment today. Ain't there no work for you fellows to do?" he said.

All the hands scattered like quail then, and her grandfather said, "You take it easy for a while. That's too much horse for you right now." He went back, stood in front of Rosa, and bit the words off. "A woman should have some gentleness in her, granddaughter, along with the toughness. I'm ashamed of you."

Rosa flushed, turned, and left, feeling the hard truth of the statement.

Riordan could scarcely move the rest of the day. That night he was so sore he could barely walk.

Ned saw him limping and said, "You know, Riordan, that big tank out there has been in the sun all day, and the water's real hot. Why don't you climb into it? I've always heard that heat was good for taking the misery out of sore muscles."

Riordan could barely turn his head to look at the tank, but he remembered how more than once he'd gotten into hot tubs to ease his aches. "You know, you may be right about that, Ned. Think I'll just go soak for a time."

"Sure, that'll set you up fine!" Ned shook his head, adding, "I didn't know Ringo had such a mean streak. He knows ain't many hands able to stay on Chief."

"I don't think it was his idea."

"Why, he's the one who put you up on that horse."

But Riordan had caught glimpses of Rosa Ramirez watching him take his fall and seeming to enjoy it. It had not surprised him, for he knew that the young woman despised him. "Oh, just guessing, Ned."

Limping out to the large tank, Riordan glanced toward the house but saw that the barn cut off anyone who might be coming from there. Slowly, with several grunts, he stripped off his filthy clothes and boots then climbed up the short ladder into the tank. He eased himself down into the water, which was very hot. Slowly he submerged himself and loosed a sigh of pleasure as his weary muscles seemed to welcome the hot bath. He kept his head above water and let the heat draw some of the aches out of his frame. For a long time he floated, thinking of what had happened. Mostly he thought of the pleasure he had seen in the eyes of Rosa when he had hit the ground with terrible force. *She really enjoyed seeing me get hurt.* The thought disturbed him greatly, for he was accustomed to women who were more gentle.

Finally he reluctantly climbed out of the tank and had put on the lower part of dirty underwear, when a voice caught him unawares.

"Don't you know our animals have to drink water from that tank?"

Turning quickly, Riordan saw that Rosa had appeared and was staring at him. He had always been a modest young man and had an impulse to climb back into the tank. A thin streak of anger touched him then, and he said, "Sorry, Miss Ramirez." He was aware that she was staring at him and saw something in her look that disturbed him. "If you'll leave, I'll put some clothes on."

Rosa laughed harshly. She had come upon him by pure accident, and her first glance of the half-naked body of Riordan had given her a shock. Now she was embarrassed and said, "Get some clothes on. We've got enough scarecrows around here." Abruptly she whirled and disappeared, leaving Riordan to stare after her.

Slowly he put on the dirty, sweat-stained clothes and returned to the bunkhouse. He found the hands sitting at a rickety table playing poker.

Ringo moved his shoulders uncertainly. He cleared his throat then said, "No hard feelings about Chief, I hope."

"Not at all."

Ringo got up and walked over to an empty bunk then gestured at a chest at the foot. "This was George Perkin's place, but he joined up with some wild riders. You might as well have his stuff. He won't be coming back for it. He was a real sharp dresser."

Riordan smiled. "Thanks, Ringo. I appreciate it."

The tension that had been in the room faded, and the card game went on as Riordan put on clean underwear and lay down with a sigh of relief. His last thought was, *That woman sure did enjoy seeing me get thrown. Wonder what she will think of next to humiliate me? Whatever it is I won't let her get to me!*

CHAPTER 13

During the days that followed her encounter with Riordan at the water tank, Rosa became more and more disgusted with him. She thought he was utterly worthless, but one thing that happened surprised her:

Her grandfather had commanded Ned to give Riordan a better horse. "Give him Big Red," he had said. "He's a fast horse. Never bucked in his life. See that the young fellow learns how to ride."

Despite herself, Rosa was interested in the experiment. She watched every day as Riordan saddled the big red gelding, who stood absolutely still as a statue for the process. Unlike other horses, he would open his mouth and take the bit without trying to bite anybody. She watched as Riordan became more and more easy in mounting and began taking Red out for rides during which he would go faster and faster.

One Thursday afternoon, Rosa went outside the house, noting that it was a lazy day and most of the work was done. She saw Ned whittling in the shade of the big walnut tree and walked over. "Where's the big dishwasher?"

"Why, he went for a ride."

"Did he get the stable clean?"

"Oh, Miss Rosa, you couldn't expect him to do that. None of these marshals ever do anything like work on these ranches. We got a new man, a young man from Mexico to take care of that."

"Where did he go?"

"I seen him about an hour ago riding out east. Didn't say where he was going. I do know he's been studying a map of the Territory and riding over it as much as he can. Looks like he wants to know the country."

"He's just riding around to get out of work. He's a bum. That's all he is."

Her nerves were on edge as she mounted her horse and rode out. She rode for twenty minutes and got to the river. Turning the mare's head, she followed a small branch of it until she saw Riordan seated under a tree. He seemed to be writing something on a tablet.

She stepped off of her horse, tied her to a sapling, and advanced until she was within a few feet of the unsuspecting man. "What are you doing?"

Riordan was startled. He jumped up, holding the pad in one hand and a pencil in the other.

"Are you writing letters?"

"I just like to get away once in a while."

"Who are you writing to?" Rosa demanded.

"Nobody."

"That sounds unlikely." She went forward and snatched the tablet saying, "Are you writing to your sweetheart?"

She looked down at the open page and received a shock. It was not a letter but a pencil sketch of the terrain that lay to the south. There was the small stream, correct in every detail, the plains, and in a bunch of high grass, a six-point buck had lifted his head, his eyes staring, looking as real as life. Far off was the outline of the mountains. "You're drawing pictures!"

Riordan looked embarrassed. "Just a hobby."

Rosa started to hand the tablet to him, but the wind caught the pages and folded them back. She looked down and saw a sketch of herself wearing her riding outfit. Her hat was pushed back on her head, and she was frowning as if she were angry.

"What do you mean drawing pictures of me?"

Riordan shrugged. "I don't know. I'm sorry. I just like to draw all sorts of things."

Rosa turned the pages and saw sketches of the ranch, of her mother standing at the cookstove, of Ringo riding a bucking bronc, her father and grandfather playing checkers. "I didn't want an artist," she snapped. "I wanted a tough man to run down some killers. I'm sick of you, you so-called marshal. Take your pictures and go back to Judge Parker."

She turned and walked back, aware that he was following her, trying to apologize. "I'm sorry, Miss Ramirez. I can promise you I won't do any more."

Rosa had reached her horse when suddenly he grabbed her from behind and swung her around. She fought loose and struck at him with a quirt she always carried, but he hardly reacted. She was shocked when he pulled his gun in one smooth motion and fired it. Twirling she saw an enormous headless rattlesnake thrashing in the weeds.

If there was one thing Rosa Ramirez was frightened of, it was snakes, and this one was a monster. Frozen with fear, even though the danger was passed, she watched until the snake finally grew still. She suddenly realized that she had struck a man who was trying to save her life. She looked at the big snake, which she knew had venom enough to kill her. "I'm sorry —"

She broke off, for Riordan had sat down and taken his right boot off. He pulled the sock down, and she saw the twin punctures. She watched, unable to speak, as he took out a pocketknife and cut a deep etch in both wounds. The blood began to flow freely. He looked up and remarked, "I guess he got me."

Rosa had always been careful of snakes, and she had never seen one any bigger than this. Suddenly she cried, "Get on your horse. We've got to get you to the doctor."

"He's at Fort Smith. I'll be dead by that time."

Quickly Rosa ran over and pulled him to his feet and led him to his horse. "Get on your horse!"

He shrugged, and she ran to her own horse and called out, "We've got to hurry!"

"There's no hurry, Miss Ramirez. I don't think there's any cure for snakebites."

Rosa rushed as quickly as she could back to the ranch. Trying to keep Riordan awake and seated on his horse impeded their progress somewhat. When they arrived at the house, she saw Ned and motioned for him to come.

Ned responded to Rosa's summons by calling out, "Ringo, something's wrong."

The two advanced, and as they did, they saw that Riordan's face was drained and pale, that his eyes were starting to turn upward. "He's been snake bit. Carry him into the house."

There was no need to pull him off, for Riordan fell right into Ned's husky arms. He hurried to the steps and called out, "Riordan's been snake bit! We need to put him in bed."

"Put him in the bed in the front bedroom," Grandfather said. He looked down. "Are you all right, Riordan?"

"I don't — feel so good."

They took him in and cleaned the blood off of his leg as he lay in the bed, but Ned said, "From the looks of those fang marks, it was a big 'un."

"The biggest I've ever seen."

Father had come in. "What gave him that cut on the cheek? That wasn't a snake."

Memory came back, and Rosa flushed, but she said nothing. She sat down beside Riordan. People came and went, and she watched his face as it began to twist in a grimace of pain. He twitched, and his arms and legs were shaking. She reached out and held him down. Finally she was aware that only her grandfather was there.

"I'm afraid he's going to die," Rosa said.

"Well, in the case of snakebites, I guess it's up to God. I've seen men get bitten and die, and I've seen some of them get well."

The only sound in the room was Riordan's heavy and uneven gasping breaths.

She suddenly felt tears running down her cheeks. "It's my fault. I was going to get on my horse, and he grabbed me from behind. I — I thought he was trying to grab me, and I hit him with my quirt." She looked up, her face twisted with grief. "He pulled his gun and shot the snake. He was trying to save my life, and I did that to him."

"Well," her grandfather said, "some things we can make up for and some things we can't. If he don't die, you can tell him you're sorry."

The doctor came, but when he looked at the leg that was terribly swollen, took Riordan's pulse, and felt the feverish brow, he said, "He looks bad, but I think he's over the hump. How long since he was bitten?"

"At least five hours, doctor."

"Well, he'd be dead by now if that were going to happen. He just needs care."

"Tell me what to do, doctor," Rosa whispered. "I'll take care of him."

When Riordan opened his eyes, he could see a ceiling and was aware that he was in a strange room. His leg was agonizing to him, and he groaned. He then turned his head and saw that Rosa Ramirez was sitting there beside him. She had been asleep, but he had awakened her when he groaned.

"You're awake," she said. She leaned over him and said, "You're going to be all right, Riordan."

Riordan was feeling miserable, but he realized that it was the first time she had ever used his name. "Can I have some water?"

"Of course." She quickly poured him a glass of water. He received it with hands not quite steady. She held his head up and helped him drink it. It spilled, running down his neck.

"That's good," he whispered. He looked down and saw his leg, which was terribly swollen. "Not very pretty, is it?"

"But you're going to be all right. The doctor said if you'd been going to die, you'd be dead already. He wants you to try to eat and drink as much fluid as you can. I've got some broth made. I'll go heat it up." She left the room.

Riordan lay there suffering the pain and

242

studying his leg, which seemed to be twice as big as the other one. "Well, ain't this a pretty come off," he whispered to himself.

Rosa entered the room with a bowl and a spoon. She said, "I need to prop you up." She put the bowl and spoon down, took him under the arms, and pulled him to an upright position. She propped his back up with the extra pillow. She fed him the broth and gave him more water when he asked for it.

Finally he said, "That's all I want." He laid his head back and shut his eyes for a moment before opening them again and looking to her.

Rosa put the bowl and the spoon down. She seemed to be struggling with the words to tell him something. Finally she said, "Riordan, when you grabbed me I thought you were trying to kiss me, and I hit you with my whip. Then I saw the snake, and I realized you were trying to save my life. I can't — All I can say is I'm so sorry."

"My fault."

"No, it wasn't. It was my fault."

"I shouldn't have drawn your picture."

"No, I was silly." She hesitated then said, "Maybe you should have been an artist instead of a marshal."

Suddenly Riordan grinned. "That's what my mother said."

Riordan closed his eyes again. After a few moments, he sensed that Rosa had risen from her position. He expected to hear her footsteps as she left the room, obviously thinking he had fallen asleep. But instead, she whispered some words, which he was sure she never intended him to hear.

"I'll never forget what you did, Riordan. Never."

He did hear her leave after her declaration. He kept his eyes closed as to avoid embarrassment for both of them, and his mind kept turning her words over and over.

Riordan was out of bed and had put on a pair of pants with the right leg split, for his leg was still swollen. He hobbled out of the bedroom and saw Frank sitting at the kitchen table. "I'm going out to the bunkhouse. I've had your bedroom long enough."

"You don't have to do that, young feller."

"I'd feel better."

Mateo and Chenoa were both in the room. They came over, and the woman took his hand and kissed it. "You saved my daughter's life."

Mateo did not speak, but his eyes spoke volumes. Finally he said, "You are a good man."

"Anybody would have done it."

As he hobbled out, Frank said, "No, they wouldn't. Some fellows would have run like a scared rabbit when they saw that big snake."

Riordan went outside and crossed the yard, limping badly. He got to the bunkhouse and sat down on the bench outside. He leaned his head back and closed his eyes, for he was still weak. He opened them when he heard footsteps and saw Ringo coming.

Ringo sat down beside Riordan and said, "What happened? We heard all kinds of stories."

"Oh, there was a snake, and I shot it."

"That's not what Rosa says. She said you pulled her out of the way and shot the snake. That it bit you instead of her. She's told everybody on the ranch what a hero you are."

"I'm no hero."

"Well, you sound like one to me. You know . . . if you can shoot the head off a snake that quick, you must be a pretty good shot."

"Just lucky, Ringo."

Ringo rose and turned to leave, calling back over his shoulder as he walked away, "Well, whatever it was, you are a hero to everyone around here now."

After a time, Chenoa brought him some cool lemonade from the springhouse. She whispered to Riordan, sounding much like her daughter, "We will never forget what you have done for us."

Ten minutes later Rosa came and gave him his tablet. She sat down beside him. He could smell the violet scent she used. "I went back and got your tablet, and when I saw the body of that snake I nearly fainted. I'm scared to death of snakes."

"Why, you shouldn't have bothered, Miss Ramirez."

"I know it's important to you. I — I looked at all the sketches." She shook her head and said quietly, "You've got a great talent. You've got the ranch and everybody else right here in this tablet. Some of the horses. All with a pencil. Maybe you ought to learn how to paint."

Despite himself, Riordan smiled. "I thought of doing that once."

"You should do it. Can I have the picture of me?"

"Why, of course."

She picked up the tablet and found the sketch of her. "Sign it and date it."

Riordan laughed. "If van Gogh had signed one of his paintings and a fellow had it now, it would be worth a million dollars. Mine won't be worth a dime."

"Still, I'd like you to sign it."

"Well, let me fill in the details." He took the tablet and the pencil.

She sat beside him, very close, watching as the pencil seemed to fly over the paper. It was almost like magic the way details appeared, and when he gave it to her she said, "Thank you, Riordan."

For a time she tried to find out a little about his past, but he had almost nothing to say.

Finally he said, "Miss Ramirez, I know I'm not what you went for. I knew that when the judge let me come. I thought by this time they'd have Heck Thomas or some of the real marshals here, but I know I'm not what you want. Judge Parker will send you some fine lawmen as soon as he can."

Rosa sat silently for a few minutes. She finally lifted her head and looked him directly in the eye, her expression revealing sincerity. "I am not good at making apologies. I am ashamed at how I reacted by hitting you with my whip. I have realized that you risked your own life to save mine." She leaned over and put her hand on his arm. "I think you're a real marshal, Riordan. Please stay with us."

Riordan was startled. He looked at her

and saw the hope and trust she was willing to place in him now. He smiled faintly, saying, "Well, maybe I will."

CHAPTER 14

The sun was falling into the west, throwing
a halo of light around the faraway mountains. Rosa had been walking around the
ranch looking for nothing really, feeling confused and a bit frustrated. She went into
the kitchen. There her mother was sitting at
the table peeling potatoes. "Let me help
you, Mama."

"Oh, I'm almost done. Sit down and talk
to me."

Rosa sighed, settled down on a chair, and
locked her fingers together behind her head.
She arched her back as if easing tired
muscles then said, "I don't really have anything to talk about."

Chenoa looked up from the potato she
was peeling and said, "What do you think
about the marshal now, the one you referred
to as only being capable of cleaning out
stables and washing dishes?"

Her mother's words brought a quick glow

to Rosa's face. She unloosed her fingers, leaned forward, and stared out the window for a moment then turned to gaze on her mother. "I don't know. He's not what I thought he was."

"He still doesn't seem like he's the kind of man to be a marshal. All the marshals I've seen around have been older men, rough and knowledgeable of the land and its harshness. You can tell that Riordan's had a different kind of life."

"Yes, he's educated, and he's a talented artist. I don't know what he's doing out here in this wild country. He needs to be in the big city somewhere making a career for himself."

"I've been watching him all the time he's been here. He's a very gentle man. If you talked to most men the way you talk to him, they would have turned you over their knees and spanked you."

"Well, I made a mistake," Rosa muttered. "He looked so awful the first time I saw him at Judge Parker's, and he couldn't ride a horse. I was expecting to get one of the better marshals or maybe three or four of them, and instead I got him."

"Well, you made him pay for it. I don't know why he put up with you."

Rosa shook her head but had no answer.

She reached over, picked up a potato, and started to peel it. But she just as quickly dropped it, saying, "I'm going to go outside. I feel like doing something, but I don't know what it is."

Quickly she returned outdoors, made her way to the corral, and for a while curried her mare, Beauty. She was a spirited mare, enjoying giving a good nip once in a while.

"Don't you bite me, Beauty," Rosa said. "I'll send you to the fort to be ridden by one of the marshals." She laughed when the mare whinnied slightly and tossed her head. "You're vain. That's what you are. You're full of pride because you're such a pretty animal."

She curried the horse carefully until her coat was shining and then turned her out to the pasture. "I don't know what to do with myself. I can't go out after those outlaws alone, and according to what Judge Parker says, it may be weeks or even months before he gets any men to send." Dissatisfied with herself, she made her way to the cook shack. She found Riordan in the kitchen cooking something. He had a huge pot on the woodstove, and she stared at him.

"I didn't know you were a cook."

"Well, no one else is doing it, and we've got to have something to eat."

"You should have asked me or my mother."

"Ah, it's no trouble. Just got this big roast and put it in to bake for a while. When it gets tender, it'll be ready to eat. Don't have much to go with it though."

"We have some canned beans up at the house. Maybe you can use those."

"Oh, that would be good. We're always hungry, all of us."

"I'll get some for you later."

She stayed for a while, watching him work in the kitchen and thinking, *If I saw another man cook, I would think he's nothing but a bore and not really a man. Somehow I don't think that about this man. He's different from everybody else.* Finally she got up, saying, "I'll bring the beans down."

Later that afternoon Rosa looked up to see Xeno Brewton riding up. Xeno had been there before. He was a horse trader, of sorts, and often bought from and sold to her grandfather. He paid attention to her, listened to what she had to say, and seemed to be understanding of what a hard time she had had.

"Hello, Xeno."

"Hello, Rosa. My, you're looking first rate."

"Thank you. Come onto the porch. My father and grandfather are up there arguing about something. They always are."

"They are a quarrelsome pair."

"Could you use some cool lemonade?"

"That I could. Thank you very much, Miss Rosa."

Rosa went to the springhouse and pulled out a jug. It was the only cool place during the hot summer months as it was dug back into a hill and covered over with dirt so that it was like a cave. She carefully opened the door, looking for snakes. She remembered that once she had opened the door and a big snake had nearly scared her to death as it slithered out. It turned out to be nonpoisonous, but that didn't matter at the time. She saw no snakes now, however; so she picked up the jug and then stopped at the kitchen and took it out to where the three men were sitting. "Who's telling the biggest lies?"

Xeno shook his head. "It's hard to tell between these two. Both of them exaggerate quite a bit."

She filled all their glasses with lemonade, poured one for herself, and then sat down. She studied her grandfather and saw that he was still looking very tired and weary. *He's not going to live much longer.* The

253

thought flashed into her mind and frightened her. She had become very fond of her grandfather and hated to think about losing him. Her eyes went to her father. Mateo was looking somewhat better. The easy living, good food, and sun had helped him quite a bit. *Maybe he'll get well. I pray God he will,* she thought.

For a while she just listened to the three men conversing. Then she suddenly straightened up as Xeno said, "There was a holdup yesterday."

"Where was this?" Frank asked.

"Just north of Big Mountain. Two armed men held up two men driving a wagon. One of them put up a fight, and they shot him. They let the other one go after they took what was in the wagon."

"What was so valuable?"

"They had some money, and the dead man had a valuable ring. I don't know how the bandits knew it though."

"This country's got more bandits than it has coyotes! Come to think of it, coyotes have more kindness about them than some of these bandits. Who were these men?"

"Well, the one that the driver recognized might be part of George Pye's bunch. It wasn't Pye himself, but he recognized one of his men. I think his name is Vernon Epps."

"Epps — He's a bad one!" Frank exclaimed.

Xeno nodded vigorously. "They're all bad. I wish they'd send the army and clean out all these thugs. They did it to the Indians. I don't know why they couldn't do it to these outlaws."

Rosa said nothing as she sat there listening to the men talk about the robbery and the killing. She left after a time. The one thought going through her mind was, *If Epps was there, probably Pye and the rest of his gang were, too.* She felt frustrated, for there was nothing she could do until Judge Parker sent a group of marshals to clean out the nest of outlaws.

Riordan was riding Red and watched as Brewton picked out a horse and paid for it. Then Riordan went up to him as he was leaving with his new acquisition.

"Hello, Marshal."

"Hello, Mr. Brewton. Did I hear right that you know something about a robbery?"

Riordan straightened up, and his eyes glowed. "Where did it happen?" He listened as Brewton described the robbery, and when he mentioned that it could have been a member of Pye's band, he grew more interested.

Brewton said, "I wish you had the manpower to go after them, but one man don't need to chase around after that bunch. See you later, Marshal."

"Take it easy, Mr. Brewton." Riordan rode slowly toward the stable. He didn't unsaddle Red, but instead he found a pair of saddlebags and went into the cook shack. He put in some bacon and several cans of beans and some day-old biscuits. Going to his bunk, he added a box of .38 shells and went back and put his Winchester in the saddle holster. He then mounted Red and rode out slowly.

Rosa had been watching Riordan from the back porch of the house since he had talked with Xeno. As soon as he rode out, she suddenly realized, *I bet he's going after Epps and his bunch.*

She went to the house and said, "Papa, I'm going out for a ride. I may be late tonight. You and Mama go on to bed."

"Don't stay out too late. The wolves might get you."

"No, they won't. I will shoot them."

Quickly she ran out and saddled Beauty. Rosa then rode out at a swift pace, headed after Riordan. She realized she had no idea what she would say to him. She was curious, however, and wanted to know if he had any plan in his mind for capturing the gang. "Come on, Beauty. Let's go."

Riordan suddenly pulled Red to a stop. His eyes were on the ground ahead, and he had a map out that showed the approximate location where the holdup had taken place. He had no idea what he would do if he saw the whole bunch. *Turn tail and run probably.* He grinned ruefully. He was weary of the life he was leading. It was actually more boring than when he was hauling fertilizer for Judge Parker. All he did now was ride around and wait. It went against his measure.

Suddenly he heard the sound of a horse approaching. "Whoa, Red." He turned around and saw Rosa riding up on her mare. He was puzzled and asked quickly, "What are you doing out here, Miss Ramirez?"

"I wish you'd call me Rosa like everybody else does."

"It doesn't sound respectable to call your boss by her first name."

"I'm not your boss. You know that. Judge Parker is your boss."

He studied her for a moment then again asked, "What are you doing out here?"

"Where are you going?" she countered.

"I'm just riding around, more or less, on official business."

"I know what you're doing. Xeno Brewton told you about the holdup, and you're going to see if you can find the men who did it."

"Well, if I could find them, I could get word back to Judge Parker. He could get up some men and bring a posse. Might catch the whole bunch."

"Your chances of sneaking up on a bunch of outlaws in the Territory aren't very good. They're all like wild animals. They have sharp instincts about lawmen. Judge Parker has already lost nearly fifty of his marshals."

"I know about that, and that's why I want you to turn around and go back to the house."

She looked at him and said, "I won't do it."

Riordan stared at her. "Miss Ramirez, I'm ordering you as an officer of the court, leave here and go back to the house!"

Rosa smiled, and then she laughed. "What are you going to do if I refuse? Tie me to a tree and leave me here, or are you going to take me back and ask my father to punish me?"

"You don't really need to be going with me. This is dangerous."

"It's just as dangerous for you. I'm going to go with you. I left word at the ranch that I might be late."

"I may not go back tonight."

"Then I won't go back either. Now let's go. We're talking too much."

Riordan threw up one hand and shook his head. "You are the most stubborn woman, Miss Ramirez, I have ever seen!" He turned, and Red obediently began walking at a fast pace.

He glanced at Rosa, who rode beside him, and could not help but think how attractive she was. He had never pursued women greatly, except for Marlene Jenson. Rosa had clean-running physical lines. She was tall and shapely, and whatever it was that made a woman attractive, she had it as far as he was concerned. He knew she was a strong-willed woman, and the thought came to him, *If she had to, she'd draw that revolver and shoot a man down and not go to pieces afterward.* Indeed, he had seen that she had a temper, could swing from extremes of laughter and softness, and he realized that there was a tremendous capacity for emotion in her. All in all she was a beautiful and robust woman with a woman's soft depth. She had an enormous certainty in her, a positive will, and he admired the vitality and imagination that she had to hold under careful restraint. He saw this hint of her will in the corners of her eyes and lips. There was fire in the woman that made her lovely and brought the rich and headlong qualities behind the cool reserve of her lips.

"Why are you staring at me?"

Suddenly Riordan flinched, and his cheeks grew red. "I'm sorry. I just don't understand women very much, I guess."

"What's to understand? I'm just a woman like other women."

"I don't think that's true. You're not really like other women . . . at least the ones I've known."

"What do you mean by that? What's wrong with me?"

"Why, nothing's wrong with you. You have qualities I admire. You have a strong will, and you have beautiful hair."

She suddenly smiled. "You think so?"

"Yes, I do. I've always liked black hair."

"Well, I've wondered about you, too."

"What about me?"

"You don't fit in out here, Riordan. You couldn't even ride a horse except for that awful one you rode to the ranch. You learned a little bit, and everybody thinks you killed that Dent Smith by accident. Everybody thinks you would be killed if you got in a gunfight. You wear a gun, but you never shoot it. Never take practice."

"Hoping I never have to use it again."

There was silence except for the clopping of the horses' hooves on the hard ground, and finally she turned to him and said, "You aren't married, are you?"

"Me? Why, no. What made you think that I wasn't?"

"You don't act like a married man. I've had enough of that sort trying to make up to me." Riordan had no answer for that, and finally she asked, "What are you doing out in this country? You don't belong here."

Riordan considered telling her the story but then decided not to. "Just wanted a change. I grew up in the city and grew tired of it."

She continued to probe, but he continued to evade her questions.

They rode for several hours, and then he said, "I think we ought to go back."

"Go back? We haven't found anything yet."

"I was going to stay all night, but that's impossible."

"Why? You afraid of the dark?" She smiled

at him, a sly light in her eyes.

"No, but it wouldn't look right."

"What wouldn't look right?"

"Why, a single man and a single woman out camping after dark. Your father wouldn't like it."

"He knows I can take care of myself. So does my grandfather. Let's find a creek somewhere and camp out."

"All right." They found a small branch of clear water. There was some grass, so they put the horses out on long lariats, and Riordan found enough wood to build a fire. The darkness fell quickly, and by the time he got the fire going, he pulled out a frying pan and said, "I brought some beans and some bacon but only one plate and one set of hardware."

"Let me do the cooking."

"You probably do it better than I could."

Soon the air was filled with the smart smell of bacon cooking and beans bubbling. It gave them both an appetite.

Carefully she filled the one plate full of beans and added the bacon to one side. She picked up the fork and said, "Things taste better cooked outdoors." She took a bite of the bacon and said, "Ooh, that's hot! We'll take turns. You take a bite, and then I'll take a bite."

He took the fork awkwardly, scooped into the plate piled high with beans, put it in his mouth, and then added a bite of bacon. They had their meal that way. Finally he said, "Aren't you sleepy?"

"No, I always hate to go to bed at night. I might miss something."

"You wouldn't miss much out here. Not much happens at night."

"I know." She was sitting across from him. She pulled her feet up and held them by putting her arms around them. The fire was burning brightly, and it caught the glow of her dark eyes. "What'll we do if we catch up with the outlaws?"

"Turn around and run like the devil. Go get Judge Parker and some marshals."

"I think that would be wise. I'd hate to see you get in a gunfight. Have you ever shot that pistol of yours at a man other than during the one fight with Dent Smith?"

"Once or twice."

"Are you any good? But you must be because you shot the head off that rattler."

Riordan shrugged. "Not the best in the world, Miss Rosa."

"Miss Rosa? Well, at least it's not Miss Ramirez."

"I think that's a pretty name."

"It's not my real name. It's just a nick-name."

He stared at her. "What is your name?"

"Rosario."

He stared at her. "That's a pretty name. What does it mean?"

"It means rose."

They talked for a while, and then she asked him, "What's your first name?"

"I don't like it, so I don't tell people what it is. Riordan's good enough."

"Pretty formal."

Finally he got the blanket rolls off of the horses and handed one to her. "I hope the snakes don't get us."

"I don't want to hear about that. Snakes scare me to death." She suddenly said, "I've been meaning to tell you something. She put out her hand, and he took it. "Thank you for all you are doing for me and my family, Riordan."

Riordan felt a jolt at the touch of her hand.

She looked at him with what could only be described as adoration in her eyes. "I've always had to be on my guard with men, but somehow I know I can trust you."

Her hand was strong and warm, and without warning, Riordan felt a warmth toward Rosa that he'd never felt for any other woman, including Marlene. At that moment the two were caught in the mystery that sometimes draws a man and a woman together — and he realized with a shock that if he suddenly took her into his arms, she would not resist.

The moment drew out, and she whispered, "Aren't you going to try to kiss me, Riordan?"

"I don't think that would be fair. I mean we're all alone, and I'd be taking advantage of you." He shook his head, saying, "Any man standing in my place would want to kiss a beautiful woman like you, but I've made a promise to myself that I'd never take advantage of any woman."

Rosa startled at his words. "You are unlike any other man I have ever known. You can explode with violence, yet there is a gentleness in you." She then seemed embarrassed at her words and withdrew her hand. "We'd better get some sleep."

They both rolled up, he on one side of the fire, she on the other, and for a long time Riordan lay there listening to the soft sound of her breathing. It was a strange situation for him. Most women he had known would not think of doing what this woman had done — spend the night, in effect, with a strange man. He knew she was afraid of snakes, but he seriously doubted that she was afraid of anything else. His last thought was, *I can't get her in a dangerous gunfight. We'll go back first thing tomorrow.*

The sun was up. Riordan and Rosa ate the remains of the beans and bacon for breakfast. He said, "Let's cut around and head back toward the ranch in a roundabout way. We might run across them."

"I doubt it. This is a big territory."

The two of them rode slowly, and they came to a long ridge.

"That's Nolan's Ridge," she said. "Nobody knows why it's here. It goes a long way."

"It's not very high."

"No, it isn't."

They attained the top of the ridge, and just as they crested the top, Riordan heard a woman's voice screaming.

Instantly be became alert and spurred Red forward, and Rosa came with him. He looked down and saw a wagon with a man lying still beside it. Two men were there, and one of them had a woman down on the ground and was tearing at her clothes.

He turned and said, "Stay here, Rosa." He rode down but was aware that she had paid no attention to him.

The sound of the horses caught the attention of the two men, and the man savaging the woman on the ground got to his feet quickly. The two of them were rough looking.

As soon as they pulled their horses up, Rosa said, "That big man there killed Blinky. He was with Pye."

"That's right! I'm Boog Powell, and I killed him. Now what does that get you?"

Riordan studied the two.

He was a huge man running to fat but obviously very powerful. His eyes were small, and he was grinning. "You two head out of here right now and you'll be all right. If you stay around, I can't guarantee your safety." Powell laughed, saying, "What you gonna do, baby face? Shoot me with that peashooter?"

Riordan made up his mind instantly. "You two are under arrest for murder."

The woman on the ground was pale, and her clothes were torn. She whispered, "They shot the driver. Didn't say a word. Just rode up and shot him!"

Riordan said, "I'm a federal marshal. I'm going to take your guns and take you in."

"You ain't takin' nothin'!" The other man beside Boog was a tall, skinny man who was grinning. "I'm Alvin Darrow. I done killed two of your marshals. You can be number three."

"He's the fastest gun in the Territory." Boog grinned. "You better not draw on him or you'll be dead in a minute."

Darrow said, "That little peashooter wouldn't hurt nobody anyway."

Riordan was aware that Rosa was beside him and wished she were not. He was willing to take his chances, but he feared for her. "You're both going back to Judge Parker. You can go alive or you can go dead. Your choice."

Darrow laughed, and he reached for his pistol. Indeed, he was fast, but before his gun even cleared the holster, Riordan drew and fired. Darrow was still standing, but there was a black spot in the middle of his forehead. He began to go down slowly as his muscles relaxed. He fell to the ground, kicked several times, and then lay still.

Boog Powell found himself looking right into the muzzle that had just killed one of the fastest guns in the Territory. "I ain't shootin'," he whispered hoarsely.

"Drop your gun on the ground, Powell."

Powell did so, and Riordan got off his horse. He picked up the two guns and tossed them away saying, "Your friend there is going to Judge Parker dead instead of alive. You try to run away and you'll arrive at the fort the same way, as I'll get you, too. And there'll be two bodies, each tied across their horses."

Riordan turned quickly and walked to the woman who was struggling to sit up, but she was crying with pain. He saw that her face was battered and bruised and knew she had taken a bad beating rather than submit. "Be still, miss. You're going to be all right."

"My side. My side hurts so bad." He touched her side, but she said, "No, no, don't!"

"I think you've got some cracked ribs there. Hopefully they're not broken. Have you got medicine in the wagon?"

"Yes, it's in a box just beside the seat."

He looked up at Rosa, who had come to kneel on the other side of the woman. "Get it, will you, Rosa?"

Rosa jumped up and ran to the wagon. She found the wooden box and brought the whole thing back. She took a brown bottle, opened it, and smelled the contents. "This is laudanum."

"Give her a big dose of that. If it's broken ribs, I know what that's like." All the time his glance kept going back to Boog Powell, who did not move. He gave the woman the bottle. She managed to gag some of the liquid down.

"What's your name, ma'am?"

"I'm Hannah Bryant. I hired the Mexican to take me to the Blackwood Tribe school, and these men just rode up and killed him without saying a word."

Rosa asked, "What kind of school?"

The woman's face was twisted with pain as well as swollen with the blows. "I'm a Monrovian missionary."

"Never heard of that church," Rosa said.

"We preach the Gospel and teach it at the same time."

Rosa exchanged glances with Riordan.

He said, "Not very wise for a woman to cross Indian Territory." She did not answer, and he said, "I'll be right back." He went over to Boog Powell and said, "Tie your friend on his horse." He waited until Boog lifted Darrow and placed him facedown on the horse, feet sticking out.

Boog started to argue, but one look at Riordan's eyes changed his mind. "All right. Just don't shoot."

Riordan said, "Now put the man you killed on the other horse." He waited until Powell had secured both men then said, "Turn around." When Boog turned around, he said, "Put your hands behind you." Quickly he pulled a cord from his pocket that he always carried and tied the man's hands securely. Then he took the lariat off the rope, made a slipknot, and stuck it over Powell's head. "I'm tying the other end to the wagon. You try to run, you'll hang yourself and won't have to hang on Judge Parker's gallows."

"You can't do this!"

"You watch me." He went back and saw that the laudanum had taken affect on the woman. Her eyes were closed, but she was still conscious. "I've got to put you in the wagon. We'll make a bed up there. Would you see to that, Rosa?"

"Sure." Rosa went to the wagon, found some quilts and blankets, and made a bed of sorts for the woman. "We'll take her to our ranch. She'll need a doctor."

Riordan carefully picked the woman up and put her into the wagon.

"You're stronger than you look." Rosa grinned at him, got into the wagon, and spoke to the mules, but then turned to say, "This makes two men you've killed. I never saw anyone who could pull a gun as fast as you. It was the same with the snake. But you still don't look like a gunman."

"I'm not." His words were spare. He saw this upset her a bit, as she said no more while she drove toward the ranch.

271

CHAPTER 15

The sun was climbing higher in the sky as they rode on. But as Riordan stared down at the woman, she was crying out with pain.

"What's wrong with her?" Rosa asked, her brow furrowed with thought.

"It's the ribs. I had some broken one time. I know what to do for it, but I've never treated an injury like this myself."

"How do you treat a broken rib?"

"You make some long strips of cloth out of a sheet or something. Then you put them around the rib cage as tight as it can stand it. It will still hurt, but nothing like it is now. You see, as it is now those cracked ribs are rubbing against nerves, but this would stop some of that."

They dismounted from the wagon, and Rosa found a muslin sheet. She took a knife out, slit it, and made a long strip about two inches wide. "Is this about right, Riordan?"

"Yeah, tear up the whole sheet like that."

Rosa finished all the strips, and he said grimly, "Let's get back in the wagon. This is not going to be fun." They entered the wagon, and he said, "You're going to have to sit up, ma'am, while we wrap your ribs."

"I can't. It hurts too bad."

"I know it does, but this will make you feel a lot better." He found a box and lifted her up, paying no attention to her cries, until she was sitting. He was in front of her, and he started removing her dress.

She gasped, and her eyes flew open. "No, you can't undress me!"

"Look ma'am, we've got to get your ribs tied up."

"No, I can't let you look at me."

"Get in the back here, Riordan," Rosa said.

He saw what she intended and instantly got up. He took his place behind the woman. He also made sure Boog wasn't looking her way either.

Rosa said, "Look, Miss Bryant, all the men can see is your back, so let me take your dress down and we'll get you tied up. You'll feel better."

The woman whimpered, but she nodded. Rosa took the remnants of the dress down, and she said, "Pass me the end of one of those strips, Riordan." She took it and lapped it over, and then holding it tight, she passed it under the woman's arm.

The woman cried out more than once, but the two kept at it.

Riordan said, "It'll have to go up over her shoulders to hold it in place."

Rosa brought the strip up between the woman's breasts and back down her back, and finally her whole body was, more or less, encased. Rosa tied it off.

Riordan said, "That's good. Take some more of this laudanum, and you can lie down."

The two got her lying down, and soon her breathing became uneven and short, but at least some of the pain was gone.

They got down off the wagon, and Rosa said, "I didn't like doing that."

"I didn't either. Broken ribs are no fun. Could you drive the wagon back?"

"Sure."

"I'll keep track of our friend out there. You want to go as slow as you can. You can't avoid all of the holes, but just do the best you can. All right?"

"Sure."

He turned and then suddenly said, "You know we're closer to your ranch than anywhere else. We can't get her to a doctor in Fort Smith. It's too far."

"No, we can make the ranch by tomorrow sometime. Maybe the medicine will help until then."

"Let's hope so," he said.

They made their way as slowly as possible. From time to time, when Hannah Bryant started moaning with pain, Rosa stopped the wagon and gave her a little more of the laudanum. "I hope I don't kill her with this."

"A broken rib makes you feel like you're dying. I remember that about it."

That night Riordan said he would keep watch on their "friend." As he kept his eye on the outlaw, he couldn't help but be impressed with Rosa, as she stayed near Hannah the entire night, offering as much comfort as she could. She was certainly a woman with many different sides to her. And he found he was interested in learning more about all of them.

It was almost dark the next evening when they arrived back at the ranch. Ringo and Ned came running out. "What's wrong?" Ned cried out. "Who is this hairpin?"

"He's under arrest for murder," Riordan said. "Lock him in the smokehouse. If he tries to get away, shoot him in the head."

Everyone in the house came out then, and Rosa explained, "We came across two men.

They'd killed this woman's driver and were attacking her."

"Who are they?" Ringo demanded.

"The live one is Boog Powell. The dead one is named Darrow."

"Darrow?" Ned said, "He's a bad one! He's killed more than one marshal, and he's faster than a snake."

"How did you get the woman away from them?" Ringo asked.

Riordan said nothing, and when Rosa saw he was silent, she said, "He told them they could go in alive or dead, and this man Darrow went for his gun." She shook her head and said in a strained voice, "He never even got it out of his holster. Riordan here pulled his gun and shot him right in the forehead. Darrow was dead before he hit the ground." The scene played over in her mind of how he pulled his gun with incredible speed and shot the man exactly where he intended for the bullet to go. She had never seen such a thing in her life, and it made her wonder more about the strange man that had come into her life.

"You shot down Darrow!" Ned said. He whistled. "Judge Parker will be glad to hear that. He was a bad 'un."

"We've got to get this woman in the house. Her name is Hannah Bryant," Riordan said. "She's a missionary."

"Bring her right on in," Chenoa said. "We'll make a bed for her in the back room where we can take care of her."

Hannah moaned as Ringo and Ned extracted her from the wagon. Ned took her gently as he could, and they walked toward the house. When they were in the room, Chenoa said, "Put her on the bed there." She turned to Rosa. "What happened? Who did all this bandaging?"

"Riordan and I did it," Rosa said. "We need to send for a doctor."

"I'll do that," Ringo said. "He ain't far from here. He had a case over at the Wilsons' ranch. I'll be back in two hours with him."

"All of you get out of here," Chenoa said.

But as they were leaving, Hannah opened her eyes and said, "Please don't leave me!" She put out her hand toward Riordan.

He hesitated then went to her and sat down. He took her hand and said, "You're all right, Miss Hannah. You're safe now."

"Don't leave me, please. I'm so afraid!"

"You just go back to sleep. I'll be here." And with that he sat down, determined to stay with the woman.

Rosa was watching. She left the room with the others, but later she came back with some cloths. "Her face is going to be swollen, but this cool water might help a little." She began to wet the small pieces of towel and hand them to her mother. When Chenoa put them on Hannah, the missionary opened her eyes and said, "Who are you?"

"My name is Chenoa. You're at my family's ranch. Don't worry, Miss Bryant, you're safe now."

"What about those men?"

Rosa said, "They won't bother you anymore. You just try to sleep."

"Could I have some water, please?" Hannah asked.

Rosa left and came back with some cool water from the springhouse.

"Let me help you sit up," Riordan said. He put his hand behind her back, and she cried out, but she sat up long enough to drink thirstily.

"That's so good," she whispered then lay back. She took some more laudanum, and soon she started drifting off to sleep, but she held on to Riordan's hand.

Chenoa said, "I'll go into the kitchen and fix something she can eat. Call if you need me." She left the room.

Rosa saw Hannah still holding Riordan's hand, and her eyes narrowed. "Looks like you've made a friend."

"I know. She's scared."

"She's a missionary," Rosa said. "That's kind of a preacher, isn't it?"

"Sort of, I suppose. Never thought of a single woman crossing the Territory with just a Mexican driver."

"It was foolish."

"I guess we're all foolish."

He sat there while the woman held his hand. She slept fitfully, and Rosa said, "What are we going to do with her?"

"Well, when she gets healed up, we'll take her to that school she's going to."

Rosa studied him. "You're a mystery man. Nobody thinks you can shoot, but you put one of the fastest guns in the Territory down quick as a wink. Where'd you learn to shoot like that?"

He did not answer, and she persisted, "You killed that outlaw so easy. Does it bother you killing a man?"

"Yes." His answer was simple but firm.

"Are you sorry?" Rosa asked.

"Yes, I'm sorry. I'd always be sorry for killing anybody."

Something about the situation troubled Rosa.

Hannah slept fitfully for a time, moaning periodically, her lips moving as she tried to say something in her half-asleep state.

Rosa watched her lips and made out the words: "Don't leave me. Please don't leave me . . ."

Riordan looked up and said quietly, "She's scared. She needs something to hang on to."

"It looks like she's going to hang on to you," Rosa said sharply.

Suddenly he looked up, and his eyes caught hers. There was some sort of anger in him, but then it turned to sadness even as she watched. "We all need someone to hold on to. I never had anybody except my mother, but I know what it feels like to need."

The doctor came, looked Hannah over, and stood up. He tested her arms and her legs for breaks. "She doesn't have any bones broken that I can tell, other than those ribs. You did a good job, Miss Rosa. Where'd you learn that?"

"It wasn't me. It was Riordan there."

"I had some banged up ribs one time. That's what they did to me."

"It's about all you can do. It's going to take some time."

"She'll be all right though, won't she?" Riordan said.

Dr. Mansfield rubbed his chin. "Physically

she will be, but there are other kinds of hurt."

His remark intrigued Rosa. "What do you mean 'other kinds of hurt'?"

"I'm sure you know. Did you ever get hurt pretty badly, not on the outside but on the inside, in your spirit? Those emotional hurts can be worse than a broken bone. I wouldn't be surprised if she clings to you. That often happens. You saved her, Riordan. Therefore, she trusts you."

"How long will this go on — this hanging on?" Rosa asked.

"Maybe forever." The doctor closed his black bag and left without another word.

Hannah stirred, and her eyes opened. "Is the doctor gone?"

"Yes, he's gone, Miss Hannah," Riordan said.

"He was nice. You'll stay with me, won't you, Riordan?"

"Sure. I'll be here. You just sleep if you can."

Rosa watched as the woman's eyes closed and her features relaxed.

She was still battered and bruised and had scars on her face, but she held on to Riordan with both hands.

Rosa smiled bitterly. *I notice she's not hanging on to me. I wonder why that is?*

CHAPTER 16

There was little they could do about the body of the Mexican who had been killed by the outlaws. Hannah had hired him but knew very little about him except that his name was Manuel. The summer was hot, and there was no possibility of keeping the body from deteriorating. They had to try to keep the body of Darrow from decaying too badly, as it had to be taken in to the judge.

Frank ordered a grave dug, and Manuel was buried quickly. A simple wooden cross with only the name MANUEL carved into it was placed on the grave.

Riordan looked down at the raw earth piled on top of the grave and studied the name. He turned to Ringo, who was standing beside him, and said, "Manuel didn't leave much behind, did he, Ringo?"

"No, but then most of us don't. A few presidents and generals, I guess, but in the war, I seen mass graves with bodies piled high and covered over with a few inches of dirt."

"But they may have left something. A child, a wife. Maybe a business. It seems wrong to go out of this earth leaving nothing behind but your name carved on a piece of wood."

Ringo said, "It don't pay to think too much about things like that. Nothing you can do about it."

Riordan turned and studied Ringo. Jukes was a roughly handsome man with a thick neck and a deep tan. He was pretty good with a gun and stuck by his friends. Aside from that, Riordan knew little about him. "I don't think that's right. I'm not much of an example myself, but my mother is. I read a book once saying the Bible wasn't true and that there was nothing to Christianity. It didn't bother me because I'd seen it in action in my mother almost every day of my life."

"Come on. Let's go get something to drink."

Ringo and Riordan walked away from the grave. Riordan felt something was wrong with what had been done with Manuel.

Rosa brought in fresh water for Hannah. Their guest was doing much better. The swelling on her face had gone down, although she had one large scratch there that would take time to heal. Her ribs were not as painful, but she was still nervous and seemed upset when Riordan was out of her sight. She had Rosa and Chenoa and Ethel to take care of her, but still she was troubled.

Riordan was sitting beside her now. They were talking about a book that both of them had read. The name of it was *Jane Eyre.* Riordan said, "There's a woman I admire."

Hannah stared at him. "She was a strong woman, stronger than most, I suppose."

"Well, of course she was only a character in a book, but the woman that wrote the book sure knew how to draw strong women."

Rosa's brow furrowed, and she thought, *I don't know what they're talking about. They know about books, pictures, and all kinds of things, and I'm just ignorant.* She set the pitcher down, picked up the empty one, and asked, "Is there anything else you want, Hannah?"

"Oh no, Riordan's taking good care of me."

"I've got to go talk to Ringo," Riordan said.

He started to get up, but Hannah reached out and took him by the hand. "Please stay just a little longer."

"Well, just a little bit."

Rosa turned and left the room and busied herself with making a batch of fresh corn bread, which her father loved. She kept looking at the door of Hannah's room, and finally Riordan came out.

He came over to her and said, "Making corn bread. Nothing better than fresh corn bread."

"Anybody can make corn bread."

"Not me. My mother could, though. She wouldn't let the cook make it. Insisted on doing it herself."

"You had a cook?"

Riordan stared at her. "Yes, we did. A good one, too. She'd been with the family, oh I don't know, fifteen years, I guess."

"Your family had money?"

Riordan had said little enough about his family, but he had no choice but to shrug and say, "My father was a good business-man. He knew how to make money." He waited for her to speak and then said, "Well, I've got to go talk to Ringo. If Hannah gets restless, tell her I'll be back after I run some errands."

"I'll take care of her. Don't worry."

Riordan gave her a curious glance and then left the room.

Rosa wondered about Riordan spending so much time with Hannah. *He needs to be careful that she doesn't become too attached to him or he'll be stuck with her for the rest of his life.* Rosa berated herself for the uncharitable thought, as Hannah had been through so much. But she couldn't help but feel a sense of loss when thinking about Hannah and Riordan being together for always . . .

Riordan crossed the yard and found Ringo helping to get a horse shod. Ned had been a blacksmith but had quit because he hated the job. Thus it had fallen to Ringo's lot. "Ringo, I've got a favor to ask of you."

"Shoot."

"I was hoping you would take Powell and the body of Darrow into the judge."

"Why don't you do it? You're the marshal. There'll be rewards out on both of them."

"Hannah's a little bit nervous. Thought I'd stay around until she got over the worst of that. That was a pretty bad time she had."

"Well, she is kind of delicate. I always like to go to town. I may have a few drinks and play some cards."

"Your sins are your own business." Riordan grinned. "Just see that the judge has the body of Darrow. And turn Powell over to him. If there's a reward, just bring it back."

After Ringo left, Riordan looked uncertainly around, not knowing exactly what to do. Finally he went back to the house and found Rosa still putting the pan of corn bread into the oven.

"You're back."

"Yeah, I thought I'd just go sit with Hannah a little bit more." He noted she gave him an odd look and said, "What's the matter?"

"Nothing. Go sit."

Riordan went in, and Hannah smiled at once. "Good. I get tired of reading, and I can't move around much."

"Well, you'll be better, but it'll take awhile. It seems like it takes ribs a long time to put themselves back together."

She made a pretty sight despite her bruised face, for she had an odd shade of red hair. It was strawberry blond, and her eyes were green, beautifully shaped, and wide spaced. Her lips were still swollen, but her features all were pleasing. She was wearing a nightgown and a bed jacket, and her head was propped up.

"Everybody's wondering what you were doing out in the middle of the wilderness by yourself. I know you said you were going to teach at a school, but you shouldn't have made that trip alone."

Hannah paused for a moment, and a pained look came into her face. "I haven't told you or anybody, but I was engaged to be married." She faltered, and tears came to her eyes. She took a handkerchief and wiped them.

"What happened?"

"He died of cholera two weeks before we were supposed to be married."

"That was rough, I'm sure. It's hard to take a loss like that. I know you cared for him a great deal."

"It — it wasn't a romantic affair. We were very good friends all through school, and we knew missionaries needed to go out in couples, so we decided to get married. Not a story like you'd read in a romance."

"Still, I know it hurts."

"Well, I decided to go alone." She paused for a moment. "Could I ask you something personal, Riordan?"

Riordan wondered what she wanted, but he still replied, "Fire away."

"Are you a man of God?"

Riordan shifted his shoulders uncomfortably and ran his hand through his hair. "That's a hard question. There was a revival in our town when I was twelve. The evangelist preached a great sermon, and I was really struck by it. I went forward and did what the preacher said, which was to call on the Lord. I did that, and I was baptized, but somehow along the way I feel as if I have strayed from it."

"You know there's a story in the Old Testament that sheds light on this. Some men had been chopping with an ax, and the head of the ax flew off and landed in a river or a pond. They went to the prophet and told him what had happened. The prophet asked where they'd lost it, and they took him back to that place. He prayed, and the axhead floated to the surface. The men picked it up. I've always thought that story meant if you lost some standing with God, if somehow you couldn't feel Him, somehow you went wrong, then the thing to do is to go back and see where you lost it, or in other words, admit what you've done wrong and make it right with God."

"I've read that story, but I never thought about it like that. Actually, I'm not sure I know how to go back. Maybe you can help me."

"We'll look for it. You can tell me the story of your life."

"Well, if you can't sleep, I will. My story is pretty dull. It would put anybody to sleep." He smiled, reached forward, and said, "You've got the prettiest hair of any woman I've ever seen. Never saw a shade of red like that."

"I've always hated my hair." Hannah smiled. "They always called me 'Red,' and I hated that."

"Well, don't. It's as pretty as any woman's hair I've ever seen."

Hannah reached up and put her hand on his and said, "What a nice compliment."

The sun was falling when Ringo rode into Fort Smith. He had spent some time there on two occasions and rode right to the courthouse. He looked out and saw that a crowd was gathered around the gallows. As he dismounted, he said, "Is there a hanging today?"

A cowboy with bowed legs and a huge chew of tobacco mumbled, "Yep, going to hang three at the same time. The judge is doing it up right."

Ringo glanced at the gallows and saw that the ropes were already attached, and George Maledon was testing them by pulling at them. He thought about Maledon, who was the official executioner. "I wouldn't want a job like that," he muttered. He went up immediately to the judge's office and knocked on the door.

When the judge said, "Come in," he entered.

"Judge, my name's Ringo Jukes. I work for the Ramirez family."

"Oh, that's where our marshal is, Marshal Riordan."

"Yes, sir, he is, and I brought two wanted men in for you."

"Well, we can lock them up and bring them to trial."

"Too late for one of them, Judge. It was Alvin Darrow."

Judge Parker opened his eyes widely. "You mean he's dead?"

"Yes, sir, he is."

"He killed two of my marshals. I wanted the pleasure of watching him hang. How'd it happen?"

"Well, it's an odd thing. All of us were a little bit puzzled about the marshal you sent out, Marshal Riordan. He just didn't seem tough enough, but he faced Darrow, and the way Miss Ramirez tells it, Darrow started for his gun, and before it even cleared leather, Riordan pulled his gun and put a shot right between his eyes."

"I wouldn't have thought that was possible! Darrow was a fast gun. Everybody knew that."

"Wasn't fast enough, Judge. Anyway, I brought his body in."

"Well, there's a reward for it. I'll give you a note, and you can draw it from the bank."

"I brought in Boog Powell, too. He and Darrow were attacking a young woman, but Darrow made a fight of it. Powell is guilty of murder, and the young woman will testify that he killed her rider. Better string him up, I say."

Ringo watched as the judge scribbled something on a sheet. He took it and put it in his pocket. "Riordan's wondering when you're going to be sending a bunch out to run that group of killers down."

"We don't have enough to send right now." Parker leaned back for a while and studied Ringo. "I didn't think I was sending a man-killer to you. As a matter of fact, I doubt if Riordan's ever shot anybody — Wait, he did shoot Dent Smith. He's got the makings in him of a man-killer. I'll see that Powell's locked up and tried for murder."

"Thanks, Judge. I'll be going now. I've got some drinking to do, and I'm going over to beat those gamblers out of some of their money."

"I would advise against it."

"I thought you would, Judge. I'm just a

hopeless sinner."

Riordan entered the kitchen, looking for Rosa. "How's Miss Hannah today?" he asked her.

"All right, I guess. She's eating more and able to get around a little bit better."

"I'd better go check on her."

"I'll go with you. I need to pick up her plate." Rosa gave him a careful glance and said, "You're taking good care of that woman."

"Well, she's fragile. Not like a Western woman, like you and your mother. She needs lots of care."

They went to Hannah's room. Riordan smiled and said, "Hello, Hannah."

"I'm glad you came. Sit down, Riordan." Hannah smiled.

Riordan frowned. "You know, you've had that bandage on long enough. It's about time to change it. It's bound to be dirty, and that's not good for you. If you'll get something to make strips out of, Rosa, we'll put on a clean one."

Instantly Hannah said, "Please, I'd much rather a woman do it."

Rosa said more sharply than she meant to, "I'll put it on, Riordan."

"Okay. I'll wait outside. Come get me

when she's all fit to be seen, Rosa."

Rosa had made up some bandages, so she helped the invalid sit up and then took her gown down. She began taking the bandages off, saying nothing.

Finally Hannah said, "I just couldn't help being embarrassed at having a man see me undressed."

"There was no choice the first time. I didn't know how to do this, and he did."

"I know, and I was almost out of it then. I didn't even know it, but now it's different." She grunted, and as Rosa drew the bandages tight, she said, "I appreciate so much how you've taken care of me. You'd make a good nurse."

"A rough one, I suppose."

"I admire the way you're able to ride and do all the things you do. I don't think I could stay on a horse."

"You didn't grow up on a ranch like I did, down in Texas."

"No, I'm a city girl. I'm anxious to get to my school."

"What are you going to teach the Indians?"

"Oh, how to read and write, and I also want to teach them about Jesus." She suddenly faced Rosa and said, "Are you a Christian, Miss Ramirez?"

"I grew up a Catholic. They tell me I was baptized when I was a baby, but with the life I was caught in, I couldn't do much about that."

"Why, it's not too late now."

"I guess I don't need to hear any preaching."

Hannah blinked with surprise at Rosa's harsh words. "I'm sorry. I didn't mean to offend you."

Rosa wanted to change the subject and steer the conversation away from herself. "What about you? You have any sweethearts?"

"Yes," Hannah said. "I was engaged to a fine young man. He died a short time before we were to be married."

Rosa stared at her. What else would this woman have to endure in life? "I'm so sorry."

Hannah replied softly, "That's all right. Have you ever been in love, Miss Ramirez?"

Rosa laughed and gathered up the rest of the bandages. "I've had to fight men off since I was fourteen." She suddenly hesitated. "I've noticed you seem attracted to Riordan. Do you like him?"

"Well, I don't know how to answer that. I'm grateful to him — and to you — for saving my life. I'll never forget it."

"I think you're more attached to Riordan than you let on. I don't usually bother to give women warnings when I see them going wrong, but you two would never be happy together."

"Why would you say that?"

"Well, you're a woman of God from the East, and he's a marshal and has a rough life in front of him. I don't think you'd ever make it." Rosa left the room, knowing that what she was really worried about was that they would make it together.

"Get up. Marshals don't need to take naps."

Startled, Riordan came off his bed in the bunkhouse and stared around. He saw Ringo and Heck and said, "Good to see you, too, Heck."

"I want to know something. Rosa says that Darrow went for his gun, but you pulled your own gun and shot him before he got his pistol out. You never told me you could do that. Course I haven't forgotten how you snuffed Dent Smith out."

Ringo said, "I didn't see it. I'm pretty fast with a gun myself. You think you can shade me, Riordan?"

"Yes."

That single word seemed to irritate Ringo. "Let's try it out."

"It's not a game."

Heck said, "I'd like to see it." Several of the hands had come in and were watching. Heck said, "You two men unload your guns. I don't want anybody shot."

"I don't want to, Heck," Riordan insisted. "It's not something you play with."

"Do what I tell you. I'm the boss around here."

With a sigh, Riordan removed the bullets from his gun, reholstered it, and then stood facing Ringo, who had done the same.

"When I shout 'Draw,' go for your guns," Heck said. Both men were still, with their hands down at their sides. The silence ran on, and suddenly Heck shouted in a stentorian voice, "Draw!"

Ringo's hand went to his gun, but even as he touched the butt, he heard a click and stared down in dismay to see that Riordan had drawn, put the gun right in his belly, and had pulled the trigger.

"I never saw a faster draw in my life!" Ringo gasped. "Let's never get in a fight, okay, partner?"

"Of course not."

"Kind of funny," Heck Thomas said. "Me and the judge were afraid to send you out here. We was afraid you might get killed."

"You've been practicin' all your life, I

reckon. Haven't you?" Ned said.

"As a matter of fact, I really haven't. But I've always been quick with my hands."

"What about it, Heck? Are we going out to get Beecher and his bunch?"

"No, we need half a dozen men if we run into the Fox. When we get the men, we'll go."

"I want to sit up, please."

Riordan had been sitting beside Hannah reading to her from a book Frank had loaned him. It was poetry, and he enjoyed it. He got up and said, "Are you sure you feel up to this, Hannah?"

"Yes, I just need to be careful."

He pulled the cover back and saw she was wearing a nightgown with a robe over it. He helped her stand to her feet and carefully placed her in a chair. "Is that okay?"

"Yes, I feel much better." She looked at him and said, "I heard about the way you and Ringo pretended to draw on each other." She hesitated. "Have you ever killed a man besides Darrow, Riordan?"

"I don't like to think about it. I had to shoot an outlaw once to save Marshal Heck's life."

"Did it bother you, killing Darrow?"

He looked at her, and there was pain in

her eyes. "Yes, it still does. I think I could have shot him in the arm, but you were there hurt, and Miss Ramirez was with me. If he had killed me, both of you would probably be dead now, too."

"It was something you had to do. Do you think you'll do this the rest of your life?"

"I don't think so."

"What do you want to do?"

Riordan suddenly grinned. "You'll laugh at this. I had ideas of becoming a painter before I got in this line of work."

"Can I see some of your work?"

"Don't really have any paintings here. They're all back East. I've got some drawings."

"I'd like to see them."

"Okay. I'll go get them." He retrieved his tablet and placed it before her.

She opened the cover and stared at the first one. "Why, that's Ringo!"

"I don't do figures as well as I'd like."

She began to turn slowly through the pages, commenting and exclaiming about his work.

She got to one of Rosa and said, "She's so beautiful."

"Yes, she is. Would you like for me to do a sketch of you?"

"No, I'm all puffy and ugly."

He laughed. "No, I can take all that out."

He took the tablet and leaned back, putting it on the table. Taking a pencil, he began to sketch.

He was so engrossed in his work he was startled when Rosa came to the open door. She watched the two for a while. A look of displeasure came over her face. She turned and left without a word.

CHAPTER 17

A week had gone by since Riordan had done the sketch of Hannah, and she was getting better every day. She could get up now, dress herself, and move around very well. She loved the sketch Riordan had made and kept it pinned to her wall.

As for Riordan, he took the bounty money that had been on Alvin Darrow and Powell and gave it to Hannah saying, "Use this for your school."

"Why, thank you, Riordan. We always need supplies for the students."

"I just wanted to tell you that I'll take you to the school when you get able."

"I think I'd better be a little bit stronger."

"Probably best. Where will you stay when you get there?"

"I — I really don't know. I think the mission board expected a couple coming out, and of course I thought William would make all the arrangements."

It was evening, and the two were standing on the front porch. Riordan often did this, sat outdoors at night, looking up at the sky and admiring the beauty displayed among the stars.

Hannah asked, "You like to watch the stars?"

"Yes, I do."

"I wish I knew the names of them like sailors do."

"I know some of them." He began to name the stars.

Finally she exclaimed, "You know so much! You went to college, didn't you?"

"I don't know as I learned all that much that was helpful."

The two were standing close together. She moved and said, "I'll be glad when my ribs get well." She inadvertently leaned against him.

He felt the soft pressure of her body. He smelled the rose scent that was in her hair, and by the light of the huge full moon, he could see her face. She had a tender expression, and Riordan did something he had not thought he was capable of. Without another word, he put his arms around her, held her gently, leaned over, and kissed her. He felt her surprise, and for a moment she resisted. Then she seemed to melt against him, and her lips moved under his.

When he lifted his head, she said, "I'm so ashamed."

"No, I don't want you to feel that way. It was all my doing."

"I don't know. I feel different toward you than I've ever felt."

"The doctor said that would happen. That you'd be dependent on me and Rosa because we helped you when you needed someone."

"I don't think that's it, but I'm ashamed that I would kiss a man so easily." She turned and left.

Suddenly Rosa's voice came in the darkness. "You comforting the patient, Riordan?"

Quickly Riordan turned and saw that she had been sitting in one of the cane-bottom rocking chairs usually occupied by her father. He hadn't dreamed she was on the porch. He was embarrassed and could not think of a thing to say. Finally he said, "Rosa, I feel sorry for her. She's helpless. She's lost the man she was going to marry, and she's afraid."

"And that's all there was to it?"

"Yes."

Rosa rose and came to him.

He was taken off guard when she reached

up, put her arms around his neck, and pulled his head down. He felt the softness of her form and was suddenly aware that old hungers had been stirred.

Her lips were soft, and she pulled him closer, and then suddenly she stepped back. "You see? You were after her, and now you're after me. If a cheap saloon girl walked by, you'd be after her, too." She turned and walked quickly away.

Riordan wanted to talk to her, and he called her name.

She turned around and came back. "What is it?"

"I loved a woman once, but she didn't want me. She was the only sweetheart I ever had. I'm not a woman chaser, Rosa. I may have made a mistake with Hannah. It won't be the last mistake I make."

Suddenly Rosa felt sorry that she had tormented him. "I apologize. I'm the one that was out of order. Just forget what happened."

But all Riordan thought about was how he was supposed to forget about holding Rosa in his arms.

Gray Hawk rode in the next day and ate as if he were ravenous.

He listened to Rosa as she explained what

had happened with the outlaws and how they had killed a man and that a federal marshal was now on the spot. She told him about Riordan.

"I've heard about Riordan. He's the one that gunned Dent Smith and Alvin Darrow down."

"Yes, he did."

"Must be some gunman."

Rosa took Gray Hawk to see her father and her grandfather.

After catching up on the news, the conversation turned once again to the outlaws. Rosa said, "I want George Pye brought to justice for killing Blinky."

"That was Powell who shot Blinky," her father interjected.

"Pye was shooting, too. He's just as guilty," she countered.

Gray Hawk's eyes suddenly gleamed. "I know where he is."

"Where?" Rosa demanded.

"He's holed up in Spivey Town. It's a rotten little hole full of bad Indians and outlaws. No decency in it."

Later on, Gray Hawk hunted Riordan down and wanted to know about the killing of Darrow. Finally he told the marshal what he had told Rosa. "Pye's and Beecher's gang are in Spivey Town, but you'd better stay away from there. Wait until you get a whole band of marshals. It's got more bad men and killers than a dog has fleas."

"Well, maybe the judge will send out a troop to clean out that rat's nest."

"It'd take a troop," Gray Hawk grunted.

"I'll send word to him. We'll see what can be done."

"You'd better tell him to get some good ones. The Fox is out there with his band. It's like a small army, Riordan."

Rosa walked up then. "I heard what you two were talking about. Riordan, you go back to the city where you belong. You're educated, and you've got a good family with money. You can't win out here."

"You're probably right," Riordan said. He said no more but turned and walked away.

The next morning Gray Hawk saw Rosa at breakfast. "Riordan rode out early this morning."

Rosa stared at him. "Where was he going?"

"Probably to Fort Smith to see the judge about getting the marshals," Mateo said.

"No, he didn't head toward Fort Smith. He rode due east headed toward the hill country."

They were silent, and it was Gray Hawk who said what they were all thinking. "I wouldn't be surprised if he was going to Spivey Town to root out that fellow who shot your hired hand."

"He wouldn't be foolish enough to do that!" Rosa exclaimed.

"Men do foolish things. He didn't ask me to go with him. We could have gotten a bunch up here, I think, but it looks like he's determined to go it alone."

Rosa groaned, and a couple of tears escaped her eyes. "I was the one that got him here to hunt up Pye and his murderers. I wish I had never done anything now."

Riordan spoke to Red, as he often did, "I'm just being a fool, Red. A horse wouldn't do a fool thing like this." He had formed a habit of talking to the big horse when he was alone. "I know I ought to get to Fort Smith and beg the judge to send at least two or three marshals, but I guess I just really haven't proved I'm as tough as I need to be. Maybe I can catch Pye out alone, just me and him. It'll be easy."

He had heard the directions and seen a map that pointed out Spivey Town. He arrived there late in the afternoon and saw that it wasn't much of a town. A few unpainted shacks and a line of businesses all built of warping boards — a general store, a livery stable, a feed store, and too many saloons for any place to remain decent.

He came to the edge of town, rode in, stopped in front of the livery stable, and dismounted. He tried to think of some way to find Pye, draw him out, and then get him alone. He was certain that if he tried to take Pye with his gang around, there would be a battle he could not survive.

Finally the sun went down, and still he could not come upon a plan. He took a deep breath and said, "I've got to do something." He started down the street, staggering, pretending to be drunk.

He stumbled into a half-breed who said, "Watch where you're going!" with a curse.

"I've got to find George Pye," Riordan mumbled. "Got some money for him."

The man's eyes narrowed. "Money? He's with his woman. Give me twenty dollars, and I'll show you her place."

"Sure." Riordan fumbled the money out and gave the man the cash.

"Come on," the man said.

Riordan followed him down a street. They stopped in front of a saloon with a sign saying THE BELLE IRENE.

The man pointed up to the second-floor window. "That's Sally's place. If George ain't gambled all his money away, and if

308

he's drunk, he'll be in her room. He ain't, he'll be in that saloon."

Riordan mumbled his thanks, and the man left.

Slowly Riordan tied Red to the hitching post. The street was almost empty now. Just a few people walking along and going into different stores. *Maybe I'll get lucky and he'll be there alone or with the woman.*

He entered the door that led to the upstairs section. When he got to the top, he saw there was a short hallway. Each wall had a door. He looked at one, and it was empty. Going to the other door, he lifted his ear and heard a woman talking and a man grunting some answers. *That's got to be him.*

He quietly opened the door, which was unlocked, and saw a woman wearing a dirty robe standing. She whirled to face him, and he drew his gun and mouthed the words *Shut up!* She turned pale and backed over against the wall. He looked at the bed and recognized Pye. He had heard the description and saw the ragged scar going down the left side of his face and down his neck. Pye was mumbling something, but his eyes were closed.

Going over to stand beside him, Riordan reached down, grabbed him by the collar, and pulled him upright. He put the muzzle of his gun to Pye's head and said, "You're under arrest, Pye. You're coming with me."

Pye woke up and started to holler, "Hey, there —"

But Riordan slapped him with the barrel of his gun and pointed it at his head. "You're going, dead or alive! Just one more bit of noise and it'll be dead. And I'm not particular. Now, get out of that bed."

Pye scrambled out of the bed. He was obviously drunk.

"Put on your boots." Riordan watched him put on his boots, and at the same time he took Pye's gun and shoved it into his belt. "We're going now. You make a sound, and I'll kill you."

Pye was rapidly sobering up. He saw the gun in Riordan's hand. He had heard of how Riordan had put a bullet exactly in the middle of Alvin Darrow's eyes. He swallowed hard and nodded.

They went down the stairs, but by the time they got to the horses, the woman had stuck her head out and was screaming, "There's a marshal here!"

Riordan said, "Pye, get on that horse." He waited until Pye mounted, and then he got on his own horse. But even as he did, the bat-wing door of the saloon flew open and five men came out. They lined up before Riordan, and one of them said, "I'm Henry Beecher. Turn that man loose, or we'll make a dead man out of you."

"I'm Riordan, Beecher. I'm taking him in."

"You're a dead man!" Henry Beecher's eyes seemed to glow in the darkness.

"That's the one that killed Alvin Darrow, Henry," one of his men said. "He's plenty fast."

Beecher shook his head and smiled. "He's smart. He sees he's outgunned. Isn't that so, Riordan?"

Riordan drew his gun in a flash of movement, and it was pointed right at Beecher's face. "You make one move or one of your men makes a move, and I'll kill you, Beecher. And then I'll take some more with me."

"You can't bluff me."

"Go for your gun, Henry. See if I'm bluffing."

Beecher's eyes opened, and he saw the expression on Riordan's face and the gun pointed at him. The muzzle was entirely steady.

One of his men yelled, "He's bluffing!"

"No, he's not bluffing!" Henry exclaimed. "He means it. He'd die, but so would some of us. Not worth it."

Riordan smiled. "That's smart, Henry. Now you get on a horse."

"You're not arresting me."

"No, I'm not, but you're my free pass to get out of here with my prisoner. You go with me until we're clear of the town, and then you can come back."

Beecher grinned sourly. "I'm supposed to trust you?"

"It's that or some of us are dead. I give you my word, you'll be the first. I give you my word also you can come back as soon as I'm clear with my prisoner."

"Don't do it, Henry," one of the men said. "He's lying."

Henry studied Riordan and finally said, "I think he's got us." He advanced, got on one of the horses, and said, "You boys wait here."

Riordan kept his eye on the men watching him and was aware that other men had come out of the saloon and were staring at him. He put himself on the far side of Beecher and Pye and said, "Let's go."

As they left town, Riordan was careful to keep his two prisoners between him and the men on the sidewalk. He felt the muscles of his back tighten as he rode out of town, expecting a bullet. None came.

They reached the town limit, and he said, "Spur those horses." They rode at a fast gallop and rode for five minutes. "This is good enough." They all pulled up, and Riordan said, "You can go back now, Henry."

Henry turned and stared at Riordan as if he were viewing an alien species. "You know I can't live with this, Riordan. I have to pay you back or I'll be laughed out of the Territory."

"You take your shot, Henry. I've got nothing against you, but if you come after me, better make sure you do a good job of it."

Beecher suddenly laughed when he saw that he was out of danger. "All right, Marshal, I'll be seeing you."

Riordan watched him go.

Pye said, "He'll kill you. I hope he does."

"I expect he'll try. Now, we got a hard ride. Let's go."

Henry rode back and found his crew milling around.

"Let's go get him," Hack Wilson said. "There's plenty of us to get one man."

"No, that would be too easy." Henry was silent for a time. Finally he smiled evilly and said, "I've got to think of a very special ending for Marshal Riordan. Something that will hurt him worse than a bullet . . ."

■ ■ ■ ■

The ranch seemed to come alive as Riordan rode in with his prisoner. He dismounted, and they all gathered around him, Ringo keeping an eye on the prisoner.

Hannah was one of them. She came and put her hand out. "You're safe," she whispered.

"For a while, Hannah."

"How'd you do it, Riordan?" Frank asked. "Nobody ever got one of the wild bunch like this."

"Well, I had a little help from Henry the Fox," Riordan said. They demanded to know his story, and he said, "It wasn't all that much. Ringo, you and Ned put Pye here under guard."

They went inside, and Frank said, "I don't know what you did, but if you made a fool out of Henry, he won't forget."

"That's what he told me, but he can't kill me but once, can he?"

"Don't say that!" Rosa said sharply. "You must be hungry. I've got some stew and beans on the stove. Sit down. The rest of you leave."

Rosa fixed him a meal, beans and a tender chunk of beef and fresh biscuits. She watched him as he ate. She sat down across from him and said, "I've said some hard things, but you did what I asked. You brought in the killer." She put out her hand, and he took it. She stared at him with a strange look in her eyes. "No man has ever kept his word to me or did what he promised. I guess I can always remember you as being one that did, Riordan."

Riordan was aware of the warmth and the strength of her hand. "You know, as I was bringing Pye back, I was thinking about you."

She stared at him. "What about me?"

"Well, there was a touchy situation, and the thought came to me that if they killed me, I would never see you again, and it made me sad."

Suddenly she smiled, and her face relaxed. She put her other hand down and held his prisoner. "You have your moments, Riordan."

■ ■ ■ ■

PART FOUR

■ ■ ■ ■

CHAPTER 18

Caleb Riordan sat in his favorite easy chair, staring across the room. His eyes were fixed on an ormolu clock. He was not studying that object but was merely giving deep thought to his son Faye.

It was a hot day. The windows were open, allowing a slight breeze to come in and stir the flowers that Eileen had set in the window. From far off came the sound of servants laughing as they trimmed the yard and worked in the flower beds.

None of this entered into Caleb's thinking, and finally he shook his shoulders together in a gesture of helplessness and looked over to where Eileen was sitting on a divan, knitting. "Eileen," he said, "Faye never writes to me." He had not intended to say this, but it had been on his mind for some time now. When Eileen looked up at him, he said defensively, "It seems like he could write his father once in a while."

Eileen smiled slightly and ceased knitting. She studied Caleb and finally said simply, "You two were never close, Caleb."

Caleb gave her a sharp look and shook his head. "No, we weren't."

"None of us were really close to Faye," Max said. He was wearing a pair of blue trousers, highly polished shoes, and a snow-white shirt. "I should think he would be considerate enough to write to us, though."

Leo looked up from the book he was reading. "Well, Max, I'm not really expecting a letter from him. I didn't pay much attention to him while he was here, and I suppose he thinks I haven't changed."

"He may be sick or hurt," Caleb said. "Surely he'd write if he were." He suddenly straightened up in his chair and passed his hand over his thick hair in a gesture of despair. Then he said, "Eileen, he writes to you."

"Yes, he does. He tells me a great many details of his work there."

"Well, why don't you read the letters to me?" Caleb complained.

"I didn't think you'd be interested, dear."

Shaking his head, Caleb growled, "He's wasting his time out there playing cowboy."

"I don't think so," Eileen said calmly. "I believe he's doing something he thinks needs to be done."

"But he can never make any money out there riding around on a horse. He's never done anything a man should do at his age."

"That's right. He never makes any money," Leo said.

"And he could, too. He could come to work at the factory."

The men waited, but Eileen went back to her knitting.

Finally Caleb got up and left the room, his back stiff with displeasure.

The carriage stopped, and Caleb and his two sons got out and started up toward the steps that led to the wide front porch. Caleb had put in a long day at the factory and was surprised when he saw a distinguished-looking man leaving the house. He was tall, well dressed, and had a pair of sharp black eyes.

"Who is that, Father?" Leo asked.

"Never saw him before."

As they passed, the man nodded pleasantly and said, "Good afternoon."

"Hello," Caleb said. He wanted to ask the man who he was, but that seemed somewhat rude. He turned and watched him go into a landau carriage, and as the man rode away, Caleb shook his head. "I don't like strange men coming to the house."

They went inside, and Eileen met them with a smile. She kissed Caleb on the cheek, having to reach up and pull his head down, and said, "Did you have a good day, dear?"

"It was all right." Caleb waited for Eileen to say something about the visitor, but she simply began chatting about what she had been doing. Finally Caleb could not refrain from saying, "We met a fellow coming out of the house. I didn't know him."

"Oh, that was Mr. Samuel Steinbaum."

The men all waited for her to say more, but she didn't. Finally Caleb said, "I don't believe I know him. What was he doing here? Is he selling something?"

"Not at all. I asked him to come. You go along and wash up. We'll have dinner early tonight."

"But why did you ask him if he isn't selling anything?"

"He's the director of the Mellon Museum of Art."

"Well, why did he come here?"

"Why, I invited him."

Leo said, "That's unusual, Mother. You don't usually invite people that we don't know."

"I've exchanged letters with him several times, so I thought I'd invite him and we could talk." She laughed and said, "Are you jealous, Caleb?"

"Don't be foolish! I would like to know what he was doing here, though."

Eileen shrugged her shoulders and said, "It concerns Faye's work."

"What work?" Leo demanded.

"Why, his painting, dear. I asked him to come and give me his opinion of Faye's paintings."

All three men stared at her, and it was Caleb who finally demanded, "Well, what did he say?"

"They couldn't be worth much," Leo shrugged.

Eileen pulled a slip of paper from her bodice. "Here's his offer on the paintings that he looked at."

Caleb stared at the paper fixedly. He did not speak. His mind seemed to be moving rather slowly. "The first one says, 'Woman With Small Girl — four hundred dollars.' " Looking up, he blinked with surprise and said, "I remember that painting. If I remember right, Faye painted that in two days."

"That's right. Not many young men make four hundred dollars in two days, do they, dear?"

"Let me see that list," Max said. The two brothers flanked their father and read down the list. They named off the paintings that they remembered and finally looked at the figure at the bottom, the total offer.

"Why, this adds up to five thousand dollars!" Leo declared.

"Yes, that's good, isn't it? Mr. Steinbaum wants to have a one-man show of Faye's work. He'll handle it all for a fee of ten percent."

"You think people will buy the kinds of paintings Faye does?" Max asked dubiously.

"Well, Mr. Steinbaum says painting in Faye's style by artists with not half his talent are selling very well."

All three men were speechless. Finally Max said, "Two hundred dollars for one day's work? Why, that's more than I make."

"Yes, I suppose it is." Eileen smiled. "Mr. Steinbaum thinks Faye has a brilliant future. He wants to act as his agent."

Caleb could not take his eyes off the list. He ran up and down it with a steady gaze, trying to find something wrong with it.

He was interrupted when Eileen said, "I need some money, dear."

"Of course. Will twenty dollars do?"

"Oh no, I need a lot of money."

Caleb had always been generous with Eileen where money was concerned, and she very seldom had to ask, for he saw to it that she had spending money at all times. "What do you want that costs so much? Some new furniture?"

"No, I'm going to Fort Smith." Eileen smiled as the shock registered in all three men's faces. "Faye needs to hear about this wonderful news — and I need to see him. I miss him so desperately."

Caleb's thinking seemed to have slowed down. He would not have been much more surprised if Eileen had said, "I'm going to the moon." The idea of her going west never had occurred to him. "Well," he said abruptly, "we'll both go."

"Let's all of us go," Leo said. "I'd like to see this world he's thrown himself into full of cowboys and guns and rattlesnakes, I suppose."

"Right," Max said. "We need a vacation."

Eileen was pleased, but she asked, "What about the factory? Who'll take care of that? You can't leave your work."

"My manager Charles can handle it. He knows as much about the place as I do." He stared back at the list and said, "I'd like to see these pictures."

Eileen was pleased. "Yes, of course. All of you, come on. I've still got them out on display."

■ ■ ■ ■

"I really need to go to Forth Smith," Hannah said.

"Why would you need to go there?" Riordan asked. The two were standing on the front porch. Riordan had come in to get something to drink, and she had joined him.

"I need to send a telegram to my superior in the church."

"I'll take you."

Rosa had been standing in the doorway and had turned to leave, but then she abruptly stopped and said, "I'll go with you. Boog Powell and Pye are going to hang for killing Blinky. I want to see it."

Ringo had arrived to stand beside Riordan just as Rosa spoke. At once he said, "I'm going, too."

"All you want to do is go get drunk," Riordan smiled. "You stay home and behave yourself."

"No, I'm going with you. I don't think you understand Beecher, Riordan. He knows people all over the Territory are talking about how you rode right in big as life and took away one of his gang. He's like a snake, Riordan. He may be quiet, but he'll strike when you least expect it. Your life's not worth a dime as long he's alive."

Riordan put up some argument, but Rosa said, "We'll take Zack and Ned with us. That'll be enough to handle Henry the Fox. I hate that name!"

"I think he sort of likes it," Ringo said. "Takes pleasure at being seen as some kind of a hero, which he is to a lot of people."

"A hero?" Hannah exclaimed. "Why would they admire a man like that?"

"Well, that's the way it is out here, Miss Hannah." Ringo shrugged. "They admire strength and courage, and you have to admit Henry's got those two qualities."

In the end, they took the whole crew except for two men.

They arrived in Fort Smith late Saturday afternoon. Hannah sent her telegrams and then joined Riordan and Rosa at the hotel for dinner. The hands spread out to various distractions. Rosa knew they wouldn't be seen again until it was time to go home.

Rosa noticed that men recognized Riordan. She heard one of them whisper to a companion, "That's Riordan. They say he's as fast as lightning with that gun of his."

This both pleased and disturbed Rosa, for she knew that Ringo was right. That Beecher would never rest until he got his revenge.

Rosa and Hannah shared a room. After

they were ready to go to bed, Hannah said, "Are you really going to that hanging?"

"Yes, I am."

"I don't know why you'd want to see such a thing."

"They killed one of my men who was liked a great deal and who had done nothing to deserve it. The poor fellow didn't even get to live his life out. Call it what you want. I want to see justice done."

There were three men to be hanged, and a crowd, as usual, had gathered.

Riordan stood beside Rosa and nudged her arm with his elbow. "Look up at the window on the second floor. That's Judge Parker," he said. "It's a way he has, so I hear. He watches every hanging from that window."

"Why would a man enjoy a hanging?"

"I don't think he does. At least that's what the marshals all say. They say he sees himself as an agent of the government dealing out justice, but he hates the hangings themselves."

They studied Parker, who was standing still, until finally they heard a murmur run over the crowd that filled the square. They watched as George Maledon led three men with their hands tied behind their backs to the gallows. He stood there and helped steady them as they climbed the few steps and then placed them very carefully in their positions.

As for Rosa, she was already beginning to wish that she had not come. It was one thing when violence explodes and somebody's shot unexpectedly. But this was different. These men were all alive and well and knew that in a few moments their hearts would stop, their blood would stop flowing, and they would be no more.

When the men were in place, Maledon said, "If you have anything to say, go ahead."

The first man was small and looked sickly. Neither Pye nor Powell spoke, and Pye seemed frozen by what was happening to him. Boog, alone of the three, did not seem to be afraid. He stared arrogantly out at the crowd and said, "Some of you deserve hanging as much as I do. Now get on with it, Maledon."

Maledon shrugged and adjusted the ropes around all three men's necks. He stepped back and without hesitation pulled the lever. The trapdoor opened, and the three bodies shot downward. As the bodies drew the ropes taut, a sigh of some sort went over the crowd.

Riordan shook his head. "Let's get out of

here, Rosa. That's enough of this."

As they left, Rosa found herself shaken. She had thought herself ready for this, but now she realized she was not. She felt sickened by what she had seen.

Riordan said, "It's too late to go home tonight. We'll go in the morning."

"All right. Suits me."

Rosa got up in the morning and saw that she had overslept. She had slept very poorly, as a matter of fact, and now wished she had not come to the hanging at all.

Hannah was already up and dressed and now turned to her and said, "Let's go get some breakfast."

"I'm not hungry."

"Well, you can have some coffee before we leave." She hesitated then said, "I'd like to go to church. Would you go with me?"

Rosa automatically began to frame a reason why she could not go, but later when Riordan joined her and Hannah for breakfast, he said, "What would you think about all of us attending church this morning? After witnessing the events of yesterday, I feel the need for something spiritual in my life."

"Okay, that sounds good." Her answer shocked even her, for she had not had any interest in being religious before. Somehow she felt the same as Riordan. She needed something like this to maybe bring peace to her heart and mind.

Beecher was sitting at the table with a bottle of whiskey in his hand. He now poured a tumbler full and drank it down. Red Lyle said "You're worrying too much about that Riordan."

"I'm not worrying about anything!" Henry snapped.

"Well, that's good. You know the best thing to do is just lay back until Riordan gets off the ranch. Just shoot him in the back. Kill him out of hand. I'll do it myself for a price if you'd like."

"You'd have to, Red. You couldn't beat him to the draw."

"Well, he may have a faster draw than I do, but he ain't faster than a thirty-thirty slug in the head."

The two men sat there drinking until Sal Maglie entered. He took his hat off, beat the dust off of it, and then walked over. "Got all of them supplies, Henry."

"You go to the hanging?"

"Yeah, I went. He went pretty good, Boog did, but he always did have nerve. You know Riordan was there with that woman, the Mexican, at the hanging, I mean."

"They were? How'd he look?" Henry said,

lifting his eyes.

"Well," Sal scratched his head, "I heard some folks talkin'. They say Riordan's sweet on the Ramirez woman.

"Can't blame him for that," Maglie said. "She's a good-looking woman."

Beecher was silent for a time. Finally he looked up, and there was a smile on his lips. "You know Riordan took something of mine. The only way I'll feel like I beat him is if I take something of his."

"Like what?" Red said in a puzzled tone.

Beecher knew none of the men understood him. He was a mystery. They knew he was deadly, and none would dare cross him, but he was a deeper thinker than any of the hands.

Now Red said, "I don't understand you, Henry. What can you take of his?"

Beecher leaned forward with his smile broadening, his eyes glittering. "Here's what we'll do . . ."

CHAPTER 19

As soon as Rosa stepped into the small wood-framed church, she felt some sort of strange pressure. Religion had played almost no part in her life. She was told that she had been baptized in the Catholic tradition when she was a baby, but as she had grown up, her life had taken a different turn. During the last year, she had been working in saloons, fighting off lustful men, and simply trying to make some sort of a life for her family.

"Come along. There are some seats," Hannah said. She put her hand on Rosa's arm, and for a moment Rosa resisted, but then it was too late. She walked with Hannah down the aisle between the two rows of wooden pews, which were already, for the most part, occupied.

A quick glance around revealed that the church was filled with men and women and children from all walks of life. Some of the men and women wore expensive clothing and looked well groomed. On the other hand, some of the men were wearing what looked like work clothes, overalls, and they had the look of poverty on their faces. Their wives wore the cheapest sort of gingham dresses, and the children were dressed as well as the parents could afford.

Moving into the vacant space, Rosa sat down. Hannah sat down beside her whispering, "I heard this preacher is a wonderful speaker. I know we're going to enjoy the sermon."

At that moment, a tall, thin man stood up and in a deep voice said, "We will now sing 'Old One Hundred.' "

The entire congregation stood up, and not wanting to be noticed, Rosa stood up with them. They sang a song that was very simple:

"Praise God, from whom all blessings
    flow;
    Praise Him, all creatures here below;
Praise Him above, ye heavenly host;
    Praise Father, Son, and Holy Ghost.
    Amen."

The song leader smiled and said, "Now we'll sing my favorite hymn, 'When I Survey the Wondrous Cross.' "

There were no hymnals, but everyone seemed to know the song. Rosa listened and found herself being strangely moved by the singing. Of course, the singing itself was not exceptional. Some of the people sang off-key and some too loudly, but the words came through to her.

"When I survey the wondrous cross
   On which the Prince of glory died,
My richest gain I count but loss,
   And pour contempt on all my pride.

Forbid it, Lord, that I should boast,
   Save in the death of Christ my God!
All the vain things that charm me most,
   I sacrifice them to His blood.

See from His head, His hands, His feet,
   Sorrow and love flow mingled down!
Did e'er such love and sorrow meet,
   Or thorns compose so rich a crown?

Were the whole realm of nature mine,
   That were a present far too small;
Love so amazing, so divine,
   Demands my soul, my life, my all."

The singing went on for almost twenty

minutes. Finally the song leader stepped back and took a seat on the rostrum.

A short, well-built man with brown curly hair and direct blue eyes stood up. "We are glad to welcome you to our church. Those of you who are visitors, feel at home. We welcome you."

He laid his Bible on the pulpit, flipped it open, and said, "The sermon this morning will be very short. I'm going to pray that if there be one in here who does not know the Lord Jesus Christ as Savior, that he or she will leave this building as a part of this family of God."

He had a pleasant look on his face. His voice was clear and carried well in the small building. "My sermon this morning," he said, "if I had a title for it, would be 'A Woman Who Found Jesus.' As a matter of fact, if you were to go to most foreign countries where paganism rules, you would find women treated worse than animals. But when Jesus came, he lifted women from a lowly status to a place of honor. This morning I want us to think about one of those women who encountered Jesus."

He picked up his Bible and began to read:

" 'And a woman having an issue of blood twelve years, which had spent all her liv-

336

ing upon physicians, neither could be healed of any, came behind him, and touched the border of his garment: and immediately her issue of blood stanched. And Jesus said, Who touched me? When all denied, Peter and they that were with him said, Master, the multitude throng thee and press thee, and sayest thou, Who touched me? And Jesus said, Somebody hath touched me: for I perceive that virtue is gone out of me. And when the woman saw that she was not hid, she came trembling, and falling down before him, she declared unto him before all the people for what cause she had touched him, and how she was healed immediately. And he said unto her, Daughter, be of good comfort: thy faith hath made thee whole; go in peace.' "

The minister closed his Bible and began to speak with excitement in his voice. He obviously believed his message and did his best to communicate that feeling. "Isn't that a wonderful story! This poor woman was unclean, for according to Jewish law any woman with an issue of blood was as unclean as a dead person. No one could touch her without becoming unclean. And for years she had sought to be healed and spent all her money on physicians but was no better."

Rosa had come prepared to ignore the sermon, but she found herself caught up with the story the minister had read. She had never heard it before, and he went on to describe the woman so well that she was absorbed in the drama of it.

"This poor woman, who had been failed by man on every hand, thought, 'If I could just touch the hem of the garment of Jesus of Nazareth, I will be healed.' Ah, now there is faith, my friends. There is faith! And you have heard how she did touch just the hem of the garment of the Lord Jesus and instantly she was healed. Bless the Lord, O my soul! That's what happens when people come to Jesus. They are healed. That's what I would like to present for you today. A savior who is Christ Jesus, the Son of God."

The minister continued discussing the story in great depth, drawing a picture of the poor woman who had struggled for so long and was so sick and how she had found healing in no place except in touching Jesus Christ.

Finally the preacher said, "Let me mention one other woman who found Jesus. It's found in the eighth chapter of the Gospel of John. 'And the scribes and Pharisees brought unto him a woman taken in adultery; and when they had set her in the midst, they say unto him, Master, this woman was taken in adultery, in the very act. Now Moses in the law commanded us, that such should be stoned: but what sayest thou?'

"The law indeed had such a verse, but Jesus did a very strange thing. He answered them not a word, but He 'stooped down, and with his finger wrote on the ground, as though he heard them not.' Finally he looked up, and He said words that I have treasured and have kept very carefully. Jesus said, 'He that is without sin among you, let him first cast a stone at her.' Well, dear friends, the Bible says that they were 'convicted by their own conscience, went out one by one, beginning at the eldest, even unto the last: and Jesus was left alone, and the woman standing in the midst.' "

The preacher ran his hand over his hair and said, "The Bible doesn't say this, but I like to think this dear woman, who was the sinner but yet a beloved sinner, came to Jesus and bowed down and held to His feet. We do know what Jesus said. He said, 'Woman, where are those thine accusers? hath no man condemned thee? She said, No man, Lord. And Jesus said unto her,

Neither do I condemn thee: go, and sin no more.' "

This story went straight to the heart of Rosa. It was as though she could see the poor retched woman ready to die for her sin, and she could hear the voice of Jesus saying, "Neither do I condemn thee: go, and sin no more." A longing somehow such as she had never known before began to build within her, and as the sermon went on, she found her hands trembling. She held them to conceal it from Hannah.

Finally the sermon ended, and the preacher said, "We're going to sing a few verses of an old hymn, and if there be one of you out there who does not yet know the Lord as personal Savior, and perhaps you are in the same condition as this woman, you have a sickness. You have sinned, and you don't know where to go. I call upon you to look to Jesus of Nazareth, the Savior of the world. He died to save sinners, and that means all of us. So come as we sing."

Everyone rose and began to sing a hymn that Rosa, of course, didn't know. She saw two people go down and speak with the preacher, then another who knelt at the altar, and she could not control the emotions that flooded through her. She stood there, her head bowed and her eyes closed, thinking about the two women that Jesus had touched. She felt tears come to her eyes, a very rare thing for her.

Finally the preacher dismissed with a short prayer.

As they left the building, Hannah, whose face was radiant, said, "Wasn't that a wonderful sermon?"

Rosa could not answer. It had been such a moving experience she did not know how to identify it. One thing she felt sure of was that her thoughts of Jesus Christ had been wrong. She had seen statues in Catholic churches of Jesus, but they were not Jesus. They were merely statues. But the man the minister had read of was living and full of love and compassion, and she knew that she would never forget this morning.

Judge Parker was poring over documents on his desk, but when the door opened and four strangers entered, he rose at once. "Good afternoon," he said. "I'm Judge Parker."

"Oh, Judge Parker, I'm so glad to meet you," the woman said. She was an attractive woman in her mid-forties with auburn hair and light brown eyes. "I'm Eileen Riordan."

"Why, Mrs. Riordan, it's good to see you."

"This is my husband Caleb and two of

my sons, Leo and Max."

Parker came around from behind his desk, shook hands, greeted them all, then turned his head to one side, and smiled. "I expect you've come all the way out here to the frontier to visit your son."

"Yes, we have. We just got off the steamboat, but we don't have any idea where to start looking, so I thought we'd come and ask you."

"Well, you're fortunate, Mrs. Riordan. Your son is in town today."

"Where has he been?" Caleb asked curiously. "We'd like very much to see him."

"I've had him stationed out on a ranch. The owners have been threatened with outlaws, and I haven't had the men to send a crew in to quiet them, so I sent Riordan." He stopped and said, "I don't even know his first name."

"It's Lafayette," Eileen said, "but everyone calls him Faye."

"Well, it's a small town. Let me call one of my marshals."

Parker went to the door and said, "Marshal Thomas."

Heck Thomas stepped inside, put his hazel eyes on the visitors, and listened as Parker explained who they were. He smiled briefly and said, "You know your son saved my life."

"You don't mean it!" Caleb said. "How did that happen?"

"I was going out to arrest a minor criminal, and I thought I'd take Riordan with me just to get him used to the Territory. When we got there, the man I wanted as prisoner had two of his kinfolk with him, both of them gunmen. One of them drew on me, and I just had time to get off a shot. I really expected to take a bullet in the head, but another shot rang out echoing mine, and I saw the other outlaw fall. I turned around and saw that Riordan was holding his gun. None of us had any idea he had that quickness or was that certain a shot."

"He — he killed a man?" Eileen asked tentatively.

"Yes, that's the way it goes out here in the Territory. Thomas, they'd like to find their son. Do you have any idea where he might be?"

"He was with Miss Ramirez fifteen minutes ago. They were in the general store. Probably still there. They seemed to be loading a wagon with supplies. I'd be glad to take you over there," he said to the visitors.

"Good. We're so anxious to see him."

"Are you planning to stay over?" Parker asked.

"Yes, we planned to make a lengthy visit of it."

"You may have trouble finding a place to stay. The hotel's full."

"Yep, we had a multiple hanging today. Two of them were killed for murdering one of Miss Rosa's hands."

"Please take us to him," Eileen said.

"Come this way. It's just down the street," Heck Thomas said as he started out the door.

"Why don't you get some more apples? I like those apple pies," Riordan said. He had been helping Rosa stock the wagon, and he picked up a large red apple. "I love apples."

"All right. Get a dozen of them. We'll have apple pie tonight. Maybe tomorrow."

Riordan obtained a sack, filled it with the fruit, and then he followed her around as she wandered through the store. "Did it bother you seeing that hanging, Rosa?"

"Yes, it did."

"I know something that bothered you worse."

"What?"

"The sermon that preacher laid on us."

Rosa shot a quick glance at Riordan.

"Well, I had never heard anything like it before. You probably grew up hearing sermons like that."

"Yes, I did, but you know there was something in that man that's not in most preachers. To tell the truth, he shook me up quite a bit."

"But I thought you said you were converted when you were twelve years old."

"Well, I thought I was, but I got away from my raising. Never got into any trouble . . . until I got out here."

They were alone at one end of the store, and Rosa said quietly, "I don't know what to think. I never thought much about God and heaven and hell, but I know they're real."

"Maybe we ought to go back and talk to that preacher, just you and me."

"No, I'd be embarrassed. I don't think God —"

"Faye!"

Riordan looked up and was shocked to see his mother, father, and two brothers had entered. His mother ran toward him, and he held his arms out. He caught her. She smelled of lemon and lavender, like always, and there were tears in her eyes. "Mother, what in the world are you doing out here?"

Caleb stepped forward. "We came out to

visit with you, son." He looked his son over, up and down. "I have to say I am impressed with you, son. You are so tan, and there's a steady look in your eye now."

"Father's right, and besides, we wanted to see the cowboy in all his glory." Max grinned.

Riordan pulled Rosa toward his family and said, "This is Miss Rosa Ramirez. I've been staying at her ranch for quite a while now."

"I'm so happy to know you, Miss Ramirez," Caleb said. He could have a gentlemanly manner when he chose, and he smiled saying, "Has this young man been behaving himself?"

"Oh yes, he has." Rosa was overwhelmed with the family. One look at them told her that they were aristocrats. They dressed entirely in the fashions of the East and were all fine-looking people. She did not see much resemblance between Riordan and his father and his two brothers, but some of his mother was in his features.

Caleb said, "I hear it's going to be hard to find a place in town. I don't know where we'll stay unless we buy a tent."

"No need to do that, Mr. Riordan," Rosa said quickly. "You need to come back to our ranch. Your son will be there. It's quiet, and you can visit as long as you'd like. Plenty of room at our big old ranch house."

"We wouldn't want to impose," Eileen said.

The entire family continued trying to protest, but Rosa said, "It will be an honor to have you. You can meet my family and have plenty of time to visit with Riordan. What do you call him? We don't even know his first name."

"His name is Lafayette, but everyone calls him Faye."

"Now you know why I don't use my first name," Riordan said. He was recovering from the shock of seeing his family, and he watched Rosa carefully and saw that she was on her best behavior.

Finally she said, "We'll have to rent a buggy to get you to the ranch. I'll go see about that. Riordan, bring them down to the livery stable when you're ready to go. I'll also let Hannah — she is a friend who has been staying with us — know that we will be leaving soon." She turned to the store owner who was listening avidly. "Fred, load these in the wagon outside, will you?"

"Sure will, Miss Rosa."

She left, and Leo said, "That's a good-looking woman. Is she Spanish?"

"Part Spanish with a little Crow mixed in."

"You mean the Indian kind of Crow?" Max lifted his eyebrows.

"That's right. Her mother was half Crow. I guess that makes her one-fourth. They say the Crow are the best-looking Indians on the plains." They stood there talking, and finally Riordan said, "Where are your bags?"

"We left them at the wharf. We didn't know where to take them."

"Well, let's go see if she's found a buggy. We'll get you out to the ranch. You'll see a side of life you've never seen before, I expect."

Marshal Swinson was outside, and he said, "Well, Mr. Riordan, I want to congratulate you on this son of yours. He don't look it, but he's got the bad men in this territory scared of him. You heard how he saved Heck Thomas's life, and he had to shoot another one that was going to harm Miss Ramirez. He was an outlaw, too."

Caleb stared at the marshal and shook his head. "He never did anything like this at home. All he did was paint pictures."

Swinson grinned broadly. "Well, you watch how the bad ones act around him. It's like they're walking around a keg of dynamite that's liable to go off at any minute.

Come along. I'll help you."

Riordan said, "Let's go. And that's enough talk about me."

Rosa and Hannah saw Riordan and his family approaching. Rosa introduced everyone to Hannah, who told the story of how Riordan had saved her, with Rosa's help, which further embarrassed Riordan.

Rosa had rented a two-seat buggy with a top. "That'll keep the sun off you, Mrs. Riordan."

"Thank you, dear. That's so thoughtful of you."

"I'll drive the buggy, and you can sit in the front with me."

"Riordan, why don't you take the wagon?"

"All right, Rosa. I will."

Rosa drove by the dock to pick up the baggage. The men loaded it in the wagon, and they all started on their way home.

Rosa and Eileen chatted easily as they traveled. They talked mostly of the countryside and what brought Rosa and her family to this territory.

Rosa finally broached the subject she hoped to elicit some new information about: Riordan. "You know I made a terrible mistake about your son when he first came."

"How is that, my dear?"

"Well, I needed help to run down some outlaws that killed one of my hired hands. I rode into town to asked Judge Parker if he had any men available. All the regular marshals were gone, so he assigned your son. You should have seen him. They had given him the hardest jobs they could find, the dirtiest."

"I know. I asked Judge Parker to do that."

Rosa looked at her. "Why did you ask him that?"

"I hoped he would get tired of it, come back, and pick up his life again."

"What was his life like back East?"

"He spent most of his time painting pictures," Eileen said. "His father and brothers were pretty disgusted with it. Caleb thought he should have gone into business with him at the factory."

"Does he still feel that way?"

"Not really. We discovered Faye's paintings are very good, just as I always thought. But of course, Caleb thought I was just speaking as a mother. Anyway, he could have a very fine career as an artist. Do you think he will stay here?"

"I don't know. You'll have to ask him," Rosa said. She slapped the line on the horses and they broke into a fast trot.

They continued to chat, but Rosa was unable to get any more information about Riordan from his mother. She really liked the older woman and could see where Riordan got some of his nicer qualities.

They finally arrived at her grandfather's property. "Well, there's the ranch," Rosa said.

"How picturesque. You raise horses?"

"Horses and some cattle. Come along." She looked back and saw that the mounted hands who had gone along for protection were following behind Riordan who was driving the wagon next to her buggy. As they approached the house, a tinge of uncertainty ran up Rosa's spine. The house was too quiet. Something was definitely wrong. "Where is everyone?" she turned and asked Riordan.

Riordan looked around. The fear in his gut reflected what he saw on Rosa's face, but he did not want her to see it from him, so he forced himself to remain calm and answer in a light tone, "I don't know. Looks vacant."

The entire party rode up to the front of the house. Before anyone could dismount, the front door opened, and Henry "the Fox" Beecher stepped out. He was wearing gray trousers and a light blue shirt with a dark

351

blue handkerchief around his neck. His low-crowned hat was shoved back on his head, and he was smiling like he had some inner amusement.

"What are you doing here, Beecher?" Riordan demanded.

"Well," Beecher said, "I've been thinking about you and about the way you took a man away from me, Riordan. Doesn't sit well with me. I can't put up with it. People are laughing at me, so I decided to do something about it."

Rosa's fear showed in her voice. "Where is my family?"

"Safe and sound. Bring 'em out, boys." Beecher's men brought out Mateo, Chenoa, Raquel, Juan, and Frank Lowery. "See. They're all right. I'm not a bad fellow. I wouldn't hurt such fine people." Beecher smiled and shoved the hat farther back on his head. "Let me show you something. You notice all my men here have guns, and I want for you to look at the barn over there. My men are going to be all right as long as your fast gun behaves himself." He pointed toward the barn and said, "Riordan, look at that second story. I've got two men there with rifles. Both of them are aimed at Miss Ramirez. You may be fast with that gun of yours, but you can't beat this hand."

"What are you saying, Henry?" Riordan asked.

"Why, I'm saying that Rosa is going with me. I'm taking her away from you as you took my man."

Riordan felt the chill of fear. "You can't do that. You'll never get away with it."

"Oh, I think I can and I will. I could have shot you off your horse, but I'm giving you a chance." He took a step forward and spread his hands out in an eloquent gesture. "Here's the way this will play out. I'll take the woman with me, and you come and take her from me like you did George. Just you. No posse. I'll give you three days. You come alone. We'll be waiting for you. You come now and see how much good that fast gun will do you."

Riordan tried to think, but he knew that Beecher was not joking. There probably were rifles aimed directly at Rosa, and the men on the porch all had their guns out. "You harm Rosa, and Judge Parker will put fifty of his marshals on your trail."

"Well, you'll have to stop that from happening, Riordan. As soon as you're dead in the dust, we'll let her go. What do you say, fast gun? From what I hear you can draw and shoot me down right now, but if you do, then my men will cut down the rest of your folks."

Riordan thought quickly and knew what he must do. "It looks like you got the best of the argument, Henry."

Beecher laughed pleasantly. "I knew you'd see it that way. Bring the horses, Wahoo."

A Mexican rode around holding the reins of several horses.

"Get on that horse, Miss Ramirez. We'll see if Riordan values you as much as he does his hide. Oh, one thing more," Beecher added as Red Lyle pulled Rosa off the buggy and led her to her mount. "You have three days, as I said, to come. After that, I'll take your woman for myself. I'll treat her right." He raised his voice, "Okay, you fellows, come out of the barn."

They all watched as two men with rifles exited. Hack Wilson was one of them. He said, "Lots of doings, Henry. I say just burn him right now."

"No, everyone says he is some kind of a white knight in armor ready to save poor folk. Let's see if he is. Come on." They all turned to ride out.

Riordan couldn't resist the itch to pull his gun. But he stopped from actually pulling it from the holster.

Rosa must have seen his action as she cried out, "Don't do it, Riordan!"

"Now, that's smart, Rosa. Your knight will come and get you, but he'll get killed doing it. All right. I'll be out there somewhere waiting for you. Three days."

Riordan watched as the men rode away.

At once a babble of voices broke out. Ringo said, "We'll have to follow them. We can beat'em, Riordan."

"No, Henry's too smart. The first thing he'd do if he saw a bunch coming would be to kill Rosa. It'll have to be his way."

CHAPTER 20

The journey Rosa was forced to make with Henry Beecher and his outlaw band was torture for her. They went at an easy trot, and all she could think was, *With every step the horses make, I'm getting farther away from home.*

"Don't worry, Rosa. I'm sure your hero will come through." Henry had pulled up beside her and was grinning at her. "After all, he is the white knight coming to save the fair princess, isn't he?" He kept up such talk for some time, and finally when Rosa simply refused to answer him or even look at him, he shrugged and said, "You'll be friendlier after a few days with us."

They rode for four hours, stopping only to rest the horses once, and finally they came into a stretch of what could only be described as badlands. There were no trees to speak of, just scrubs hardly higher than three feet. The land rose slightly into hills, which they had to ride around. Overhead, the sky was a dull gray, and the feeble rays of a waning sun cast the entire location to Rosa into a grim light. Finally they pulled up, after crossing several arroyos and making their way through several canyons, some barely wide enough to permit the passage of a horseman. Henry spurred his horse and came back to her. "Well, there it is. See, up on that hill there. There's your castle, Rosa."

The "castle" was a weather-beaten frame house with rusted tin for a roof. There was a porch running the length of the building, the roof of which was propped up by six-inch saplings. There was a run-down look about the place. The barn was leaning, and it received the same kind of treatment as the roof — six-inch logs dug into the ground and pushing against the top kept the whole structure from falling. The fences were in bad shape, barely good enough to keep the herd of horses that looked up and whinnied as they approached.

When they reached the house, Henry stepped out of the saddle, reached up, and pulled Rosa down. "Don't be bashful, sweetheart. This is your new home."

Rosa felt the strength of his arms as he pulled her up the steps, and when he opened the door, several chickens came fluttering out, clucking and ruffling their feathers. "Maybe you can do a little housekeeping. Me and my boys, we're not much at that." Beecher smiled. He pulled her inside, turned back, and said to his men, "Unsaddle those horses and grain 'em and see that they have plenty of water drawn for them. They've had a hard trip."

Rosa glanced about noting that it was about as unlovely a room as she had ever seen. The floor had been painted some bright color once but now was a leprous gray, scarred by spurs and with boards nailed over holes to keep the livestock out, which it had failed to do. The room had a cast-iron stove at one end with the stovepipe wired together and the door to the oven sagging. A three-by-ten-foot table served for meals she supposed, and some of the dishes from the last meal were still there with the food hardening and flies swarming everywhere.

"We don't stay here much, so we don't keep it up," Henry said.

He came close to her, and when he stood directly in front of her looking into her eyes, Rosa felt a trace of fear. She knew this man was ruthless, that he thought nothing of killing any more than the other members of his band. Now she forced herself to stand straight and meet his gaze. "It looks like a pigsty."

Beecher laughed suddenly. "I like a woman with spirit, but you can clean it up. Make yourself handy while we're waiting on Riordan to follow us here. Come on. I'll show you where you'll stay."

He walked across the room, and she followed him. There was a hallway, with rooms on each side, she supposed.

Beecher walked to the end, opened a door, and said, "Right in there, sweetheart."

Rosa moved inside the doorway and was disgusted. "This place is filthy!" She stared at the bedstead with broken springs and a mattress losing its padding. There was a washstand with a chipped pitcher and bowl, and a bucket over in the corner.

"Well, it's not the Waldorf, but you'll like it here. I'm going to have to leave you awhile now. I'll have to lock you in. Not that I think you could get away. If you try to run away, Rosa, it'll just make it hard on you. You saw what the land is out there. From up here on this hill, we can see ten miles, so just make yourself comfortable." He waved toward a chair that was broken but had been fitted with sticks and boards to make it sit up. "I'll be back, and you can cook a good supper for us." He looked at her and said, "I guess you're pretty scared."

Rosa looked at him. "I know you'd do anything, Henry, so of course I'm scared."

"I'm not such a bad fellow," Beecher said, his eyebrows rising in surprise. "As long as I get my own way, I'll look out for you." He waited for her to reply, and when she said nothing, he turned and walked out.

She heard the door close, and then she heard a bar being dropped to prevent her from opening the door. Quickly she walked over to the window, which was barred. The bars were so close together that there was no hope of wiggling through them. A child might do it but not a grown woman. She looked out over the landscape and noticed that with the exception of one clump of three walnut trees grouped together over to her left, the trees had all been cut down. She lifted her eyes and noted that the house was up on the highest point around. The land fell away for miles, it seemed, and she realized that Beecher had chosen this place because, with a lookout, no one could ever take the man off guard.

She turned and for a long time paced the floor, which was rather dangerous because it had broken boards that she could step through. The thought came to her that maybe she could remove the boards at night

360

and crawl down under the house, but she found they were nailed securely, and she had no tools to remove them.

Finally Rosa sat down in the patched-up chair. Her mind was in a state of confusion. She tried to calm herself, but everything she could think of had a grim ending. *Riordan will come,* she thought. Then immediately she whispered, "Don't do it, Riordan! They'll kill you!" Realizing the futility of speaking, she simply sat in the chair. After a time, she heard the men laughing and banging in the next room and dreaded when she would have to go out and be subjected to their crude talk and manners.

She surprised herself when she suddenly began thinking of the sermon that she had heard. She had a good memory, but this was different. It seemed she could hear every sentence that the minister had spoken. It was a relief to think of something other than Henry Beecher and his murderous band. She thought about the scripture that the preacher had read, the woman with the issue of blood, and how she had sought Jesus out, and how she touched Him and was healed instantly. She thought of this for some time, and then her mind moved to the other illustration, the woman caught in adultery. Rosa had a vivid imagination at times, and she could almost see the scene. The woman being dragged before Jesus, before the whole town, she supposed. She thought about how the men had insisted that she be killed. Rosa went over the whole scene, thinking about how the men had left and Jesus stood up and asked the woman where her accusers were. *She must have been weeping. She says, "They're gone." Jesus then says, "I do not condemn thee," and the woman reacts with tears to that,* she thought.

The noise from the other room grew louder, and she knew soon she would be called out to cook for the men. She was used to being around rough men, but always she had had control of them. These men had control of her now, she realized. She was totally at the mercy of Henry Beecher, and it was not beyond him to throw her to his men for their entertainment.

She forced herself to think again. *I'm like that woman taken in adultery. I haven't done that, but I've been a sinner all my life. If I could just hear Jesus say, "Neither do I condemn thee," I think I'd be the happiest woman in the world,* she thought. She remembered the invitation that the preacher had extended. He had said at one point, *"A person can find God anywhere. In the middle of the desert with no one there, in a crowded room, on the streets. It doesn't matter. It's when you believe that He's the Son of God and you're ready to yield your life to Him. That's when He'll say, 'Neither do I condemn thee,' and you'll become a part of the family of God."*

Suddenly the door rattled and opened, and Henry said, "Come on, sweetheart. You can do some cooking for us. We butchered some beef. Reckon you can cook steaks, can't you?"

Knowing that she had no choice, Rosa got up and walked into the room. The men were leering at her. She walked over to the stove at once and began cooking their meal, ignoring them as best she could.

Riordan knew his father was a man accustomed to being able to solve any problem, but as Caleb Riordan watched Henry Beecher and his men disappear into the distance raising huge dust clouds, he must have felt totally helpless. Riordan understood the feeling all to well.

"We've got to do something!" his father cried out desperately. "We've got to go back to Fort Smith and get a posse!"

"That won't do, Father," Riordan said. "You heard what Beecher said, and he's just cruel enough to do it, too. He'd kill Rosa in a minute if he saw a band of marshals coming."

Eileen came over. "But you can't go after them alone. They're all killers. You're just one man."

Riordan put his arm around his mother and said softly, "Well, it's not what I'd like to do, but the question is — is it the right thing to do?"

Mateo Ramirez said, "Go get my daughter. You can do it." He looked sickly and pale in the fading sunlight.

Chenoa came to stand beside her husband and said, "That's asking too much of anyone, Mateo."

"No, it's not," Riordan said.

The ranch hands all stood watching the drama. Ringo finally said to Riordan, "They can talk all they want to, but I can tell you right now I know you and you are going after that girl."

"I think you're right, Ringo. I don't think you can get her, Riordan. No offense, now. You're fast with a gun, but there's too many of them, and you can bet they'll be holed up in a safe place."

"I need a little time to think," Riordan said.

Chenoa took charge. She introduced herself and her family to the new guests. "Now, everyone come into the house, please. I know you are all tired and hungry. We'll fix something to eat and then try to figure out what to do."

Riordan turned and walked away from the house. He was aimless, for it mattered little where he went, as the situation wouldn't change. Riordan had never faced such a dilemma as this. He tried to think of a way to get Rosa back, but Henry was too clever. *He knows he's got me, and he knows I'll come. I don't think I can do it by myself, though.*

Finally he arrived back at the house. Twilight had come. There were sounds of talking in the house.

Riordan looked up and saw Hannah coming out to the porch. "What are you going to do?" she asked in a solemn tone.

"I know I've got to go after her, Hannah."

"I knew you'd say that, but I want you to know God before you leave."

"It may be too late for me."

"No, you've got a good spirit in you. You told me how you made a profession of faith when you were a boy and that you'd gotten away from it. I think you've been in God's family all this time. You just need to come back."

"How do I do that?"

Hannah moved closer to him and put her hand on his arm. "You remember the story in the Bible of the Prodigal Son? How he went bad, went away from home, and ruined his life? And what did he do?"

Riordan smiled briefly. "He decided he'd had enough eating with the hogs and wanted to go home and just tell his father what he had done and that he was sorry."

"You remember it well. And what happened when he got home? Did his father curse him and tell him to leave?"

Riordan dropped his head and thought. "No, the Bible says, if I remember correctly, the old man looked up and saw him when he was a long ways off, and he ran to meet him. He threw his arms around him, and the boy tried to tell him how badly he had messed up his life. The old man wouldn't listen to it, though. He said, 'Kill the fatted calf. Make merry for this, my son, was lost but now he's found again.' Something like that."

"That's very close to word for word," Hannah said. "But you need to come back to your Father, too. Don't you see?"

Riordan had been touched by the sermon much in the same way that Rosa had. He said quietly, "I need God. I know that."

366

"We'll pray, and you must dedicate your-self to Christ. Will you pray with me?"

For a moment Riordan seemed to be swayed between two choices, and then he whispered. "I've got to."

The two bowed their heads, and Hannah prayed fervently a long prayer, an encouraging prayer. Finally her voice fell away.

Riordan was silent for a moment. Then he said, "Lord God, I'm not worth anything. I haven't served You, but I want to." He went on to confess about his life away from God. Finally he said, "Lord, I want to be in Your family, so just like that wayward boy that came to his father, I come to You." He waited for a long time.

Hannah didn't speak. The two of them were totally silent.

Then something happened. Riordan had been disturbed and confused, his thoughts like the waves of the sea without purpose. But now there seemed to be a calm that was creeping into his heart, and he realized that this was what he was looking for.

"God's welcoming you home, isn't he?"

Riordan's throat was thick, and he could barely speak. He felt the tears in his eyes. "I may not have much life left, but whatever I do have, I give it to God."

■ ■ ■ ■

The next morning Riordan ate breakfast with the family. When they were almost through, he spoke to them as a group. "I've got to go get her. You all know that. There's no other choice."

Caleb said, "Son, you're just finding yourself, and I'm just discovering what a good son you are. You can't throw it all away."

Riordan rose to his feet and looked at his father and his brothers. "I wouldn't be a good son if I let Beecher have Rosa, would I now?"

No one said a word in answer.

Riordan finally said, "I prayed last night for the first time, really, in years, since I was a boy. I told God I would do whatever He commands, so now I'm going to do it. I'll be leaving in a moment, as soon as I get saddled."

Caleb said, "I can't think. I've always been able to fix things, but I can't fix this."

"I think God is fixing it," Eileen said. "Come. We'll all pray while he is gone and trust God for the outcome."

They all went out to the corral, and Riordan began strapping the saddle down on Big Red.

His mother came to him, and when she looked up at him, he saw that there was pride in her eyes. "I'm proud of you, son. You might not live through this, and that would be a terrible tragedy for all of us, but I know you're doing it because you love that woman. Is that right?"

"Maybe I do. I'm not really sure yet. But I'd go even if I didn't."

Caleb had been silent for a while. Finally he said, "You know. I don't know how this is going to turn out. I always wanted a son that was strong, and I didn't think you were, Faye, but now I see that you are stronger than all of us." His voice took on a bit of sadness and regret as he added in a whisper, "And I wish I'd been a better father to you."

Riordan had to hold back tears. He simply hugged his father and said, "I love you, Father."

He then shook hands with his brothers and was amazed, as he thought he saw tears in their eyes.

He turned to his mother last. He looked straight into her eyes, communicating how much he loved and appreciated her. He kissed her on the cheek, stepped into the saddle, and then rode away at a fast pace.

CHAPTER 21

Riordan straightened up stiffly and resisted the impulse to turn around. He had been riding steadily, looking down at the ground for signs of Henry Beecher's passing. When he had the eerie feeling that he was being watched, he tensed up, waiting for the gunshot, to feel the bullet crashing into his spine.

Suddenly a voice said, "You'll never make it this way, White Eyes."

Twisting around the saddle, Riordan saw Gray Hawk, the relative of the Ramirez family. He was riding a big lanky bay without a saddle but with a twisted rope for a bridle. Riordan had seen him only once, but he was not the kind of man that one forgot. His skin was bronze and drawn tightly around his face, making his high cheekbones more prominent. His eyes were obsidian, as black as night.

Riordan was surprised to see a little smile

twist the corners of his mouth upward. "What are you doing here, Gray Hawk?"

"Tryin' to keep you from getting killed." Gray Hawk kicked his horse and rode up even with Riordan's gelding. "You don't think you can find Beecher by yourself, do you?"

"I'm going to try."

"You're going to get yourself killed, as I said. Now I'm going to help you."

Riordan felt the tension leaving his muscles and said, "Well, I guess I can use all the help I can get. I'm no tracker."

"I am. Best tracker in my tribe. I can help you find Henry, and we can get the woman. We could even kill Henry if you want."

"I don't really want to kill anybody."

"That's not what I hear about you. You've killed a couple of men."

"Sometimes a man has to kill to save."

Gray Hawk glanced down at the ground and said, "Pretty easy tracking to here, but this ground gets hard farther on past those draws. Takes a good eye to follow their trail. Besides, I think Beecher probably is going to do a lot of dodging around to throw you off for a while."

"I don't think so. I think he wants me to find him."

"Maybe you're right. He's made it pretty

371

clear that he's going to kill you."

"I guess he'll have his chance."

The two rode along silently, Gray Hawk glancing down at the ground from time to time. They did hit hard ground quickly, and more than once he had to get down, lead his horse, and lean over, scrutinizing the hard earth carefully. "They came this way." He straightened up and looked off into the distance.

It was a hazy day, and Gray Hawk did not speak for such a long time that finally Riordan said, "Well, what are you thinking?"

"I'm thinkin' I must be crazy helpin' you commit suicide like this. If they get you, they'll get me, too."

"I'm hoping that God will keep us safe."

Gray Hawk turned and stared at Riordan. "You're a Jesus man then."

"Yes, I am. I didn't always act like it, but that's what I am, a Jesus man."

A broad smile came across Gray Hawk's face. "Well, from what I hear it's good to have God on your side. Did you notice the trail turned back there, about a quarter of a mile headed over toward those rocks?"

"No, I didn't notice."

"You better start noticin' or you're going to find yourself dead."

"Do you think their hideout is that way?"

"No, not in a hundred years. He's just moving around. As a matter of fact, he's probably got somebody watching us right now. They could knock us right out of the saddle."

"Well, it'll be dark soon. If they don't kill us before we get there, maybe we can do something."

Gray Hawk shook his head. A sober look flitted across his bronze face. "I don't believe in happy endings."

"I do this time," Riordan said grimly.

Rosa had cooked several meals, for it had been two days since they had arrived at the house. None of the men had offered to touch her, but that was because Henry had warned them against it. He hadn't warned them, however, against making crude jokes at her expense. She had been exposed to rough male talk before, but nothing like this. Gritting her teeth, she determined to show no sign that she was afraid.

"These are good pancakes, Rosa," Henry said. She had found supplies enough to make pancakes, and they had blackstrap molasses to pour over them. She had been working hard, for they ate like starved wolves. "You'd better sit down and eat some yourself."

"I'm not hungry," she said.

"Do what I tell you," Henry said. "I don't want a sick woman on my hands here."

Rosa put the last pancake on a tin plate and picked up a fork and a knife. She sat down as far away as she could get from Henry, who grinned and said, "You won't always be so standoffish."

"Yes, I will." She cut the pancake up and poured syrup over it, but it might as well have been sawdust. She was exhausted, as she had slept very little. When she wasn't cooking or trying to clean up some, she felt alternately calm and uneasy as she thought of the sermon she had heard. She had the feeling that she was under some sort of magnifying glass and that God was looking at her to see what she would do.

Henry finished his pancakes, drained his coffee cup, and said, "Get me some more coffee, Sal."

Maglie got up, moved to the stove, and brought the coffee back. It was thick and black, and Henry drank it without any sugar or cream. He was studying Rosa and said, "You know, Riordan is a tough fellow, but I've got the feeling that he's smart as well."

"What does that mean?" Rosa asked.

"Why, it means that he'll never come for you. He'll run to Judge Parker and get a big posse. That's what any man would do with any sense. I get the feeling he's sweet on you. Anything between you two?"

"No." She felt this was the wrong answer, but she could give Henry nothing to build on. "All I want is out of here," she said.

"Well, you heard my terms. Riordan comes and we knock him off, then I'll see you get back to your family. You see, I'm not such a bad fellow."

Wahoo Bonham, a short, barrel-shaped outlaw with a round face and a short beard, giggled. He had a strange high-pitched giggle that sounded ridiculous from such a muscular man. "Maybe you ought to marry her, Henry. She's a better cook than anybody else and keeps the place clean."

"That's just like you, Wahoo," Mordecai Bailey said. He was as tall and lanky as Wahoo was short and round. He had only one good eye, the other covered by a black patch. "You don't have to marry her. But, maybe one of us could do the marrying if you do. I thought about becoming a preacher once. That ought to qualify me."

"You, a preacher?" Hack Wilson said. "You're about as far from a preacher as a man can get."

"What about you?" Wahoo grinned. "You'd make a pretty good preacher, a nice-looking fellow like you. Got an education. You ought to quit this robbin' and stealin' and shootin' and get you a job as a preacher in some town. They got an easy life."

Hack shook his head. "Not for me. I don't believe in God."

"I do." Everyone suddenly turned to look at Henry. He was staring at his men and said softly, "A man's a fool not to believe in God."

"Why, Henry, you never said nothin' about having a religion!" Wahoo said in astonishment.

"No, I never said anything because I don't have any, but you just go out sometime and look at the stars. No, there's a star-maker somewhere, and I'm pretty sure it's the one in the Bible. I'm not scared of dyin', but I don't like to think about when I have to meet God and give account."

Sal Maglie said, "My grandpa was a preacher. He was a good man. He believed in God all the way through. I can't forget about him."

The talk went around the table.

Finally Rosa got up and began to collect the dishes. No one ever offered to help wash them, but she didn't expect it.

Henry watched her and waited until the men started a card game and then went over to where she was standing by the dishpan washing the sticky plates. "Rosa, I don't want to see you disappointed. I keep men watching, and as soon as they see that posse, I won't kill you like I said I would. But you'll be my woman. There's plenty of places in this territory to hide. I'll keep you until I get bored with you, and then I'll pass you along to one of my men."

"He'll come for me." Rosa was astonished at the assurance she felt as she said this.

She saw that Beecher was surprised as well. "You believe that in spite of everything?"

"I do. I'm not a Christian woman, but I believe in God, and I know Riordan's family is praying for him . . . and for me."

"Well," — Henry yawned and stretched — "they'd better be good prayers." He went over and joined the card game. When she finished the dishes, he got up and said, "Come on. Get on to your room." He walked with her, and when he unlocked the door, she started to step in, but he grabbed her instead. His strength was frightening. He held her to his chest, his eyes inches away from hers. "You're a good-looking woman. I never had much of a weakness for women, but I like you. If he don't come tomorrow, you'll be mine."

"I'll never be yours!" Rosa tore away and stepped inside the doorway.

He stared at her then laughed and pulled the door shut.

She heard the bar fall into place. Rosa paced the floor, and fear came like an armed man. She had never known fear like this, and she was thinking of what Henry had said about God. *He's not afraid to die, but he's afraid to face God and give account.* The words came floating back to her, and she slumped down on the side of the bed, put her face in her hands, and suddenly began to weep. She was not a weeping woman, but things had fallen apart, and now here in this darkness, with only the candlelight flickering, she knew that she had reached the end of her resources. She wanted to run and scream, but there was no place to run and no point in screaming. The beast that held her there would merely laugh at her.

Finally she grew quiet, but the words of the minister's sermon came floating back to her again. She remembered a great deal of it, and the part that stuck in her mind was when Jesus spoke the words *'Neither do I condemn thee.'* That was what caught her attention, that Jesus, the Son of God, didn't condemn that woman who was obviously a sinner. She thought on that for a while, get-

378

ting up from time to time and pacing the floor. She leaned against the wall, put her head back, and shut her eyes. "I can't go on like this," she whispered. "I've got to believe God."

She walked over to the bed, knelt down, and began to pray. The words were hard to get out. She'd never had so much trouble, but she had no practice. She nearly gave up, but she kept thinking, *That other woman took a chance. She didn't know Jesus would help her. She was desperate.* And then it came to her, and she realized that she was fully as desperate. Finally, weary, she whispered, "God, I don't have any right to ask You for anything, but I'm reaching out to You, just like that sick woman. She needed physical healing, and I need the other kind. I sinned against You terribly. There is no reason why You should forgive me, but I'm asking You to do that. Do for me what You did for that woman."

She grew quiet then and waited. From time to time she would try to pray again, but there was a stillness that had crept into her soul now. "Lord, I don't know of anything else to do. That preacher, he wanted people to believe in Jesus and to follow Him and obey Him, and, Lord, that's what I intend to do. No matter what happens tomorrow, I'm going to follow You." She lay on the bed then and after a time grew utterly still. She could hear a night bird crying out and a coyote singing its plaintive song way out on the prairie, but all she could think of was herself and God.

Time ceased to exist, but there came a moment when she whispered, "Lord, I don't deserve it, but I feel that You've done something in my heart. I'm still a prisoner, but I know somehow that I can ask You and You'll help me and Riordan. Get us out of this terrible situation." She fell asleep then, exhausted emotionally, and lay as still as if she were paralyzed.

Riordan and Gray Hawk had tracked Henry's party to a difficult place. Actually Gray Hawk had done the tracking. He had passed over ground that Riordan could not see a single mark on. It was hard, stony ground, but the Indian had eyes apparently like a microscope.

"How do you know we're following them?" Riordan asked.

"Because Rosa's horse had one shoe off. Ringo was going to put the shoe on. I've been followin' that track. She won't be far from Henry or his men."

They were paused at the foot of a hill. It

was late afternoon, and the rays of the sun were feeble. Gray Hawk said, "Well, there it is. That's where they are. There are their horses in that corral."

"Well, there are at least six or eight of them. How do we go about this?"

Gray Hawk laughed silently. "I got you here. Now it's your turn. You're the tough man with the fast gun. You tell me what you want, and I'll do it."

Riordan had been thinking ever since they had paused and located the band. The house was on a rise, and he realized they would have a scout out on a moonlit night. They could spot anybody coming from any distance. He stared over at the large barn. As he stared, the door opened, and Rosa came out carrying a bucket. At the sight of her Riordan felt a sudden gladness. "She's all right."

"Yes, but look. They're watchin' every move she makes."

"We'll have to wait until dark. Wait until they all go to bed."

"That part's easy. What's the next part?"

"I'll think of something."

The sun went down, and the night creatures began calling softly. It was easy to spot the scout, for he made no attempt to hide himself.

They waited, listening to the noises from the house. Apparently the men were gambling and drinking.

"Maybe they'll all get drunk and pass out," Gray Hawk said.

"No, they won't do that. I don't know what to do, but it'll come to me."

"You've got a lot of confidence. I don't know if we're going to do any good here at all except to get ourselves killed, and I'm not ready for that yet."

They did not speak often, but slowly the night wore on. The noise in the house ceased, and it was past midnight when Riordan said, "Here's what we'll do. We've got to create a diversion."

"A diversion? What do you mean?"

"We've got to get them out of the house, all except Rosa. I'm sure they've got her locked up. So here's what I've come up with. I want you to go over to that guard out there by the barn. He's got to be put down."

"You want his scalp?"

"I wish you didn't have to kill him, but if he gives the alarm too soon, we're done. You go in there and, except for Rosa's horse, let the horses out at a walk. Bring Rosa's horse back here to me."

"And then what?"

"Then you go set fire to the barn, and when it's burning good, fire off a couple of shots."

Gray Hawk chuckled. "You white men have crooked minds. What's going to happen then?"

"The men will come to put the fire out, and when they do, I'll go in and get Rosa. You come back and meet me here, and we'll get out of this place."

"It's too complicated. It'll never work."

"It's got to work, Gray Hawk. Now get to it."

Gray Hawk disappeared, silent as a shadow. Riordan sat there. The house was clearly outlined in the moonlight. He had been all the way around, and he saw that there was one window with bars on it. "That must be where she is. I hope they all get out of there so I don't meet any of them."

Time seemed to stand still, but finally Gray Hawk came back leading a horse.

"Tie him with ours, Gray Hawk." He waited until the Indian had tied the horse, and then he said, "Now, go back and set the barn on fire. Let it get to blazing fairly well, then fire off a couple of shots and holler and then run back here as quick as you can."

"And you're going in?"

"I'm hoping they'll all come to put the fire out so that the barn won't be burned up with the feed."

Gray Hawk was enjoying all this. "This is the kind of life I like, lots of entertainment." He disappeared again into the darkness.

Fifteen minutes later Riordan saw a flickering light and knew that it was the barn. It grew higher and higher, and then he heard several shots and somebody hollering. He knew it was Gray Hawk. He straightened up and moved in closer.

The door opened, and men began tumbling out. Henry was yelling, "Get the horses out of there. They'll burn up! Put that fire out!" They all ran toward the barn.

Riordan knew his moment had come. He made a dead run for the house. Glancing over his shoulder, he saw the men fighting the fire. He burst in with his gun in his hand, but the house was empty. "Rosa, where are you?" he shouted.

"Back here!"

He ran to the sound of her voice and saw the barred door. He ripped the bar off, threw it down, and opened the door.

Suddenly she was in his arms. "I knew you'd come, Riordan," she said weeping. "I knew you'd come."

"I had to come, but let's get out of here.

384

They may come back any minute."

The two fled, and when they got back to the horses, Gray Hawk was there. He was grinning and said, "You're a good man, Riordan. You should have been an Indian."

"Too late for that. Let's get out of here. Gray Hawk, could you take us another way? They won't be able to follow our tracks tonight, but they'll pick them up in the morning. By that time we'll be gone."

The Indian nodded and jumped on his horse.

Riordan and Rosa mounted up. He looked at her and said as he picked up his lines, "I came to realize I couldn't live without you, Rosa."

She gave him a smile and moved her horse closer. When he leaned over, she kissed him. "Let's get out of here," she said. "We'll not get another chance."

CHAPTER 22

"Looks like it might rain tonight," Riordan remarked, looking up at the sky. "Those clouds look like they've got some rain in 'em maybe."

Rosa shifted in her saddle and glanced upward. "I hope it does. It'll wash out any tracks we make." She looked over her shoulder and added, "I keep thinking I'll look back and see Henry and his bunch right there, coming at us."

"I don't think so. Gray Hawk gave them a false scent to follow. They'll follow it for a while, and then they'll figure out that it's not us. But they will be coming after us. You know that."

The two were riding in a canyon that twisted and turned, and when they emerged at the far end, they found a small stream with what looked like good, clear water. "We might as well wait here. We can't travel tonight, and besides, the horses would give out."

"I'm pretty tired myself . . . Faye." She grinned at him.

Giving Rosa a quick look, obviously due to the use of his old name, Riordan nodded. "I am, too. We've got a little food left in here. Let's tie the horses and let'em feed on that grass. We'll leave before daylight in the morning."

The two stepped off their horses and removed their saddles and blankets. Then they staked the two, using lariats to tie them to the tops of young saplings. They were separated so that each of them had plenty of grass, and they began chomping at once hungrily.

"I'll break some of that dried wood off of that fallen tree. You look through the saddlebag and see what we can come up with. It won't be much."

"We'll make out." Rosa watched Riordan as he moved away toward the dead tree that had fallen and began breaking small branches off. Then with a sigh she pulled off his saddlebag and found two cans of beans, an end of bacon, and a quarter of a loaf of bread, which was already hard. *We'll soak it in the beans with juice,* she thought.

Thirty minutes later they were both seated before the small fire. Rosa was heating the beans up in the skillet. She had added some water to make it more like soup and was dropping the bits of bread in. The bacon was frying in another pan and sent a tingle of smoke upward.

Rosa looked up and followed its track then remarked, "Look. There's just one star in the sky. I wonder where the rest of them are."

"They took the night off." Riordan grinned.

Rosa knew he was weary and tired, and worried for her. She knew that Henry would kill them both if he found them.

"That's Venus," he said, nodding his head toward the star.

Rosa looked at him and asked, "How do you know that?"

"Oh, my head is packed with useless knowledge. Venus is called the evening star. Anytime you look up at night and all the stars are gone except one, that's Venus."

"I wish I knew as much as you do. It must have been nice to go to school and then go on to college."

"I was bored out of my skull most of the time," Riordan said. He picked his fork up, stirred the beans, and cautiously lifted a few to taste. "Still not hot enough," he said. "I like my food hot."

The two sat there in silence. From far off came the mournful howl of a coyote.

"That sound always makes me sad," Rosa said.

"Well, he's probably having the time of his life. Coyotes have an easy life. Something to eat, a little water to drink, and a little family life to make little coyotes. We should have it so good."

Rosa shook her head. "I don't think anybody has that easy a time in this life."

"No, I don't think so either."

She glanced at him and studied his face carefully. "Something happened to me at Henry's house."

A look of concern hit his face. "What did he do to you?"

"No, nothing like that. I mean something spiritual."

"Well, that's a great thing. I gave my life to God before coming after you. I have felt so much freer since then."

"Well, I feel so . . . guilty still."

"You mustn't do that. My grandfather used to say, when you ask forgiveness for a sin, God always gives it. That's in the Bible, in the book of First John. 'If we confess our sins, he is faithful and just to forgive us our sins, and to cleanse us from all unrighteousness.' You can take that to the bank. God Himself said it. Grandpa said, too, that you could take your sin out in a boat in the ocean, drop it in the deepest part, and then put a sign up somehow out there that says 'No Fishing Allowed.' "

"I think the beans are done. We have one plate."

"You take the plate, and I'll take the pot."

She divided the meal up. She had a spoon, and he had a fork.

"Bacon's about done. Wish there was some more of it."

"You know. I want to do something, Faye. I know families pray over food before they eat it. I've never done that, but I'd like to start."

"Well, go ahead and start. We did it all the time at my house."

"You do it then."

"All right." Riordan bowed his head and said simply, "Lord, we thank You for this food, we thank You for every blessing, and we ask You to give us safety, in Jesus' name. Amen."

"Amen," Rosa echoed him. "Is that all there is to it?"

"That's it. You don't think God expects a long oration for a blessing over food, do you?"

"I don't know. I don't know anything. I

don't know how I'm going to live the kind of life I know a godly woman does."

"You *are* a godly woman, Rosa. That's what God made you when you called on Him." He took a mouthful of beans, moved it around in his mouth, and then immediately began to make a face. "These are hot!" He took a sip of water from the canteen that they shared and said, "I've been having thoughts myself about how I started out with God when I was just a boy, but I got away from it somehow and got interested in art. Things were so easy at our house. Never wanted for anything, but I see now that I did. I needed God, and I wasted a lot of my life."

The two continued to eat the beans and the bacon, washing it all down with cool water from the brook.

Finally they sat back, and Riordan said, "We'll wash the pot and the frying pan in the morning. I'm too tired."

Rosa put two more small pieces of wood on the fire. She listened to it crackle, and the movement sent fiery sparks upward. "Look. They look like tiny stars going up to the heavens."

"They do, don't they? Here. We're going to have to make some arrangements." He got up and went to where he had thrown his saddle and got the blanket he carried behind the cantle and brought it back. "Here. Let's sit on this. It'll be more comfortable." They sat down close together.

Rosa was very aware of his presence and his arm pressing against hers. "I have to tell you that I haven't been a good woman."

"You don't have to tell me, Rosa."

"I guess I do. I want you to know. A man came into my life, and I thought he loved me. He said he did." Her voice was unsteady, and she looked down. The light from the fire flickered on her face, and she added, "He was unfaithful and left me, and I grew bitter. I'm like that woman that preacher preached about, the one that committed adultery."

"Well, that's all over now. Both of us have made a decision to serve God. I guess we're at some kind of fork in the road, and we've got to be sure we don't take the wrong way."

"How can I be sure what God wants?"

"Lots of scriptures talk about that. It says to wait on the Lord. Don't rush ahead. Pretty hard for some of us to do."

They fell silent for a time.

Rosa broke the silence, "I think Henry Beecher is going to come for us."

"No doubt. He's that kind of man."

She turned to him suddenly and put her

hand on his forearm. "I think you need to go back East, Faye. He couldn't get you there."

"One thing I've learned is that you can't run from trouble. You have to trust God and face it. Sooner or later things come back to haunt you."

"Faye, you've led such a simple life. I don't know what could haunt you."

"You know, Rosa, when people talk about the big sins — murder, adultery, theft — that's not been my problem. I've been troubled by the spiritual sin."

"What kind of sin is that?"

"Something that you do that's wrong, but other people don't see it. God says it's wrong, but it's on the inside of you. People could look at you and never know it. Like envy. You could envy somebody's possessions. Nobody would know it, but that's a sin. So I've had trouble with sins on the inside."

She was quiet for a long time. "I still think you ought to go back East. You can be a great painter."

"I'll probably be a painter wherever I am. I've grown to love this country, Rosa. I didn't think I would. It looks so barren to some people, but I like it. That's the way God made it. And there are plenty of subjects to paint. Indians, for example. Nobody is really doing that."

"But Henry will hear about it. How would you feel if you had to shoot him?" A long silence passed, and Rosa could see that he was thinking hard.

Finally he said heavily, "I don't want to kill anyone, Rosa. I'd rather save someone, and that's all I can say." He thought for a while and then added, "My mother asked me why I had to leave to come after you. I told her I had to do it because it was the right thing to do . . . and I thought, too, that I might be falling in love with you."

Rosa grew absolutely still. She did not know what to say, for no man had ever affected her like this.

Finally he reached over and pulled her so that she turned to face him. "Rosa, I can only tell you what's in my own heart. For me, you are the only woman on earth. I love you for your beauty, but that's not who you are. That may fade sometime, as it does for all of us, but I tell you what. When this beautiful dark hair is white, I'll still love you, and when this strong figure is dim and bent with age, I'll love you even more than I do now. After you've lost the bloom of life, I'll love you, Rosa, for you're the one woman, I think, that God has made for me."

Rosa was moved. She leaned toward him, and he brought her to him with a quick sweep of his arm. When he kissed her, she felt the desperate hunger, a feeling that came to her as it never had before. She knew she had this power over Faye, this way of lifting him out of the ordinary, to touch the vague hints of glory a man and woman might know.

She moved to catch a better view of his face, and when she saw the heaviness of his lips, she thought she knew what he was telling her. And something like a pair of shears seemed to cut a restraining cord.

He put his arms around her and drew her into himself.

Even though he was saying all of these wonderful things, she was not yet completely sure of him, of how he felt, and she had a dread of making a mistake with him. For a moment, she watched him. She felt no anger and offered no resistance.

He lowered his head and kissed her again.

It was what Rosa wanted. She could sense that he felt the luxury of it as well. For her, it was a need that she could neither check nor satisfy. She knew the pressure of his arm and his mouth was too much for her, yet her own arms were tight about him, holding him as he held her.

Finally, with an effort, Riordan removed his arms and ended the embrace. He said simply, "I want to spend the rest of my life with you, Rosa."

She was shaken by the kiss, and she said, "Your family wouldn't like that, and I'm not sure I could live in the East. People would make fun of you for taking a Spanish woman, especially one who is also part Indian."

"I think all couples have to make some adjustments when they come together, but God will help us. And if I could have my way, I'd live out here half of the year. Buy a ranch with some peace and quiet where we could come and be close to your family. And then have another home in the East where I could go to visit my family."

"You think that's possible?"

"I think it is. We'd better get some rest. Well, we only have one blanket. You wrap up in it."

"No." She smiled. "We'll share it. I trust you, and I never thought I'd trust any man."

They lay down on the blanket and pulled it around them.

Rosa felt him relax as he fell into sleep. She whispered, "I love you, Faye." Then she went to sleep, a smile fixed on her face.

■ ■ ■ ■

"Did you get Hannah on her way, Ringo?" Eileen asked.

"Yeah, I hired four men to take her to her new post. With that many watching her, she'll be fine. Shame to waste a good woman like that. She'd make a fine wife."

"She's doing what she thinks is right," Eileen said. They had finished breakfast, and no one spoke for a while, but she knew they all had the same thoughts — that Faye might be hurt or even dead. Eileen said, "I want us all to pray for Faye. He's come a long way, but he's in trouble, and I want us to ask God to keep him."

She bowed her head, and the other members of the family did the same. Afterward the men left, and Eileen turned to Chenoa. "What do you think about my son marrying your daughter?"

Chenoa gave Eileen a direct look, and there was pain in her eyes. "You can't know what a hard time Rosa has had. She had to give up everything that she wanted to keep the family together. We would have starved, Eileen, if she hadn't helped us. She had to work in a terrible, despicable saloon just to make money to feed us."

"I treasure her for that, Chenoa. She's a fine woman. All she needs is to let God come into her life." The two women had begun to grow close during the Riordans' brief stay. Eileen had never been around people of the Ramirezes' class, but she saw fine things in all of them. "You know, Faye loves Rosa, whether he fully realizes it yet or not. How would you feel about it if they married?" she asked again.

"We're from two different worlds, Eileen."

"I know, but if they love each other, God will make a way."

Riordan and Rosa were so happy to see the familiar ranch come into view. As they rode closer, Riordan saw Ringo and knew the hand recognized them. He ran into the house, and Riordan imagined his telling all inside that their loved ones had returned.

Sure enough, there was a stampede as everyone rushed outside.

When Riordan and Rosa dismounted, Caleb grabbed Riordan. "Son, you're back! Thank God, you're back!"

Riordan was shocked. His father had never shown this sort of appreciation or love for him. It seemed to sink down into his spirit. "I'm back, and I'm all right."

"As I told the boys and Eileen, the first

thing I want to say is how proud I am of you. You are a real man, and I'm proud to have you as my son."

Eileen was standing close. Riordan put his arms around her and saw the tears in her eyes. "You brought her back, son."

The Ramirezes were gathered around Rosa, all of them trying to hold back the tears. Rosa could not.

"He brought you back," Juan said. "I didn't think anybody could."

"He saved me, but I think I knew already what kind of a man he was."

"Come on into the house," Chenoa said. "The food's ready. I know you two are starved."

"We're pretty hungry." Riordan smiled. "Your daughter's a pretty good cook, but even she can't make beans and bacon burnt over a campfire taste very good."

They all went to the table, and when they were all gathered, Rosa said, "There's something I must tell you. While I was being held at Beecher's house, they locked me in a room. I had time to myself, and I began to grow afraid. Not of what Henry would do, but of what I had been." She went on in a steady voice, and finally she said, "So I asked God to save me, and He came into my heart and gave me peace."

"Well, hallelujah!" Chenoa said. "That's wonderful news!"

Leo demanded, "How in the world did you do it, brother?"

"Well, it was mostly Gray Hawk. He found me and guided me to them and helped me get her away." He went on to tell the entire story. When he finally finished, everyone agreed what a wonderful thing it was that God had delivered them.

Finally Riordan said, "One other thing I want to make clear. I haven't had a chance to talk to you, Mateo, to ask you to give me your daughter as my wife, so I'm asking you now, you and Chenoa. I love her, and I always will."

His announcement brought smiles and cheers and applause and congratulations.

Finally Caleb said, "We'll be happy to welcome you and your wife to our home, won't we, Eileen?"

"Of course we will. We love her already."

Caleb nodded. "I've been critical of you, Faye, but I'm so proud of you now I'm about to bust."

Suddenly Mateo said, "What about Beecher? He'll be after you for besting him again."

"I don't want to take a man's life, and I'm not going to do it unless he absolutely makes it necessary." He shrugged and said, "I'm handing in my badge as marshal, and Rosa and I are going to start a new life."

Rosa came and stood beside him.

He put his arm around her and looked down at her. "Well, we've got everyone's permission. Now all we need is somebody to marry us, and we'll have our whole life together."

CHAPTER 23

A slight breeze brought some comfort from the heat of the day as Caleb and Eileen sat on the front porch. They had spoken for a long time of the problem that Faye was facing, but no matter what, they could think of nothing that seemed certain to bring a solution.

Chenoa came up and leaned against one of the pillars of the post. She gazed out into the distance and said nothing.

The silence grew so heavy that finally Eileen said, "What's troubling you, Chenoa?"

"I'm worried about Rosa and Riordan."

Caleb instantly said, "You're worried about their marriage."

"Yes. Your son is a fine man, and we all have the utmost respect for him, especially since he risked his life to save our daughter, but I'm not certain that the marriage between them would be a good thing."

Caleb shifted uneasily in his chair and

glanced over at Eileen. Finally he said, "Why would you say that? Faye can give her a good life."

"We're hoping he'll go back to the East with us," Eileen said. "He's becoming well known as a painter and could make a good living for her. Besides, we would help them."

Chenoa turned and faced them both. There was a troubled look on her bronze features, and she said reluctantly, "I think it would be hard on Rosa because white people look down on other races."

Mateo joined them now. He stood beside his wife and listened intently to what was being discussed.

"I think that depends on the people," Eileen said. "Some dislike other races, but others have no problem with people of different ethnicities."

Mateo said, "If they lived here, it would be different. No one makes anything of a white man who marries a woman who has Indian blood, but it would be different in the East."

"You can't know that, Mateo," Eileen said quickly.

"You know it's so, though, don't you?" Mateo said, his dark eyes fastening on Eileen. "You've seen it happen, I'm sure."

Eileen glanced at Caleb, knowing both of

them had the same thought. They both had memories of people from their social class marrying outside the white race. Even though it was a European race, there were still problems.

"Rosa would be unhappy among the rich, white people," Mateo said. "Many would not accept her. You know that's so."

A silence fell across the four of them, and finally Chenoa said, "Will your son want to take our daughter to the big city?"

"I haven't heard the plan, Chenoa," Eileen answered, "but I've got a plan of my own."

Caleb instantly turned to face her. "What kind of a plan? You haven't said anything to me about it."

"I have my secrets, and besides, nothing may come of it. Let me think on it a little."

Riordan and Rosa came in from a ride. They dismounted, tied their horses to the rails, and started into the house.

"Let's go get something to drink," Rosa said. "I wish we had some ice. At least the water will be wet."

The two went inside.

Rosa went out to the springhouse and brought in a cool pitcher of water. "We've got enough lemons and sugar for lemonade."

"Sounds good."

Rosa made the lemonade efficiently and handed him a glass. "You always had ice available in the city, didn't you, Faye?"

"Pretty much. I don't miss it all that much, though." He drank several swallows and said, "There. That washes the dust down."

They sat there talking idly, and finally he reached over and took her hand. He looked at it.

She watched him, wondering what he was thinking. Her hand was strong and showed signs of work.

He smiled at her and tightened his grip on her hand. "You've got strong hands," he remarked. "I like that. How do you feel now?"

She smiled and said, "For the first time in my life, I'm content, Faye. I never knew where I was going. All I could see was another day in that vile saloon where I had to fight men off. But now it's different."

"I'm glad, but you still looked concerned about something. Please tell me about it."

"Well, I'm a little worried. If we stay here in the Territory, it'll be simple."

"You mean nobody pays any attention to

intermarriage here."

"That's exactly right," Rosa said. "But if we go to your home in the East, some people would be unkind. I'd bring shame to you."

"You think that bothers me?" Riordan said at once. He extended his other hand and held her in a grip. "I love you, Rosa, and if we have to live at the North Pole, that'll suit me fine."

She laughed and shook her head. "I don't want to live in all that ice."

"Our parents have talked about this."

"What do they say?"

"Well, they say that they're so glad to have me back alive they'll be happy to see me married."

The two sat there sipping the lemonade.

Finally Rosa said, "We haven't had time to think about it. I'd like to get you away from this place. Somewhere it will be safe. Beecher won't stop until he kills you, Faye. You know that."

"That's the kind of man he is. I hate to run, though. It seems cowardly."

"It's either that or face him, and you said you didn't want to shoot another man."

"I don't. I don't want to ever kill another human being. So I talked to my mother, and we've come up with a plan. She is a very wise woman."

"What sort of plan?"

"We'll get married, and then we'll go to the East, but not for very long at our home. I'd like to go somewhere in the Smoky Mountains. It's beautiful there. We could have a fine honeymoon." He grinned. "Did you know that the Bible says that when the Hebrews married, the man didn't go to work for a year?"

She stared at him in disbelief. "What did he do?"

"The Bible says he just made his wife happy."

Rosa suddenly laughed. "I like that a great deal. Yes, we'll do that. You can just please me for a year."

"I'm serious, Rosa. We'll go to the Blue Ridge Mountains, and we'll do two things. We'll have a great time just being in love with each other and enjoying the scenery and just being together. And I'll be painting, and you'll be in my schoolroom."

"What does that mean?"

"Well, there are ways that Easterners have that you'll need to know about. Nothing too difficult — what to wear, what utensils to use at a meal, things like that."

"You consider yourself an expert in women's clothing?"

"Oh, definitely!" Riordan grinned broadly then dropped Rosa's hands and rubbed his palm across his chin. "I could teach you which fork to use. We'll be among some high-class people there. So when we go back to my home, everyone will fall in love with you, just as I have."

"It sounds too good to be true."

"Well, here's what I'd really like to do. I'd like for us to have a house here somewhere. Not a fancy one. Just someplace we could come. I love the West. I'd like to do some painting here of the people, the cowboys, the Indians, even the outlaws and the marshals. We could spend half our time here and then have a house somewhere close to my parents and go spend time with them. That way both families will have their grandchildren close. By the way, I'd like to have a great number of children. We'll talk about that. How do you like my plans, sweetheart?"

"I love them!"

"Good. Now about these children. I'd like to have at least four. You can have them one at a time or all at once. . . ."

The house was busy with people getting ready to make the trip to Fort Smith. Riordan had gotten up that morning and said,

"I want to get rid of this badge. It's like a weight on me."

"You sure you want to do this?" Mateo said. "It's quite an honor to be a marshal."

"Yes, they're great men, but it's not for me, Mateo. I want to give this badge back to Judge Parker and put this gun away for good."

"I think that's wonderful." Eileen beamed.

"You've proven what you are — a real man." Caleb nodded. "Now, it's time to move on to a new life. I love the idea of you two spending half your time close to us, and half here. That'll make all of us happy. Won't it, Mateo?"

"I think we'd all better take the hands with us," Rosa said.

Instantly Riordan looked at her. "You're thinking we might run into Henry along the way and his bunch?"

"I think he'd like nothing better than to catch you out alone."

"All right. We'll all go. Just leave a few hands here to take care of things."

They left as soon as they had finished packing and made the trip in record time. When they pulled the buggies up in front of Judge Parker's office and tied their horses, Riordan went upstairs at once. His parents and Rosa followed.

They found Judge Parker at his desk, as usual. He rose at once and said, "Well, Marshal, I'm surprised to see you." He came around and shook Riordan's hand. "The whole Territory is talking about how you took this young lady away from Henry."

"It was mostly Gray Hawk," Riordan said.

"Well, in any case you got her back. I was trying to scrape a big posse together to go after her, but you never know about Henry. He might have killed her just out of spite."

Riordan reached up, unpinned his badge, and said, "I appreciate you letting me serve with you, Judge Parker, but I'll be leaving now. We're going back East for a time."

"Well, I think that may be a good idea. Sooner or later we'll catch up with Beecher. Nothing would please me better than to see him hang on that gallows out there."

"Judge, I want to thank you for taking care of my boy," Eileen said.

"Why, it's more like he took care of us." Parker smiled. "I'll be losing a good man, but you were meant for a different kind of life. Besides, it's good that you're leaving the Territory. Beecher won't ever forget you made a fool of him. I've been talking to Heck Thomas. We've got a number of marshals available. They're going to leave soon and run the Fox into the ground. We'll get

410

him. Don't worry about that."

"Thank you, Judge. I'll see you again before we leave."

"Write me when you get settled. I'd like to see some of those pictures of yours sometime."

"I'll paint one and ship it to you." Riordan smiled.

They made their good-byes to the judge and went back to the street.

"You feel better now, Faye," Rosa asked, "I mean not being a marshal?"

"It was getting to be a heavy thing. They're noble men, most of them, but just not for me."

They were headed for the restaurant, both families, and suddenly a shock ran through Riordan, for Henry Beecher stepped out of an alleyway. He had his gun drawn, and it was pointed directly at Riordan.

"Don't move, Riordan. I've got my men posted along the street."

"You're making a mistake, Henry."

"No, my mistake would have been if I tried to match draws with you. I've heard about that draw of yours, and I don't care to test it."

"I don't have a gun on me, Henry."

"I don't believe that. You always have a gun."

411

"Not anymore I don't, and I'm not a marshal anymore."

Beecher scowled. "I know you've got a hideout somewhere."

"No, I don't. I don't ever want to shoot anyone else."

"You're a liar!" Beecher shouted. "I'll give you a break. I count to three, and on 'three' you go for that hideout."

Judge Parker's voice came, "Beecher, you're under arrest."

Beecher looked up and saw Judge Parker leaning out the window. "You won't get me this time, Judge. All your marshals are gone out on a job. I found that out. I'm taking Riordan out."

"You'll hang if you do."

Beecher merely laughed. His eyes were alight. It was the kind of situation he liked. "All right. On the count of three. One — two —" On the count of two, Beecher fired.

Riordan thought he could feel the hiss of the bullet passing close to his ear. He did not have time to move, but he suddenly realized that there was another gunshot right on the heels of the first. He saw a black spot appear in the center of Beecher's forehead. Beecher's eyes went dead, and he simply collapsed, dropping his gun in the dust.

Riordan whirled and saw that Ringo was

pulling his gun up. "You owe me for that one, Riordan." Ringo grinned. "I'm going to claim the reward on this scoundrel, and then I'm going to have me a high time."

"He died like he lived," Caleb said. "A cheat and a liar."

Beecher's men began to scatter. They mounted their horses and rode out.

"Well, they'll break up now. Henry was the brains of the outfit," Riordan said. He turned to face Rosa and saw her face was pale. "Don't be afraid. It's all over."

Rosa whispered, "God kept you from killing him."

"Yes, and I'm thankful for it. All I want is you and some peace."

"You can have me, and we'll see about the peace." She giggled.

A crowd was gathering. Some were bending over Beecher, but Riordan said, "I don't want to see him. Let's get out of here. We're safe now. God has answered our prayers for peace."

Rosa and Riordan got out of the buggy and stood looking at the small cabin. "Not much of a honeymoon spot."

"But the mountains are so beautiful," Rosa said. She turned to look at the rolling hills that seemed lost in a blue haze. The air was clear, and the forest was thick. "This is such a beautiful place."

"I'm glad you like it."

"Whose house is it?"

"Well, it's ours for a week." Riordan reached over and put his arms around her. "I've got just one week to teach you how to be a good wife."

Rosa laughed and threw her arms around him. She drew him down and kissed him and said, "It's going to take longer than that for me to teach you how to be a good husband."

"Come on. Let's look at the inside." They went to the door, and he opened it then turned and suddenly swept her into his arms. "An old custom. The groom always carries the bride over the threshold." He walked inside and put her down. They stood looking around. "Looks like a palace to me."

"Plenty of peace here. That's what you wanted, Faye, me and peace."

"Right."

They found another door and saw a large bed. "This is the bedroom. I hope you like it." He smiled at her. "You'll be spending a lot of time here."

She hit him on the shoulder, laughing.

"I'll go bring the things in. You can cook me a fine meal while I rest up. Getting mar-

414

ried is hard work." He looked thoughtful then said, "Which case has the white silk nightgown my mother bought you?"

"Never mind. Just bring it all in. I think I'm going to wear my old flannel gown. It's sort of ratty, but after all, you should have to work to get the white silk one."

They suddenly reached for each other, and he kissed her gently and then with fervor. "We're going to have a wonderful life."

"Yes, and four beautiful children — one at a time," she smiled.

They clung to each other as they rested in the peace God had provided. A peaceful place to begin their married life together, a peace from having to fight outlaws, and the most important peace . . . the peace residing in each heart given to God in faith and love.

ABOUT THE AUTHOR

Award-winning, bestselling author, **Gilbert Morris**, is well known for penning numerous Christian novels for adults and children since 1984 with 6.5 million books in print. He is probably best known for the forty-book House of Winslow series, and his *Edge of Honor* was a 2001 Christy Award winner. He lives with his wife in Gulf Shores, Alabama.